THERE'S ONLY ONE WAY
THESE TWO ARE GOING
TO GET ALONG...

THE
HARD
WAY

MICHAEL J. FOX

A HOLLYWOOD ACTOR.

JAMES WOODS

A NEW YORK COP.

UNIVERSAL PICTURES Presents

A BADHAM / COHEN GROUP · WILLIAM SACKHEIM Production A JOHN BADHAM MOVIE

MICHAEL J. FOX JAMES WOODS

'THE HARD WAY'

STEPHEN LANG ANNABELLA SCIORRA and PENNY MARSHALL

Music by ARTHUR B. RUBINSTEIN Film Edited by FRANK MORRISS TONY LOMBARDO

Production Design by PHILIP HARRISON Directors of Photography DON McALPINE, A.S.C. ROBERT PRIMES, A.S.C.

Story by LEM DOBBS and MICHAEL KOZOLL Screenplay by DANIEL PYNE and LEM DOBBS

Produced by ROB COHEN and WILLIAM SACKHEIM Directed by JOHN BADHAM A UNIVERSAL PICTURE

DOLBY STEREO
IN SELECTED THEATRES

UNIVERSAL.
AN MCA COMPANY

©1991 UNIVERSAL CITY STUDIOS, INC.

THE HARD WAY

A novel by J.R. Robitaille
Based on a screenplay by
Daniel Pyne and Lem Dobbs
Story by Lem Dobbs and Michael Kozoll

J

JOVE BOOKS, NEW YORK

THE HARD WAY

A Jove Book / published by arrangement with
MCA Publishing Rights, a Division of MCA, Inc.

PRINTING HISTORY
Jove edition / March 1991

ISBN: 0-515-10654-2

Jove Books are published by The Berkley Publishing Group,
200 Madison Avenue, New York, New York 10016.
The name "JOVE" and the "J" logo
are trademarks belonging to Jove Publications, Inc.

PRINTED IN THE UNITED STATES OF AMERICA

10 9 8 7 6 5 4 3 2 1

THE HARD WAY

ONE

THE INNOCUOUS CHRYSLER PULLED QUIETLY TO THE curb and came to a stop not far from a dimly lit phone booth. In the long shadows of the night, it was impossible to tell exactly what dark color it was painted. That was on purpose. Maybe once, when someone else had owned it, it had been a gleaming dark green or coffee brown, polished and cared for. Now the finish was simply dull. The car had a few dents— nothing distinctive, certainly nothing as noticeable as a blown headlight or a rusted bondo spot. It blended in.

He was careful about that kind of thing. There would be nothing to draw attention to him, at least not until he wanted it. A dark, inconspicuous car, a quiet, unobtrusive demeanor, black clothing, head to foot—it added up to nothing. A chameleon, he could move through the city unseen until he chose to be visible.

Even this one risky act, stopping in a red zone, was a carefully calculated gamble. After all, *everyone* in New York used these off-limits parking spots, simply because there wasn't enough room to breathe or walk in safety in the city, let alone park a car. And it wasn't as if he'd be there for long. What he had to do wouldn't take much time at all. Considering the consequences, it was a downright stroll in the park—an anonymous, deadly stroll in the park.

He smiled a thin, private smile. Some people needed flashy cars, glittery women, Emporio Armani suits. Some people

1

needed gold and diamonds dripping from their arms and necks and ears. Not him. He would have all the attention he needed soon enough. And he only required one simple, streamlined accessory for it. He put his hand softly on the gun that rested on the cracked vinyl seat beside him.

It was a unique weapon, designed to his own specs, fitted with a laser sight. Excellent for night work. He thought of it as his special friend, a one-of-a-kind weapon created just for him. It had been put together from the flotsam and jetsam of other guns, guns that hadn't been used the way they should have been used. The way he had used, and would use, this one.

He popped open the glove compartment and pulled out the amyl nitrate he kept there. He broke the capsule open under his nose, snorting in the heady fumes. The heart-jumping drug rushed right to his brain. It galvanized him: he was on. He smiled again, thinking about his mission. Everybody knew that people got what they deserved. And he was just what they deserved. He was fate; he was omnipotent.

His heart and brain going triple time, he picked up the gun and caressed it. Then he jammed a clip into it and thrust the gun down into the pocket of the thin, black leather coat he wore.

"Time to party," he murmured, yanking open the door and slipping fluidly out onto the pavement. There was only one thing left to do before the big show.

The phone booth's dim interior light shone like a beacon, signaling him to come. Yes, this part of the mission was dangerous, but what the hell? He shrugged his shoulders, telling himself that this little bit of recklessness was part of the high. He slid into the booth and picked up the receiver, then dialed 911.

The phone rang and rang. Damned New York cops, he thought. They couldn't even answer the emergency line. As he listened and waited, his restless attention was caught by a billboard resting against a nearby building, waiting to be

2

hoisted up. It was a mammoth ad for a new movie called *Smoking Gunn II*.

He touched the weapon in his pocket like a talisman and stared at the billboard, appreciating the irony of the situation. The movie star in the ad had his own gun, too. He studied the face on the billboard with disgusted amusement. The actor's boyishly handsome face, his twinkling eyes and charmingly cynical smile all belied the weapon in his hand. Joe Gunn looked about as dangerous as a kitten. Then he was distracted by the click on the other end of the line.

"New York Emergency," a disembodied voice said. "Please state your name, number and address, and the problem you're having."

"It's not the problem I'm having," the man in the phone booth said genially.

"Sir?"

"It's the problem *you're* about to have," he continued in an odd lilting voice. He could feel his brain expanding, could feel his power growing.

"Sir?" The voice was growing more puzzled.

He wasn't fooled by stalling tactics. He couldn't leave them time to trace this call; he couldn't spend the time he'd like to spend teasing and hinting . . .

"I said," he repeated, his voice soft and menacing, "you've got a problem."

"If you'll please . . . "

"Have you ever heard of the Party Crasher?" he whispered.

There was a nervous pause on the other end. "If this is a joke . . . "

"Shut up!" His tone turned abruptly to a snarl. "This is no joke. It's me. And I've got a clue for you. A location . . . "

He could hear the sharp intake of breath as the woman on the other end realized he was who he claimed to be.

"Sir . . . " She recovered quickly. "Please tell me where you're located, and I'll try to help . . . " He was right, he thought smugly—she *was* trying to keep him on the line.

3

"The Power Plant," he interrupted her. "But you don't have much time, because I won't be there long." He laughed softly. "Tell your cops to look for the man . . ."—he looked down and smiled— " . . . wearing black."

Then he gently replaced the receiver and walked purposefully toward the glittering nightclub where he had a job to do.

TWO

DETECTIVE SKATE CAIN BRACED HIMSELF WITH ONE hand against the dashboard and one on the window, and waited tensely for what had to be the inevitable crash. The sedan in which he was riding veered sharply around a corner, coming so close to the sidewalk that it barely missed hitting a fruit stand and three shaken pedestrians.

"Would you please . . . ," Cain began through clenched teeth.

The driver didn't seem to hear him. "Dammit!" John Moss shouted, pounding on the steering wheel hard enough to shake it loose, as he braked abruptly behind a fancy Mercedes prowling for a safe place to park.

Moss stuck his head out the window. "Move it or lose it, you stupid dickhead!" he screamed, accelerating around the Mercedes. He yanked at the steering wheel, zigzagging dangerously close to a small Honda that was double-parked in a No Parking zone.

"John . . . ," Cain began again.

"Let's go, let's *go*!" Moss yelled to no one in particular, as he managed to push their unmarked blue vehicle through yet another space where there didn't seem to be one.

"Moss!" Skate Cain yelled, feeling the sweat begin to bead on his forehead, "for Christ's sake, *watch* it, would you *please*?"

"I *am* watching it!" Moss insisted with a quick glance over at the passenger seat. "If I wasn't, we'd be in a dangerous situation, Skate!"

Oh, right, Skate thought. Of course. Pleading with Moss when he was fired up, he reflected gloomily, was just like carrying coals to Newcastle, or whatever that phrase was that meant you were doing something for nothing. Moss didn't really hear a thing you said—he was tuned in to his own driving forces.

Cain was thrown abruptly back against the seat as Moss stomped hard on the brakes, just in time to avoid barreling into the back of a truck. Not surprisingly, he swore again. "*Go*, asshole, for Christ's sake, whatya think the goddam gas pedal is *for*?"

He pulled out from behind the truck with a screech of rubber, and Skate saw a rush of oncoming traffic. "Oh, no," he muttered, "this is it." He closed his eyes. Was it Hail Marys or Our Fathers? he wondered. And would it make a difference?

"You can open your eyes, Skate," he heard Moss say.

Cain did, and saw that somehow, with a combination of skill and recklessness, Moss had managed to swing their sedan back into its proper lane in time to avoid the fatal head-on waiting to happen.

"See?" Moss grinned ferociously at his partner. "No problem."

"Right," muttered Skate Cain. "And they wonder why cops are under stress."

John Moss was the most intense man—no, strike that, Cain thought, skip the gender—Moss was the most intense *person* he had ever had the luck—good or bad, he wasn't sure which—to encounter. And when you wore the badge of the NYPD, and your job was facing down dealers and killers and pimps and junkies on a regular basis, that was a radical statement.

Moss was also his partner, and that, Cain reflected, brought about its own particular set of problems. It wasn't that you couldn't trust Moss: you could trust him implicitly. It was just that you never, *ever* knew what the hell he was going to do next. Cain figured Moss *himself* probably didn't know what he was going to do next, either. The guy seemed to operate on instinct and adrenaline. He was like a grenade, Cain reflected unhappily, with its pin pulled halfway out. But that was part of what made him such a damned good cop.

Cain's reverie came to an abrupt end as they once again screeched to a bone-shaking halt, behind a catering van that was stopped, its engine running, right in the middle of the street. They were so close to it that Cain thought he could probably count the screws on the van's taillights, should he so desire. He shuddered.

"Moss . . . ," he began.

But John Moss didn't even hear him. He had already stuck his head out the sedan's open window and was busy berating the owner of the van. "What the hell do you think you're doing, standing there?" he screamed. "It's *D* for *Drive*, shit-head!"

The driver of the van, leaning casually up against the vehicle, shrugged and pointed to the curlicue letters of the catering sign painted in pastels on its side panels. Cain figured that the silent gesture must mean that white uniformed minions from the catering company were even now unloading amazingly expensive platters of decorative food with unpronounceable names and strange tastes for some upscale party. And why *not* double-park a van for such a good cause?

"I don't give a rat's ass if you're delivering poodle pâté to Jackie O!" Moss shouted. "Get that thing out of my way!"

The driver shrugged again and casually flipped Moss the bird.

Cain thought, uh-oh, as he watched Moss's face go from its normal abnormal intensity to something that looked as though it was lit up in one of those forties horror movies.

"That does it . . . " Moss seethed as he pushed open his door and started out of the car, all long legs and arms and anger.

Time for damage control, Cain thought. "Whoa, buddy,"

7

he said, reaching over quickly and pulling his partner back into the sedan with a viselike grip. "Don't want to be doing that, Moss," he warned, shaking an admonishing finger in his face. "Remember what happened *last* time you got into an unauthorized street brawl?"

Moss settled reluctantly back into the driver's seat, his taut, angular face sullen. "Yeah," he muttered. "I remember."

"And you don't really *want* to go back to walking a beat, John, do you?" Cain continued calmly. It was a whole lot easier to be calm and rational when Moss didn't actually have his foot on the gas pedal.

Moss snorted in disgust at the thought. "That's right, Skate," he said derisively, "that's real nice—just go ahead and rub salt in the wound."

Cain shrugged equably. "I just don't want to see you get into any more trouble," he said.

"Oh?" Moss turned his fierce brown eyes on Cain. "Why not? At least then you could get yourself a *normal* partner."

Cain grinned. "No, thanks," he said, "I'm having way too much fun."

Moss shot him one of his patented looks of suspicion, but Cain just shrugged innocently.

"Besides," Moss muttered, "what the hell would an *authorized* street brawl be?"

"Ask the Captain," Cain suggested mildly, and belched. Jesus, he thought, he really needed some Tums. He really needed a scotch to wash down the Tums. He really needed not to be in this car with John-the-maniac-Moss driving. "Hey," he said brightly, as if the idea had just occurred to him, "why don't you let me drive?"

"Whattaya, crazy?" Moss shot back in disbelief. "I wanna get there tonight, for Christ's sake!"

"I'll get you there . . . ," Cain began.

But Moss was lost in his own private snarkdom. He glared at the van driver, who had casually lit a cigarette and was scuffing the pointed toe of his black boot against the pavement.

8

"Lookit that asshole," Moss muttered. "There oughtta be a law against driving without a brain!"

Suddenly, he leaned down and reached for something. Cain saw with relief that it wasn't any kind of weapon. And just as quickly, his relief turned to dismay.

Reaching outside the window, Moss stuck the revolving red police light on the roof of the sedan and grinned at his partner, his lean wolf's face triumphant.

Then, as the light began to turn and flash, he stuck his head out the window and screamed at the van driver, who was staring at the red light, mesmerized. "Police business, dickwad! Let's move it before I dump you in the back of this car and haul your ass down to the station!"

The van driver, forgetting all about his urgent culinary business, promptly leapt into his vehicle and pulled away, while a stream of oncoming traffic slowly split to allow the sedan through. But even now, under the best of circumstances, they still moved along in fits and starts.

"Oh, for Christ's sake, Moss," Skate Cain said to his partner, "take the damned light off the car! You know you can't do that!"

"Why not?" Moss replied, concentrating on the traffic. "We're cops, aren't we? And we're in a cop car, aren't we?"

"Because it's not police business, John, it's a date!" Cain exploded. "A goddam *date*!"

Moss accelerated forward, careening through a red light, sending cars in all directions screeching to noisy halts. Horns blared. People screamed. Skate Cain winced.

"This gets reported, what are you gonna tell the Captain?" he demanded. "You gonna say, 'Sorry about the forty-five people I killed, Cap, but I was *horny*'!"

Moss ignored the jibe. "I have to be there on time, Skate," he said seriously. "This is important, this is our second date!"

"Big deal," Skate muttered.

"It *is* a big deal," Moss insisted. "Since my divorce, not one chick has stuck around for a second date, not one!"

"Maybe that's because you still refer to them as chicks," Skate suggested.

Moss's brow furrowed in a moment of introspection between near crashes. "I don't know," he mused. "They always *say* they don't like my being a cop, but maybe it *is* something about my personality . . . " He stuck his head out the window and screamed at a honking car, "Up yours, asshole!"

"Oh, Moss," said Skate with a smirk, "surely not your personality."

"But Susan's different," Moss continued obliviously. "She really could be the *one* . . . I even stopped smoking for her."

"What's that?" Cain asked pointedly, gesturing toward the unlit cigarette that Moss had been clutching for the past fifteen minutes.

Moss glanced down and tossed the offending object out the window. Catching the look on his partner's face, he said defensively, "I didn't *light* it! Oh, hell, never mind, I don't know what I'm doing explaining a woman to you, anyway. You're happy if you find one with all her teeth and no hair on her back . . . "

"Moss, watch out!"

Moss screeched suddenly to a halt as something huge blocked the car's path. "What the . . . "

A billboard operation had completely blocked off the street. Cain watched with mild interest as a man on a crane began to hoist up into the air a mechanical arm holding a huge plywood cigarette.

Moss slammed the wheel. "What the hell *is* this, a goddam conspiracy?"

"Nah," Cain said calmly, "it's a billboard." He glanced up. "Oh, lookit, it's the new Nick Lang movie, you know, that tough guy he plays—Joe Gunn. God, I love that guy."

"I *hate* the sonovabitch!" Moss fumed. "I hate anybody who gets in my way, and he's in my way."

Just at that moment, the radio crackled to life.

"Fourth Squad Lieutenant, we've got the Party Crasher at

10

the Power Plant on Forty-sixth . . . "

Cain and Moss exchanged a look. The Party Crasher was a maddeningly elusive killer, a man who taunted the police with phone calls and then killed his victims almost right under the cops' noses. There wasn't anyone in the city that the cops wanted more than this self-styled serial killer.

"Jesus, we're practically there!" Cain exclaimed. "Let's go!"

What little color there was drained out of Moss's feral face. "No," he groaned, "not tonight!" He looked up at the billboard and glared at the cynically smiling Joe Gunn. "Why don't *you* take care of this, you hotshot asshole?" he snapped. "You've got a big gun!" Then he slammed the car into reverse.

Cain felt his neck jerk from the impact. "Moss . . . ," he began.

But Moss was all business now, intent on backing the car up as fast as he'd driven it forward. "Forty-sixth," he muttered. "Shit, shit, shit, shit, shit . . . !"

He spotted a tiny space in the traffic, which looked as though it might barely accomodate a kiddie car, and somehow maneuvered a fast 180-degree turn, peeling out with a screech. Cain automatically flipped on the siren, and they wailed back into traffic, passing the astonished van driver again.

"This time it's for real," Cain assured him.

THREE

THE POWER PLANT PULSATED WITH THE SOUNDS AND lights of a busy, hip club making a fortune from watered-down drinks, ear-splitting music, and the clientele's ongoing hope that they might find people to go home with that night.

"Lookit this," Moss said, disgusted, as he screeched to the curb.

"Yeah," Cain agreed, "the fucker couldn't have picked a better place to get lost, could he?"

Moss was already out of the car, hand on his weapon. "That, too," he said, "but I was talkin' about these people! *Christ*, where the hell do they all come from?"

Outside, people dressed in every conceivable outlandish outfit waited to get in. Suburban explorers, urban sophisticates, borough wannabes—everyone in line had one goal in mind: to look hip enough to make it inside and be seen. The bouncers had seen it *all*; they weren't impressed by bribes, lies about knowing the musicians, or faked industry credentials.

Cain shrugged, surveying the crowd with a practiced eye. "There's Grainy," he said, cutting efficiently through the surging throng.

Except tonight, the bouncers knew, there was something a little strange going on. It had to do with the drab, boxy sedans that had suddenly converged on the place, and the people who spilled out of them. Their outfits were decidedly unhip, their collective purpose too obvious—from their intent expressions to the telltale gun bulge noticeable on each of them. The crowd seemed oblivious.

"Okay, let's find this asshole this time," Moss and Cain heard Grainy, a tough, grizzled veteran of plainclothes work, say. "I'm sick of this shit."

A youthful cop named Billy grinned, a smile that was filled with the tension of the situation. "I know, Grainy," he said. "We're all sick of it. And now you're gonna tell us that they just don't make psychos like they used to, right?"

Pretty China, who looked more like a streetwise urchin than an undercover cop, winked at him. They had heard Grainy's stories before.

"Damned straight," Grainy said bleakly. "I mean, what's with this schmuck, he gonna call us up every time he's about to kill someone? It's fuckin' unnatural!"

"The man likes an audience," Moss said, joining them. "Keep your eyes open."

"Here?" Billy scoffed as a brunette bombshell squeezed past him, dressed in just enough leather to make it legal for her to be out in public.

Despite the joking and camaraderie, each of the officers knew that there was only one reason to be here: the Party Crasher, a new breed of killer who played them like a violin. And they were determined to catch him before he killed again.

Cain continued to scan the crowd, while Moss focused on face after anonymous face, willing the Party Crasher to show himself.

"Grainy," Moss said, "you check out the back. China, Billy, you stay here in front."

Billy looked offended. "So we stand around outside pullin' our puds while you and Cain go in after him and get the glory shift?"

Moss's intense eyes narrowed. "Cheer up, Billy," he said, "he might kill somebody out here."

China intervened before the two could escalate the argument. "Billy," she said sweetly, "I don't have a pud. You think you could pull yours twice for me?"

"Let's go," Grainy said, cutting through the banter. "Let's do it."

The plainclothes cops scattered to their respective assignments. Moss and Cain, tension radiating off them, flashed their badges at the jaded bouncers and made their way through packed bodies into the Power Plant.

Over the deafening sound of the music, Moss glanced back over his shoulder at Cain and shouted, "At least he shouldn't be too hard to spot. He said he was dressed in black."

Then, as they emerged onto the packed dance floor, Cain stopped abruptly and elbowed Moss in the ribs. "Great clue," he remarked.

"Shit," Moss seethed, surveying the crowd. *Everyone* was dressed in black. "What is this, the fuckin' Inquisition?" he yelled.

"It's fashion," Cain yelled, looking down at his Levis and white shirt. He and Moss were the ones who stood out—the only people in the entire place who weren't wearing black.

"Let's make a quick go-around," Moss shouted. "Maybe there's something else about this guy." He pointed in one direction. "You go that way, I'll hit the dance floor—meet up on the other side of the bar."

Cain nodded and moved away, disappearing into the sea of bodies.

Moss elbowed his way rudely across the dance floor full of squirming, gyrating bodies, arms and legs and hair flying wildly. Moss didn't even want to *know* what various body parts were being pressed and jostled against him. He certainly didn't want to see the coke being snorted right out in the open, or a hand-rolled joint of something being passed back and forth between a couple of wild dancers.

"Shit," he muttered, "goddam freaks, shit, shit, shit . . . "

In a back hallway, right off the dance floor, he spotted a drug deal in progress—cash for crack. "Shit," he muttered again.

Under normal conditions, it would have been an easy, automatic bust. But not now—there was no time to worry about it. His sharp, narrowed eyes swept the crowd around him, looking for a clue, a hint, a telltale expression, anything that would reveal his quarry to him.

"Anything?" he screamed to Cain when they met up at the bar, packed three-deep with bodies.

Cain shrugged and shook his head in frustration. "You think he's pulling our chains?" he yelled.

Just at that moment, Moss found himself looking into the dark, fearless eyes of a man who stared unwaveringly back at him. The man wore a long black leather coat and had a gaze like an anaconda. The hair went up on the back of Moss's neck, and some sixth sense told him that he had found his quarry.

"Cain," he yelled, reaching for his gun.

The man in the black coat, still holding Moss's gaze, reached down and came up with a gun. Faster than Moss could believe, the man swiveled gracefully in place, sighted the drug transaction in the hall, and fired two shots directly into the dealer's chest.

A bloody arc exploded as the man was thrown violently back, and the hall was suddenly sprayed with red. The recipient of the transaction panicked and began to scream at the top of his lungs. Even over the din of the club, the action in the hall drew the attention of the crowd. Instantly, people reacted, stampeding in all directions, tripping over each other to reach the club's exits, howling in alarm.

Peripherally, Moss saw the band members dive to the stage, saw the bartenders disappear behind the bar, saw the milling action of the terrorized crowd. He and Cain shoved their way through, displaying their weapons.

"Outta my way, shithead!" Moss elbowed a dazed by-stander roughly in the neck. "Out, out!" He screamed as he ran.

"Come on!" Moss shouted over his shoulder to Cain. "We're gonna lose him!"

16

He shoved viciously through the wall of bodies and flew out the door onto the street. Outside, he stopped in his tracks, looking keenly around. He was unable to see or feel the maniac anymore.

Moss flagged Billy and China. "Where'd he go?" he demanded, his eyes darting restlessly into shadows and doorways, each spot a possible hiding place for the maniac.

Billy shrugged helplessly.

"Goddammit!" Moss exploded. Now official blue-and-whites had pulled up to the scene, making the panicked crowd even more skittish.

Moss knew this had all the potential to turn into a fiasco and a riot all rolled up in one. He had to spot that bastard, he had to *get* this guy . . .

"There!" he shouted, as he saw the black-coated figure of the Party Crasher slipping around a corner.

"Moss, wait!" China shouted, but Moss was off, running at breakneck speed, heedless of backup or cover.

Legs pumping, lungs straining, Moss raced after the Party Crasher, screaming. "Stop, you bastard!" he shouted, as they dashed across a crowded parking lot. "Police! Halt or I'll fire!"

He saw the Party Crasher hesitate for a split second, as if something had gone wrong with his plans. Then he did something completely unexpected: he leapt into the cab of a city tow truck.

"Jesus Harry Christ!" Moss exploded, as the surprised tow-truck driver scrambled out from under the old Chrysler he was fastening to the winch.

"Hey!" the driver screamed. "What the hell do you—"

Moss knocked the man roughly out of his way as he raced past. "Police!" he yelled. "Get down!"

Moss jumped for the driver's side door as the Crasher ground into first and stomped on the accelerator.

The truck jumped forward just as Moss's fingers grabbed at the door handle. The door swung wide, taking Moss with it. He could barely hang on, scrambling frantically to get a better purchase on the door as he ran alongside the moving truck. Then he spotted Cain, coming around the corner from the other direction and heading straight for a collision with Moss's door.

"Watch it!" he screamed.

The warning came too late. Cain got whacked by the open door, and went flying backward onto the pavement. Moss, clinging with one hand to the frame of the open window, the other to the frame of the door, swung in a pendulum motion as the truck sped up.

"Stop the truck, asshole!" he screamed. "You're under arrest!"

Moss saw the Party Crasher point his gun in his direction. With superhuman strength, Moss managed to pull himself partially into the cab, just far enough to reach over and knock the gun from the killer's hand. It went skittering under the bench seat as the Party Crasher swung the truck abruptly right, throwing Moss's body back outside the cab again.

"Fucker!" screamed Moss, hanging on for dear life.

Straining with the effort, Moss once again got his body partway into the cab. The Party Crasher made a stabbing motion at the panel on his door, and Moss suddenly found his hand pinned, as the window came all the way up. He bellowed in pain.

The Party Crasher grabbed a tire iron from the seat beside him and began flailing away at Moss. The door swung back and forth wildly, with Moss barely managing to hang on, as the killer veered the truck all over the street. Moss tried valiantly to dodge the tire iron, but he could feel the occasional blow that landed, could feel himself getting battered and bloody. The Party Crasher landed a particularly effective whomp on his fingers, as the truck veered wildly to the left.

"I hate reckless drivers," Moss muttered through clenched teeth. Anything to keep his mind off the pain that was threatening to overwhelm him.

Suddenly, he saw the welcome sight of Billy's car in pursuit. Billy and China, their faces grim, had their weapons drawn and were trying to get a bead on the killer. With his free arm, Moss waved frantically at them. "Keep comin', Billy!" he screamed. "Shoot the bastard! Shoot him!"

Billy pulled the car alongside Moss. "I can't!" he shouted. "You're in the goddam way!"

"I don't care!" Moss screamed. "Kill this asshole!"

Just then, the killer whipped the truck violently to the right and around a corner. The towed Chrysler whipsawed like an off-balance water-skier, and flipped directly into the path of Billy's car.

There was no room for Billy to maneuver, no time to stop, and Moss saw Billy's sedan crash and crumple from the impact, then buckle from behind as the next blue-and-white in pursuit smashed heavily into the back of it. It folded up like an accordion.

Moss watched helplessly as all his backup came to a dead halt, and he grimly held on as the out-of-control tow truck headed into Times Square, pedestrians and homeless people scattering before its reckless path. Struggling, Moss finally managed to smash the window with his gun, and ignoring the jagged glass that cut into his hands, he got a better hold on the door. But the impact had jolted the gun loose from his grip. His only means of defense was gone.

"You won't get me!" the killer said, a crazy grin on his face. "You'll never get me!"

"You crazy fuck," Moss screamed, "I've *got* you!"

"Just watch!" And the Party Crasher headed straight for a giant billboard waiting to be hoisted. With a terrific crash, he barreled the truck through the sign. Moss and the door he was clinging to were ripped from the body of the truck.

There was a huge bang as the truck impacted with the giant, three-dimensional hand of Nick Lang as Joe Gunn. Moss tried to cover his head as everything exploded in a shower of truck parts and sign limbs.

Moss found himself clinging to Joe Gunn's huge cigarette,

19

which was still intact, halfway up the sign. He watched in incredulous shock as the tow truck swerved away and disappeared into the night. Then, with a crack, he felt the mechanical cigarette break, and he was dumped unceremoniously on the ground.

"Moss! Are you all right?" He could hear Cain's worried voice.

Moss shook his head to clear it, then crawled out from under the rubble of the sign. His arm was killing him; he thought it might be broken. His side felt caved in, and he was scraped and bleeding from a dozen places. And the Party Crasher had gotten away. Again.

Moss looked up at the still-intact face of Nick Lang, smiling smugly down at him. "Fuck you," he said.

FOUR

"NO ONE TALKS THAT WAY TO JOE GUNN . . . " NICK
Lang's face filled the screen in Technicolor glory. His voice,
his expression, the slight curl of his lip said it all—Joe Gunn
was everyone's hero; he was masculine confidence personi-
fied.

The camera pulled back slowly, and you could see all of
Lang as the super hero, the character he had made so famous.
He was practically bursting with self-confidence and perfectly
outfitted for the part in ripped and artfully smudged Banana
Republic togs.

"Especially," he said, his hazel eyes deadly serious, "with
a lady present."

Now you could see the jungle that surrounded tough Joe
Gunn, and the incredibly built woman he was talking about.
She was *also* outfitted in Banana Republic clothing, but most
of it seemed to have disappeared back along the trail. Now,
expanses of tanned flesh were stretched provocatively out,
gleaming through cunningly placed tatters. She was tied to a
rack and dangling in midair over a bed of sharpened stakes.
It wasn't exactly clear *why* she was in such a position, but it
was clearly a lethal situation. And the imminent threat from
the crowd of Ninjas that surrounded the pit was evident to
everyone. Including, apparently, Joe Gunn, who promptly
waded into the throng and proceeded to dispatch about forty
Ninjas without even breaking a sweat.

21

"Very nice," remarked Angie Greenburg. "This is very good, Nickie."

"No it's not," muttered Nick Lang sullenly.

"Yes, it is," she insisted. "I'm your agent, I know about these things. Now be quiet and watch."

Nick Lang and Angie Greenburg were in Nick's luxurious pool house, watching this latest promo on a forty-six–inch Sony.

An announcer's voice said, over the death-dealing action on the screen, "Look who's back in town! Where there's fire, there's smoke. Where there's smoke, there's Joe Gunn. He hates bad guys!"

Joe Gunn snarled at a Ninja, who snarled back.

"Gunn!" yelled the Ninja, "I'm gonna kill you!"

"I *hate* this," Nick Lang said.

"Shut up," said Angie.

"He loves bad girls!" exclaimed the announcer, as the scantily clad actress flashed a little more silicone.

"Gunn!" she pleaded, "you gotta help me!"

"This time," said the announcer, "he's tracking a killer halfway around the globe! From the East . . . "

The scene switched to Joe Gunn in Japan, decimating what looked like half the Yakuza.

" . . . to the West . . . "

The West was Los Angeles, where sleazy, well-dressed mob types bit the dust as Joe Gunn dispatched bullets with a steely demeanor and God on his side.

"Oh, Christ," groaned Nick Lang, "I really can't stand this."

"Shush!" hissed Angie, intent on the promo.

"He's not just good, he's the best!" the announcer exclaimed. "He can't be stopped . . . not in war . . . "

Joe Gunn's car crashed into a brick wall, and the hero leapt out, faced down four black-masked bandits, and blew them efficiently away.

" . . . and not in love . . . "

The dangling victim, now freed from the rack but no better

dressed, fell into Joe Gunn's arms. "Oh, Joe," she sighed, "you're the best."

"Are those tits real?" Angie asked curiously.

"How the hell would I know?" Nick Lang snapped.

"Well, you were close enough to them," Angie said pragmatically.

"Not off the set I wasn't," Lang replied.

As a building was blown to smithereens on the screen, the announcer wound up to his fever-pitch finale. "Nick Lang is Joe Gunn . . . in *Smoking Gunn II*. You can't keep a good man down. Rated PG."

As the credits flashed on the huge screen, something else flew by and flashed. With a resounding crash, the big screen exploded.

"Oh, that was very good," Angie said, nodding calmly, "very mature."

Nick Lang pulled his striped robe tighter around himself and paced like a caged lion. He lit a new cigarette off the butt end of the one he had been smoking and fumed, his boyish, handsome, all-American face set in an angry mask.

"It's crap, Angie! Utter, absolute crap! And you know it!"

"Nick . . . ," Angie began placatingly.

He flashed her a warning look, his hazel eyes shooting sparks. "It *is*. It's just one more big-box-office, go-in-one-end-out-the-other piece of crap!"

"Well," Angie said mildly, changing tack, "it might not be Shakespeare, but you didn't have to throw your People's Choice Award, anyway."

A middle-aged Hispanic woman wearing a tidy uniform and a seen-it-all expression entered the room quietly, carrying iced drinks on a silver deco tray.

"Thanks, Maria," Nick Lang said, reaching for one. He turned his attention back to his agent. "When are you going to come to me with something that has *substance*, Angie?"

"Nick . . . "

"Something with *relevance*," he said.

"I know what it means," Angie said calmly, reaching for

23

a tall, iced glass. "Thank you, Maria."

"For Christ's sake, Angie, I want to do something with meaning, something that doesn't have a Roman numeral in the title! You ever hear of *Hamlet II*? *War and Peace: The Early Years*?" He continued to pace.

"They made *Henry V*," Angie joked.

It didn't work. Nick was on a roll.

"I'm good," he said. "I'm not just another pretty face . . . " He paused to glance in the mirror. "When am I going to get the chance to play someone real, someone who can reach out and touch the audience with raw, honest emotion? Someone who cares about something that *matters*?" He took a sip of his drink and made a face. "Maria," he protested, "*this* isn't Evian!"

He handed the glass back to the maid and stalked outside, fuming. Angie followed, matching him step for step, as he headed past the black-tiled lap pool and the manicured tennis courts toward the huge white neoclassical house.

"So what's this really about, Nick?" Angie demanded, tugging on his sleeve. "Is it me? Is that it? The agent who mismanaged you all the way to number one at the box office?"

"You know it's not you," Lang replied peevishly.

"Okay," Angie said, "fine. You want something that matters, I can understand that. Let's *talk* about something that matters, Nick, let's talk about . . . "

Nick sighed wearily as he chorused the words right along with his agent, " . . . 1.2 billion dollars in combined ticket sales . . . "

"Not to mention," Angie continued without breaking stride, "seven million dollars above the line, pay-or-play, plus twelve percent of the gross. And this." She gestured to the grounds, the house. "The house that Joe Gunn built for Nick Lang— it's not too shabby, is it?"

"That's not the point . . . ," Nick began, but it was Angie's turn to rant.

"And that People's Choice Award which you just now so cavalierly tossed into your five-thousand-dollar screen," she chided him. "For God's sake, Nickie, people love you!

You've never been bigger, not in earnings and not in popularity! Christ, your movies are even bootlegged to Lybia!"

"Oh, that's great, Ange," Lang said in disgust. "Congratulations to me, I've cornered the terrorist market!" He stopped in midstride and stared at her earnestly, with those eyes that could melt hearts around the world. "I'm tired of playing cartoons, Angie." He sighed. "It's time to grow up, but you don't want me to grow up, the studios don't want me to grow up . . . "

"Nick, that's just not true . . . "

Suddenly, looking very young, he stamped his foot. "Goddammit," he yelled, "I'm the only one who wants me to grow up!"

"You've managed quite nicely to parlay that youthful cuteness into a fortune," Angie reminded him. "It worked on the series, and it works in the Joe Gunn movies. What's the problem?"

"The problem is that I am a thirty-year-old *man*," Nick said through clenched teeth. "And I'm ready to play my *age!*"

Angie trailed along with a sigh, as Nick stalked off, heading into the house. At least he hadn't said he was ready to act his age, she thought. What the hell was she going to do about this latest whim?

"Nick," she said, "you've got the respect of your audience, of your peers, of the filmmakers who . . . "

Nick paused in his living room, a huge, open-spaced room with the kind of Pacific view only really big money can buy. He didn't seem to notice either his surroundings or his agent's words. "I want to grow up," he insisted again.

Angie looked sharply at him, then said crisply, "Okay, Nickie, let's cut through the crap here."

Nick shot her a wounded look.

"It's that part," she said, "isn't it? That . . . cop. You still want to play that . . . what's his name, Tony the Bandana, right?"

"DiBennedetti!" Nick corrected her through clenched teeth.

"Tony DiBennedetti! And you're damned right I want that part!"

"I think you're obssessing about this part," Angie warned him.

"It's *not* obssessing!" he insisted vehemently. "What actor in his right mind wouldn't want this part? A *real* part, a cop who worries about making the rent, who struggles every day to keep his head above water, who bleeds when he gets shot, who vomits when he gets sick . . . "

Angie made a face. "Lovely," she remarked. "You want to puke on screen. What a challenge!"

"What is it, Susan?" Nick said, distracted, as his assistant stuck her head around the corner.

"Simmons's wife had the baby," she said, "Cedars. Should I send the usual wine and cheese basket or a silver teething ring?"

Nick paused. "Wine and cheese," he said. "He didn't mention me in his AFI speech." He turned to Angie. "*See?*" he said.

"See *what?*"

"This is the kind of part that would give me prestige," he insisted.

"You want to be mentioned in an AFI speech? That's *prestige?*" Angie said incredulously. "Come on, Nickie, let's be sensible. Your movies make people happy!"

"Happy," Nick repeated in disgust.

"Yes, *happy!*" Angie insisted. "There's nothing wrong with that! And call me crazy, but I just don't see America coming out in droves to watch you vomit!"

"Come on," Nick said, heading for the circular stairs, "I've got something in the media room I want you to see."

"Besides," Angie continued, trailing after him, "you *know* they want Mel Gibson for that part. And he wants to do it. The director's out of town for two weeks, but when he gets back, it's a done deal."

"Two weeks," Nick muttered.

He was quiet for a moment, and then his face lit up with a

sudden inspiration. "Perfect," he said gleefully. "That's just enough time!" He turned to Angie and grabbed her arm. "I wanna test for that part," he said earnestly.

"*Test?*" Angie's voice rose to a screech. "No! Absolutely not! No!"

"Angie . . . "

She glared at him. "What are you *talking* about? Are you *nuts*?"

Nick didn't reply directly. "Come on," he said, pulling her along with him up the stairs and into a room stocked with pinball machines, games, electronics, video equipment, audio equipment—a teenager's dream, a mother's nightmare. Nick's playroom.

"Test!" Angie repeated, still in shock. "Test?"

"Angie, listen to me!" Nick said. "I've made up my mind, dammit, this means—"

"No, *you* listen to *me*!" she interrupted him. "You cannot, I repeat *cannot* test for a part. It's a giant step backwards, it's . . . "

"I'll pay for the damned test myself . . . "

"It's not the *money*, Nick, it's the message it sends out, the wrong kind of message in this town . . . "

" . . . All I want is a shot at this part . . . "

" . . . They'll think you're desperate . . . "

" . . . and it's the part of a lifetime, and I know just how to get it . . . "

" . . . and they'll try to get you for less, for a *lot* less!"

They both paused for a breath. Nick jumped in first, shoving a tape in the VCR. "Angie, enough—just *watch* this! I got it off the dish last night after the Mets game. It's some kind of sign, I swear!"

"Sign?" Angie echoed in disbelief. Goddam actors and their superstitions.

She sighed and turned her attention to the screen, which was showing a tape of a mike being thrust into a man's face. The background was New York, and it was obvious from the devastation and the revolving red lights that some kind of cop-related event had just occurred.

"Lieutenant," a newsman began, "this makes four times now that the Party Crasher has killed someone *after* alerting you to the crime. And now he's gotten away again. Care to comment?"

The plainclothes cop with the mike in his face glared. He was certainly an intense-looking individual, Angie thought—what presence. What eyes; they were almost feral. What bone structure . . .

"Why don't you go tie your *bleep* in a knot?" the cop snarled.

Lang punched his remote, freezing the tape on John Moss's snarling expression.

"Well?" Lang demanded. "Isn't that incredible?"

"Uh . . . ," Angie said, thoroughly puzzled, "isn't *what* incredible?"

Lang looked at her as if she was crazy. "*Research*, Angie . . . look at that face, look at those eyes . . . "

"I'm looking," Angie agreed. It was difficult not to look at this cop. Not that he was what you would call traditionally handsome or anything, but . . . "I could probably get him work," she mused. "Heavies, character stuff . . . "

"It's *him*, Angie," Lang insisted excitedly. "That's my character, that's the face of the man who has tasted fear and swallowed, who's been to the edge of the abyss and contemplated the blackness there . . . "

Angie blinked. "Nickie, I think you're getting a little carried away about a five-second news bite . . . "

Nick didn't hear a word. "I want to go to New York tonight," he said. "Tomorrow at the latest. Get the studio to set it all up. I wanna spend the next two weeks with this guy, eat, drink, sleep with John Moss. I wanna taste his world, get into his skin . . . "

"Nickie . . . "

"Angie, look at him!" Nick's face was animated, intent. "John Moss *is* Tony DiBennedetti! Don't you see? If I can learn to be John Moss, I can get that part!"

28

Angie paused to try to collect her thoughts. It was difficult to stop Nick when he was high on an idea, and she had to admit that this might indeed *be* research if Nick was Bobby De Niro or Daniel Day Lewis. But Nick was Nick, and this was . . . ridiculous. This was commercial suicide.

That, however, would definitely be the wrong approach. "Nickie, sweetie, listen to me," Angie began patiently. "I understand exactly what you're saying here, but it's reality-check time. Think about your schedule. You cannot, I repeat, *cannot* leave L.A. right now. Your movie opens on Friday. I've already booked you on Johnny and Arsenio . . . "

"And I've already done Regis, Geraldo, and Oprah!" Nick said succinctly. "Just tell the infotainment shows to run the old interviews. All anybody ever *really* wants to know about is that paternity suit, anyway." He looked earnestly at her. "Come on, Angie, this is *big*!"

Angie sighed. It didn't look as though there was going to be any way around this one. Nick would have to go through with this crazy charade. Unless . . .

"Nickie," she said calmly, "you forgot something."

"What?" Nick said, still staring at John Moss's face, frozen and glaring, on the screen in front of him.

"What if this cop doesn't *want* you tagging along with him?"

Nick turned to stare at her, his hazel eyes wide and astonished at the mere suggestion of an idea so patently silly. "Come on, Angie," he scoffed. "Get real. It's a great plan, it's . . . uh, *professional*! Two pros exchanging ideas. Of course he'll want to do it . . . He'll probably be more excited than I am!"

FIVE

"THIS IS A JOKE, RIGHT? SKATE PUT YOU UP TO this, right?" Moss stood in front of Captain Brix's desk and stared quizically at him.

"No, Moss, it's not a joke," the Captain replied. "It's your assignment."

"Guarding an *actor*?" Moss said, his voice filled with disbelief.

"Not exactly guarding," the Captain replied. "It's more like teaching him the ropes, it'll be a snap."

Moss's silence was ominous. "This really isn't a joke?" he repeated.

"Nope," said Captain Brix.

"Over my dead body!" Moss exploded. "No way, not a chance!"

The Captain stared at his most recalcitrant officer and shook his head wearily. "Moss," he said, "look at you." He pointed. "You've got a broken arm in a plaster cast . . . "

"It's my *left* arm," Moss pointed out. "I'm right-handed."

" . . . You've got a couple of broken ribs," the Captain continued, as if Moss hadn't spoken at all.

"They don't hurt," Moss insisted.

"Moss, you're a mess. You are in no shape to work."

"But I *want* to work," Moss said. "I mean this in the most respectful way, sir, I really do, but no way, no way in *hell* am I gonna baby-sit some candy-ass actor with an ego the size of Trump Tower, just so he can get his rocks off playing cops and robbers! That's bullshit detail—you know it and I know it—and besides, I'm smack in the middle of a murder investigation!"

Moss stood before Brix's desk and glared like a caged wildcat. His spirit quite clearly hadn't absorbed the same battering that had been delivered to his body.

Brix, however, hadn't risen up the ranks for nothing. He glared sternly back. "Moss," he said, "hear this. You are off the case."

"Off the Party Crasher?" Moss said, his eyes widening in disbelief. "That's impossible! I'm the most—"

"No *arguments*!" Captain Brix shouted. He forced himself to calm down. "The condition you're in, hell, if it weren't for this Lang character's request, I'd make you report sick and just stay home!"

"Oh, Jesus, Captain!" Moss said angrily. "If it weren't for that little bastard, my arm wouldn't be broken in the first place!"

"*What?*" Brix looked utterly confused.

"The billboard . . . ," Moss began. "Oh, never mind, that doesn't even matter." He leaned forward over the Captain's cluttered desk and came as close to pleading as John Moss could. "Dammit, sir, you can't pull me off the Party Crasher, not now! He's playing a game with us. He's popped four people right in front of us and he's laughing all the way to the armory!"

"Moss," Brix said wearily, "for once, you are going to have to listen to me. You are off the case. You are in no condition to take this guy on."

"But I *have* to," Moss insisted. "I saw this guy, close up and personal, Captain. We stared at each other, eyeball to eyeball. And believe me, what I saw, well . . . he's no garden-variety lunatic. He's . . . well, you know what I saw in his eyes?"

Captain Brix shook his head. "No, Moss," he said wearily, "I don't."

"I saw pleasure," Moss said somberly. "He's gone, Captain. Way gone. And he's gonna do it again and again until I—that is, until *we* bring him down!"

Brix shook his head. "I'm sorry, Moss, but this order comes straight from the Mayor. I guess this little candy ass has some kind of pull."

Moss tried another tactic. "Okay, tell me this—how's this guy whose face is plastered all over the city gonna hang around and not draw a crowd?" he asked. "He'll endanger everyone he's near, *hell*, he'll endanger *himself*!"

Brix sighed. "He's going to be incognito," he said.

"You mean, like . . . disguised?" Moss said in disbelief. For a moment, he was shocked beyond words. "What the hell does he think this is, a fuckin' *movie*?"

"Moss . . . "

"He gonna bring along his hairdresser? His makeup artist? Maybe his *set decorator*?" Moss's voice seemed to rise one decibel per word.

"Calm down," Brix said. "I don't know exactly how he's planning to pull it off, but he's got to blend in, just be another cop. And he certainly can't do it if everyone knows he's Nick Lang."

Moss was lost in thought, the wheels churning fast. "What if they . . . just find out, I mean, like his disguise falls off or something?"

Brix glared. "If Nick Lang's disguise falls *off*, Moss," he warned, "I will hold you personally responsible and you will be forced to walk a beat again. Got it?"

Moss shrugged sullenly.

"And," the Captain continued, "from now on, there's no Nick Lang. He's Ray Cazenov."

Moss snorted in derision. "Cute," he said snidely.

" . . . and the official word is you are breaking in a new partner while you're incapacitated. And whatever you do, don't, I repeat, *don't* get him too close to any action."

"Right, he's made of glass, he'll break, that's it?" Moss said, sarcasm dripping from his words.

Brix shrugged. "I don't know what he's made of," he said, "but I do know that if he so much as gets a scratch on him, the Mayor's gonna have our butts for breakfast."

"Captain . . ."

"No, Moss," Brix said firmly. "This is an order, and you are dismissed."

Moss had no choice. He saluted and walked out of the Captain's office, smoldering, his psychic temperature rising with every breath and step.

"An actor," he muttered under his breath. "A goddam baby-sitting job for a goddam actor."

He turned a corner and saw a trash can. "I don't believe this is happening to me," he murmured, and then, without thinking, launched a swift kick into the metallic container. It felt good, so he did it again.

"Damned broken arm!" he swore, kicking the hell out of the trash can. The clatter was beginning to draw some attention. "Damned broken arm, damned Party Crasher . . ." With this last damnation, his kick knocked the can on its side.

"Damned actor," he swore under his breath, and kicked the can so hard that it went rolling merrily, noisily, down the linoleumed hallway, out of reach of his foot.

Somewhat mollified, Moss turned away and promptly bumped straight into a pretty, bemused-looking woman who was being escorted around the corner by a uniformed cop.

"Susan!" Moss exclaimed, suddenly mortified. "Uh . . . hi! I mean . . . I didn't expect to see you . . . here, that is. Uh, this morning, that is."

"Hello, John," she said calmly. Her expression turned to concern. "John, your arm! What happened?"

"Oh, this," Moss shrugged it off. "It's nothing, it's just a bone chip. Listen, Susan . . . "

"John, I can't really talk now," Susan said, "I'm on my way to a counseling session. I just came by to tell you I got all your messages last night, and I would have called you at home but . . . " She looked down, a tinge of embarrassment on her face. "I . . . lost your number. Actually," she corrected, "my

34

daughter lost it, but it was probably an accident. Anyway, I don't think she'd do something like that on purpose."

"Oh, yeah, of course not." Moss nodded, not believing it for a second. He didn't really know very much about kids, but he knew enough to believe that they were capable of all kinds of sneaky, underhanded, heinous actions, especially if they sensed their parents were headed into romantic territory.

Susan looked relieved. "Anyway, I didn't want you thinking I was mad or anything like that. I mean, not that I wasn't a little disappointed when you didn't show up, and yes, I admit that for a bit I did wonder if you could possibly be one of those Cro-Magnon jerks who stand people up for no reason, so I went out and that's why I wasn't there when you called, but . . . "

"Uh huh," Moss said, his head spinning. He really liked this woman. He hadn't been exaggerating when he talked to Skate Cain, but God, she could overexplain everything. That, he reflected, was probably a part of this whole therapist thing, something he didn't have the least interest in. "Well, at least you got the messages."

Susan smiled. "And then I saw you on the news, and I was glad Bonnie was already asleep." Her smile widened into a grin. "I read lips," she said.

Moss shrugged defensively. "Hey, I was quoted out of context. Reporters, you know, they can be real assho—uh, irritating."

Susan smiled knowingly. "Well, look, I've got to get going, John. I just wanted to see how you were doing. It's not as if I expected to pick up where we left off, like dinner tonight at eight instead of last night at eight . . . so, well, see you later."

She turned to go, and Moss put his arm on hers as her intent dawned on him. "Say, uh, Susan, what *about* tonight?"

Susan tried to look surprised. "What about it?"

Moss shrugged casually. "Dinner?" he asked. "About eight?"

Susan grinned. "Well, now that you mention it, I don't have any plans."

Moss felt relieved. "Good. I'll give you a call later, okay? Figure out a place?"

"Great," Susan said briskly, all business now. "I'm looking forward to it."

He watched her walk away, confused once again by the workings of the female mind. Then he shrugged and headed for the muster room.

Inside the gathering place, the usual chaos reigned. Cops in uniform, cops in plainclothes, undercover cops looking like bums and bag ladies and hookers, they all gathered there, buying junk food from the vending machines, drinking endless quarts of coffee, and chattering about their latest collars, cases, divorces, and test scores. Moss automatically went for the coffee pot and, holding his cup awkwardly in his left hand, poured himself some of the thick, bitter brew.

"Moss," China said consolingly, "I'm sorry you got yanked—it's not fair. And to get stuck breaking in a new guy, jeez . . . " She shook her head in sympathy.

Moss nodded. "It's the pits," he agreed.

Billy wandered over and chimed in, "Yeah, and especially after you got such a good look at the rat-bastard psycho, too."

Moss could feel his fury rising again. He wanted this collar, and he deserved it. There was no way, he thought, no way at all that he was going to back off. No matter what he had agreed to with the Captain. After all, he reasoned, it wasn't as if he had really agreed to *anything*. He'd been, well, *coerced*. Moss ignored the conversation around him, as he tried, once again, to get into the killer's head. What drove him? Who was he? And why did he hand out warnings the way Hansel and Gretel left a trail of breadcrumbs, assuring himself an audience before he struck? Maybe he was an ex-cop, Moss thought, maybe . . .

"You must be Cazenov," he heard Grainy say. Startled by the name, Moss blinked and came back to reality.

36

He turned slowly in his tracks and studied the young man who stood just inside the doorway to the muster room, a young man who exuded enough attitude for a platoon of South Bronx homeboys.

It was him all right, Moss thought grimly, but . . . different. Nick Lang had gotten rid of his trademark longish, finely styled ginger brown hair. The hair was now dark and cropped almost punk spiky. The cute, youthful face that made girls flock to see Joe Gunn was partially hidden behind a dark, bushy mustache. The tight, tattered jeans, the strap-jangling motorcycle boots, the black leather jacket and the Ray•Bans, the toothpick being worked around in his mouth . . . Holy Jesus God, Moss thought, he thinks he's fuckin' James Dean or something. It was worse than he had dreamed.

"Cazenov?" Grainy repeated.

"Fuckin' A," Lang replied, with a cocky grin. "That's me."

Well, thought Moss, *that* hadn't changed, that famous cocky grin. Moss hated him on sight. Moss thought nastily to himself that Mr. Lang-Cazenov had a real lesson in cockiness and attitude coming his way. This was the asshole from the billboard, the asshole who had ruined his chance to bring in the Party Crasher, the asshole responsible for the cast on his arm, the asshole who was now about to try to put a crimp in his career by attaching himself like some leech to him, Moss, while he was allegedly disabled. Sorry, Captain Brix, he thought fleetingly, but this just ain't gonna work.

Meanwhile, the cops around the room surveyed the newcomer with jaded eyes. For all they knew, he really *was* a rookie. He certainly had that know-it-all attitude, which they all figured would be smashed to smithereens in about one week on the job. In the meantime, they would be tolerant. And amused.

China walked over to him. "I'm China," she said, holding out her hand.

Lang shook it. "Say hey," he said casually.

What? thought Moss.

"You know," China said thoughtfully, "has anybody ever told you that you look a little like that actor . . . what's his name?"

"The one on the billboard?" Moss inquired helpfully.

Lang threw a glance in his direction, and Moss thought he saw a flicker of recognition behind the dark glasses.

"Yeah," said Grainy, "that guy, you know, Nick Lang."

Lang smiled a self-satisfied smile. "One or two people have . . . ," he began.

"You really do, kind of," China said. "But you're a lot . . . shorter."

Lang looked startled, then shrugged it off. "Well . . . ," he said.

Before Moss could see how Lang was going to extricate himself from this, Cain stuck his head in the room. "Okay, ladies," he announced, "tea time's over. Party Crasher briefing in the squad room."

The cops gathered up their belongings and trooped out. As Moss began to file out automatically with the rest of the cops, Cain stopped him with a look. "Sorry, pard," he said apologetically, "but Brix let it be known in no uncertain terms that you aren't in on this one anymore."

Moss stopped, fuming in his tracks.

Cain nodded in sympathy. "I know," he said, and then, lowering his voice, he indicated Lang with a jerk of the head. He said, "And look what you got stuck with. Jesus, talk about bad luck."

Then he was gone, and Moss was left alone in the room with Lang, who swaggered up to him. "I heard what that guy said."

"Yeah?" Moss said. "So you've got ears, how unusual. Congratulations."

Lang shrugged off the sarcasm. "Well, you know what they say, if it wasn't for bad luck, I wouldn't have no luck at all. Seems to apply, huh?"

"What the fuck are you talking about?" snapped Moss. He was feeling positively molten, a volcano about to erupt any second.

Lang looked startled. He pulled his sunglasses down an inch and peered at Moss, wide-eyed. "Hey, Moss," he said in a low, confidential voice, "calm down, it's me." He extended his hand. "Nick Lang."

Moss looked at Nick Lang's hand as if it was a coiled rattlesnake. Then he reached out with his own hand and, with one quick motion, ripped the fake mustache off.

Nick Lang yelped in pain.

"Don't worry," Moss assured him, "I know who you are."

SIX

THE HEAVY DOOR THAT LED TO THE BOOKING AREA flew open with a bang and John Moss strode through, eyes steely and fixed. In his wake, the shorter, hipper Nick Lang, aka Ray Cazenov, struggled to keep up.

"Hey, Moss!" Lang said, as they passed through the bustling hallway, which led to a wide open area full of cops and perps. "Moss!"

John Moss just kept walking.

"You know something?" Lang said, sort of hopping along beside him. "That was a really good idea back there."

Off Moss's blank look, Lang hurried on, "You know, ripping the mustache off. I mean, really, who was I gonna fool with that phony-looking thing anyway, right? And besides, it was itching me like a son of a gun." Lang chattered on, seemingly oblivious to Moss's lack of response. "You wanna know something? I honestly can't remember being this jazzed about anything since the Golden Globes. You knew I won one of those, didn't you? Oh, well, I guess that kinda stuff doesn't matter so much here, like here in the real world, huh?"

Moss wheeled around a corner, Lang dogging his footsteps, talking a mile a minute. "I mean, think about it, a cop like you, teachin' me the street, the two of us comparing scars." Lang paused for a breath, then barreled on. "And you know, you might not believe this, but I've had a coupla tough scrapes, myself. In fact, my stunt double on *Smoking Gunn II* had the flu for two days, and I had to do my own action scenes—took an elbow in the face; my nose musta bled for a good ten minutes."

Two plainclothesmen filed past, leading three handcuffed hookers behind them. One of the girls, dressed in a gold lamé string bikini bottom and a vinyl jacket, winked at Lang, who swiveled in his tracks.

"Whoa . . . ," Lang said, walking backward, his eyes glued to the retreating threesome, "this place is really great, you know. I mean, for a method actor to be here, to get the look, the textures . . . "

He turned to address Moss and just barely missed colliding with a huge, unshaven bum in layers of filthy clothing.

" . . . the smell," Lang said, a little less enthusiastically. Then he recovered and hurried to catch up with Moss. "I mean, it's just like a movie, it's so *real* . . . "

Moss banged through another door, this one leading to a stairwell. He still hadn't said a word.

"And hey, Moss," Lang said earnestly, "don't worry about me fitting in around here, okay? Like doing something I shouldn't, saying something stupid . . . I really worked on this, came prepared. I mean, I did my homework—read up on police procedure, leafed through a coupla Joseph Wambaugh books, got the lingo down and everything."

A uniformed cop clattered by them on his way down the stairs.

"Yo! Homeboy!" Lang called out.

The cop shot Lang a peculiar look, threw a covert glance of pity in Moss's direction, and kept going.

Moss continued up the stairs, Lang keeping pace a little breathlessly. "And I've been working out, too. My trainer's had me on Nautilus *and* Aerobicise, so there'll be no problem keeping up."

Moss flew through a door leading to another hall, and then another door, which banged back, smacking Nick Lang hard enough to make him stumble as he found himself in the men's room.

Lang took a quick look at himself in the fly-specked mirror, ran a hand over his spiked hair, and caught up with Moss at the urinals, just as Moss unzipped his pants.

"You know, Moss, I noticed that I'm the one doing all the talking here. I guess that means you're not much of a morning person, which is fine. I can relate to that, it's in character. I mean, I'm the same way before Esperanza brings me that first cup of cappuccino. Decaf, of course. My nutritionist is trying to get me off caffeine . . . whoa! Careful there, buddy!"

Lang had to jump back as Moss turned, nearly spraying him. Moss zipped up and slammed out into the hallway again. Lang checked himself in the mirror on the way out.

In the hall, Lang kept on as though there were two people participating in the conversation, while Moss barreled straight ahead with intense purpose written all over his lean, set face.

"So . . . here's the thing," Lang said. "I was wondering . . . in the interest of maximizing the reality of the experience, learning absolutely everything there is to know about being a cop . . . do I get a gun?"

Moss finally turned to look at Lang, and his expression was somewhere between blank and manic.

"Well, come on, you know," Lang said cajolingly, "for realism!"

Moss wondered fleetingly if he should simply strangle the little idiot right there. After all, he was disguised. Maybe they would never know he was really Nick Lang. Maybe it would be worth it, even if they did.

Lang continued, sublimely unaware. "I mean, I *am* supposed to be a cop, and it's not like I'd actually use it or anything. Although," he said thoughtfully, "bullets might be a good idea . . . just in case."

Moss shot him a look of horror, and pushed open a door. He blocked Lang pointedly with his body, and slammed the door shut behind him.

"Oh." He heard Lang's voice penetrating the pebbled glass of the door top. "You need some time alone? I can relate to that."

43

Moss strode to the Captain's desk and came to an abrupt halt, his body language reading red alert. He leaned forward and hissed at the Captain, "Not if you tied my tongue to your tailpipe and drove me eighty miles an hour naked across a field of broken glass."

"Moss," Captain Brix said calmly, "what a pleasant surprise."

"Not if you stuck bamboo shoots under my fingernails and wired my balls to an electric light socket . . . "

Brix sighed. "Why is it I find myself hoping against hope that this unexpected visit doesn't have anything to do with your current assignment and a certain actor?"

Moss exploded. "I gave the little dick a chance!" he said.

"What chance?" Captain Brix consulted his watch. "Five, eight minutes?"

"I got all the way to the bathroom and back!" Moss yelled. "He doesn't belong here! He belongs back in never-never land, with his maid and his stunt doubles and his nutritionist and his astrologer and his personal trainer and, for all I know, the guy who wipes his butt after he takes a dump! But he doesn't belong here with me!"

Brix shook his head. "Forget it, Moss," he said. "I'm not in the mood to hear any bullshit about a perfectly simple assignment. You're going to do this gig, and that's it. Period. Not up for discussion."

Moss leaned forward farther and smiled. It was not a pleasant smile. "Guess what?" he said.

"What?" the Captain repeated resignedly.

"He wants to carry a loaded weapon," Moss said softly.

Brix's eyes narrowed. "Send that little jizzball in here," he snapped.

Moss's smile had started to turn from malicious to triumphant when there was a knock at the door and Nick Lang stuck his spiky coiffed head inside the office, flashing that famous charming smile.

"I'm sorry . . . excuse me, Captain Brix? I'm Nick Lang.

44

I hope I'm not interrupting something important, but I just wanted to say hi, since I understand you're the only one in on our little secret. By the way, the Mayor sends his regards."

Moss bit back his smile and watched expectantly, waiting for the fireworks to happen. Well, diplomatic fireworks, given Brix's rank and all, but still . . .

Lang moved forward to stand beside Moss and stuck out his hand. Brix shook it. Moss was suddenly suspicious. Why did Brix look so . . . friendly? Why did he suddenly seem so . . . happy? Why was his handshake so limp and . . . oh, for Christ's sake! *Nervous?*

"I can't tell you how much I appreciate all the effort and all your help in coordinating this," Nick Lang said, all grateful charm.

Brix looked as though he'd just seen God. "Oh," he said modestly, "it's nothing."

"Really?" Moss said through clenched teeth.

Brix ignored the interruption. "I can't tell you how . . . happy I am, I mean, my wife is just such a fan of yours. I mean, we're *both* such big fans!"

Moss thought, Why don't you just lean over and lick his phony biker boots?

"Thank you, Captain," Lang said, all sincerity and puppy eyes. "I know that I couldn't do it without people like you. In fact . . . ," he paused to pretend to think and snapped his fingers, "you should come to L.A. for the premiere of the movie. I'll roll out the red carpet for you and your wife!"

"Really?" Brix looked embarrassed and pleased.

Moss felt like throwing up.

"Hell, yes!" Lang said heartily. "You know what? You guys—you and your wife—you can stay at my place!"

There was a heartbeat of a pause, during which Moss was pretty sure Captain Brix was going to have a heart attack and go straight to Hollywood Heaven.

Finally, Brix said, as if he hadn't heard right, "In your *house?*"

"I insist," Lang said graciously. "You'll love it. It's just a modest little spread, but the jacuzzi is terrific, and the tennis court—you do play tennis?—was designed by the guy that redid Forest Hills."

"That sounds wonderful!" Captain Brix said heartily, as if this kind of invitation was an everyday occurrence. "You know," he said to Lang, "your disguise is really quite good."

"Think so?" Lang beamed.

"I wouldn't have known you at all if you hadn't introduced yourself," the Captain assured him.

And I'm the Queen Mother, thought Moss.

"Well," Lang said modestly, "it's not as if I did it all by myself. I had expert help, and they deserve every bit of credit they can get. Of course," he added, "the general *look* was my idea."

Moss couldn't take it anymore. "Captain," he said, feeling his jaw begin to lock up, "what about what we talked about?"

Brix did an excellent job of pretending Moss wasn't in the room at all. He just sat there and beamed at Nick Lang.

"Great," he said. "Terrific. And listen," he turned very serious suddenly, "if there's anything, and I do mean *anything* at all that Lieutenant Moss or I can do for you while you're here . . . "

That was it. Moss couldn't take another fawning word. He turned abruptly on his heel and stalked out the door, slamming it emphatically behind him.

He slouched against the wall outside Brix's office, fuming helplessly. Brix was star-struck, and that meant he was star *stuck*. Jesus, he thought in disgust, who would have thought this could happen to him?

He looked up as the door to Brix's office opened and Nick Lang, beaming with self-congratulatory pleasure, came out. He joined Moss without seeming to notice Moss's displeasure.

46

"Look," Lang said in a conciliatory tone, "I've been thinking about it and . . . we can forget about the gun."

Moss looked at him quizically, the way he might look at a caged banana slug or something in a carnival sideshow labeled as Martian droppings.

"Really?" he said.

Lang nodded. "Yeah. Actually, I think it would be better to maybe wait a day or two."

"A day or two?" Moss echoed. "That long?"

"Well, yeah." Lang apparently had no ear for sarcasm, Moss thought. Either that or Moss was losing his touch.

"Why so long?" Moss prodded him.

Lang's brow furrowed. On him, it was cute. "Verisimilitude," he replied.

"*What?*"

"You know," Lang shrugged, "truth, reality . . . "

"I'm not sure I get this," Moss said.

"It's all a part of the method," Lang assured him. "I really shouldn't have a gun right now."

"I'll second that," Moss said with false geniality.

"After all," Lang continued, oblivious to the implication, "I need some time to really learn the part. I figure, oh, a day or two to get the cop thing down pat."

Moss had felt himself starting to get explosive again when, suddenly, something about Lang's words set a bell of recognition off in his head.

"The gun!" he exclaimed. He started off at a jog.

"Hey," Lang said, keeping up with him, "where are we going?"

Moss smiled at him. Again, it wasn't a pleasant smile. "The next logical place, *partner*," was all he said.

SEVEN

LANG FOLLOWED MOSS AS HE HEADED TOWARD the set of double swinging doors in the Medical Examiner's office and shook his head in apparent admiration of Moss's choice of destination.

"This is *perfect*," he said enthusiastically, "the morgue! You know, the cop in my film—well, it isn't exactly my film yet, but that's the whole purpose of us being together, so I can get that part . . . "

Right, Moss thought, I knew there had to be a reasonable explanation somewhere for this cosmic dog turd of a joke being played on me.

" . . . he has to ID his best friend at the morgue, it's a very heavy scene. Challenging." He reached into an inside pocket of the leather jacket and pulled out a tiny microcassette recorder. "I gotta make some notes."

They came through the doors, and Moss, accustomed to the singular stench of the place, kept on walking. Lang paused in midstride, swallowing hard. He looked around at the mess—corpses in various states of disassembly, everywhere, some stacked on top of each other; instruments in disarray, left lying casually by the bodies. The tiny recorder dropped unnoticed from his hand.

"Jeez . . . ," Lang murmured, putting a handkerchief up to his nose.

Moss noticed with glee that Lang's face seemed a bit paler than it had a few minutes before. Unfazed by his surroundings, Moss walked over to the middle of the room, where Grainy stood, observing Felix Addams, the Medical Examiner, as he worked on a body.

Moss indicated the clutter and the mess. "Little thick in here, Felix, don't you think?"

"Backed up," Felix said, without even looking up. "Busload a' Shriners flipped over. Who's your friend?"

Lang gave a feeble half wave, clutching the side of a gurney. "Ray Cazenov," he said from behind the handkerchief.

Felix peered up for a second, his light eyes magnified behind thick glasses. "Hey," he said, "anybody ever tell you you look like Nick Lang?"

"Uh . . . ," said Lang.

"But . . . shorter," Felix said, turning his attention back to the corpse in front of him. "I like that guy's movies," he continued cheerfully. "I counted fifty-six bodies in *Smoking Gunn*, can't wait to see the sequel."

"Felix," Moss cut in impatiently, "you done the guy from the Power Station yet?"

"This is him." Felix nodded toward the corpse he was working on. "Or is that this is *he*?"

"Whatever." Moss shrugged as he surveyed the body clinically. The chest wounds were the only colorful thing left about the pallid dead man. Moss and Grainy watched, unaffected, as Felix began to probe the wounds with a pencil, dictating into a recorder as he pushed and prodded.

"Two clean chest wounds an inch apart," Felix said. "Entered point-blank range . . . center of mass, very professional . . . unusually large entry holes . . . "

There was a clatter as Nick Lang fainted dead away, his body coming to an awkward rest on the floor, right next to a corpse on a stretcher.

"Sensitive sort, your new partner." Grainy grinned at Moss.

"And look at this," said Felix, turning the body over and continuing to probe, "this circle pattern around his spine, looks like acne . . . "

"Glaser safety slugs," Moss said, recognizing the pattern. "That makes sense. I got a look at the perp's gun, ramp 'n' throat job, heavier barrel."

Grainy nodded. "And the shell casings they found didn't have stamps on them."

Felix looked up briefly. "Nothing to do with a gun like that but kill people." He shrugged and went back to work. "The guy knows his weapons."

"Or," Moss said thoughtfully, "he knows somebody who does."

Lang began to come around. His eyes fluttered open and he spotted the corpse lying next to him. Stifling a yell, he scrambled up abruptly. He casually stretched and yawned, trying to look utterly unaffected by his surroundings. "Jet lag," he said. "Guess I must've dozed off."

A few minutes later, Moss and Lang were back in Moss's car. Moss was weaving skillfully, if dangerously, through the congested traffic. Lang, still pale and queasy, was breathing into a paper sack. He flinched as Moss swerved to avoid a collision, laying on the horn and screaming at the driver next to him.

"Guess cops can drive as fast as they want to, huh?" Lang asked weakly.

Moss veered sharply to the right and screeched around a corner, barely avoiding three pedestrians in a crosswalk.

Lang gulped, trying to keep his nausea at bay. Finally, he broke the silence. "Seems to me," he said, "there's a pattern developing in our conversations . . . I talk, and you ignore me." There was no response from Moss, and Lang continued on. "Okay, Moss . . . maybe it's time we aired things out between us. I'm sensing that you're not entirely happy with this situation."

Moss, jerked back from an emerging suspicion about the origins of the gun, narrowed his eyes. He glanced over at

Lang, deadpan, but said nothing. His eyes were flat and cold. Then he looked back at the road. He pulled a cigarette from his pocket, thought about lighting it, and tossed it in the street instead.

"I can respect that," Lang assured him. "But the fact is, there's a lot we share, and we're more alike than you seem to think." Moss felt himself tense but remained silent. How long could this schmuck babble before he got the hint?

"Really," Lang continued earnestly, "an actor approaches acting by getting to the emotional truth of the scene. It's a lot like a cop investigating a case." He paused expectantly, but there was only stony silence in the car. "Moss," he said finally, "I'm here because you're the best at what you do, you're a genuine heavyweight, a kind of Yoda among cops."

Moss shot him an incredulous look.

"Little guy, big ears?" Lang said, trying to joke. It fell flat. "Look," he continued doggedly, "whatever you think about me, I have all the respect in the world for you. I just want you to know that, to know where I'm coming from."

That was it. Moss tried to control his rage, but enough was finally enough. "Look, dickwad," he exploded, turning to Lang, "I don't give a rat's ass where you're coming from! The only thing I care about is where you're *going*!"

"Good, this is good," Lang said, nodding in satisfaction. "Now at least we're talking."

Moss felt his blood pressure zoom. "Where do I drop you off?" he said through clenched teeth. "Plaza, Regency, where? Just give me a name."

Lang looked surprised. "I'm staying with you," he said.

There was a beat of thick silence before Moss managed to say, *"Me?"*

"Uh huh," Lang nodded.

"When my asshole learns how to chew gum," Moss said flatly.

"Now look," Lang said, beginning to get angry. No one treated him this way. "I've got my bags in the back; this was all arranged!"

"Not with *me!*" Moss exclaimed. "No one arranged jack *shit* with *me!*"

"Listen, Moss . . . "

"No, you listen, you little fuck!" Moss yelled, completely out of control. The car swerved dangerously. "You pulled some strings and got me yanked off a priority case just so you could get your rocks off being around cops! But I've got a job to do, and I'm gonna do it, and I don't have time for anyone in this car who isn't either a cop or the Party Crasher!"

Lang's eyes widened as he stared at Moss's livid face, with the bottom line of the situation finally dawning on him. "So *that's* what this is really about, isn't it?" he demanded. "That's why you went to the coroner's. You're still going after this guy." His face lit up with excitement at the prospect. My God, he thought, this was better than even he had anticipated, a real murder investigation. A real pursuit of a real killer! And he was *in* on it!

Moss glanced over at him coldly, all the fire of his anger tamped down again. He couldn't believe he had just slipped and let this little jerk in on the secret. "Just give me a hotel name, or I bounce your ass out at the next light."

But Lang had a card to play now. "I don't know, Moss," he said genially. "You really think that's such a good idea? Personally—and you're free to disagree with me, of course— but personally, I sense that Captain Brix wouldn't be very *happy* if you did that. You know, us being separated like that, and you being back on the case. I mean, you *were* told to stay off it, right?"

Moss shot him a laser look.

Lang shrugged, his face a mask of innocence. "Not that *I'd* tell the Captain anything. I mean, if you can't trust your partner, who *can* you trust?" He smiled blandly over at Moss.

Moss told himself this was it—a death sentence. His short hairs, he thought, steaming in silence, were being firmly clutched in Lang's hands. But there had to be a way out, didn't there? Then it struck him: if he couldn't get the actor off his back the way he had planned, maybe he could just *scare* him off.

Lang seemed to be content with his temporary victory. He sat in smug silence, watching the progressively deteriorating pockets of the city as they rode through them. Moss smiled grimly as he turned the car into the worst section yet, a dark canyon of buildings—run-down, abandoned, gutted, and burned; hideouts for junkies, shooting galleries, drug dealers' paradise. It was an urban war zone, littered with trash and stripped auto shells. Few people came out even during the day.

There was one ostentatiously incongruous note, however, on a block that otherwise had the ambience of Beirut: a pristine, cherry red 1990 Cadillac, showroom clean and bright, parked right in the middle of the block.

"What's *that* doing here?" Lang asked as Moss pulled up and parked right across the street from the car.

Moss didn't bother to reply. He pulled out his gun and checked the clip, then shoved it back under his jacket. Lang, following suit, reached back and opened one of his bags. He pulled out a badge and a small gun in an ankle holster.

Lang saw Moss stare in disbelief as he strapped the gun to his leg. "Oh, this? No problem," Lang assured him. "I got these from props. The gun's rubber, it's just to help me get into character till I get the real thing."

Moss blinked. "Great," he said flatly. "Dickless Tracy."

Then, with great effort, Moss pulled himself out of the car, wincing as the pain from his cracked ribs shot through his torso, reminding him of his limited mobility. Holding his side, he straightened up and surveyed the gutted street. Lang emerged from the passenger door as Moss went to the trunk. He popped it open, took out a baseball bat, and swung it

54

casually in his hand as he started across the street. Lang followed eagerly.

"Hey," Moss said, glancing over at him. "You stay here."

"What do you mean?" Lang protested. "I wanna come."

Moss gave him a look that brooked no argument. He pointed back at the car. "Stay!" he barked.

Lang walked sullenly back to the sedan and watched as Moss disappeared into the dark cavern of a seemingly abandoned tenement. "I sit and roll over, too," Lang muttered to himself.

He slouched resentfully against the car, wondering if he was going to miss the really good action, wondering why Moss had such a hard-on about him. After all, it wasn't as if the cop could actually do anything in his present condition. Most people would be flattered to have Nick Lang tagging around after them asking questions.

Lang glanced around at his war-zone surroundings and began to perk up. This was a new world for him. This was John Moss's world, and even more important, this was Tony DiBennedetti's world. Nick Lang, on the other hand, had never seen anything like it before. He perked up a little more. After all, he was here to do research, wasn't he? And this was research at its grittiest—this was real, this was texture, this was down-and-dirty true-life stuff; best of all, it would all go into making him a gritty, true-life cop on screen.

Lang held up his hands and, putting thumbs together and forefingers straight up, made three sides of a square with his fingers. He framed the scene, turning this way and that, "panning" the street with his make-believe camera. He got into it a little more, turning left to frame a burned-out building with gaping holes where its windows used to be, turning right to frame some particularly colorful gang graffiti scrawled on a wall.

As he swung around again, he was startled to find himself face to face with a raggedy street person, standing not two feet from him. Lang gasped and jumped back. The man's hair was matted and greasy; his clothes, layer after layer of filthy, tattered rags. His face was streaked with dirt and, Lang thought, God knew what else. The man just stood and stared at Lang, his dark eyes unreadable.

Lang forced himself to remain calm. After all, this was just another person. This was all a part of the experience.

He flashed his famous, charming smile at the man. "Hi," said Lang. "How ya doin'?"

The man stared at him silently for a few seconds, as if considering his reply. Then a grin split his filthy face, revealing a few blackened teeth and dark gaping spaces.

At least, Lang thought, repressing a shudder, he's smiling.

The raggedy man finally spoke. His tone was matter-of-fact, almost cheerful. "I might have to kill you later," he informed Lang, still smiling.

EIGHT

MOSS PICKED HIS WAY QUIETLY THROUGH THE RUB-
ble that lay strewn around the remains of the tenement. Moving
like a cat, he avoided the broken hunks of plaster, the bottles
and rusted cans, the occasional syringe—anything that might
make noise, that might reveal his presence here before he
wanted it to be known. This was the territory of a gang called
the Dead Romeos, and Moss, who had encountered them on
more than one less-than-legal occasion, knew the advantage
lay with surprise. Especially when you were outnumbered.

He followed vague sounds up a filthy flight of stairs
and moved carefully down a hallway, keeping close to the
graffiti-covered walls. As he approached the door at the end
of the hall, he could hear the sounds of laughter. He thought
this was a perfect place to be ambushed, but he resolutely
pushed the thought aside.

"Hey," he heard a young man say from behind the door,
"you hear what the bitch said? I say, let's waste her."

Oh, well, Moss thought, so much for preparation time. He
set himself in position, and ignoring the jab of pain from his
ribs, he took a deep breath and kicked the door in.

Six gang members stared at him in amazement, jumping
to get up, to get away.

"What the fuh?" said one of them, his eyes darting
from Moss's badge to the bat he brandished and back
again.

57

One young man made a quick break for it, but Moss intercepted him, jabbing his bat through the rotten plaster of the wall and clotheslining the guy at neck level. The kid crashed into the bat and fell gasping to the floor, clutching his neck.

It was then that Moss noticed the large-screen Sony blaring "The Love Connection." He realized the bitch he had heard about, the bitch they wanted to waste, was a contestant on the show.

Moss pointed at the television. "What'd she do, pick the wrong guy?" Then he glanced down at the kid still on the floor. "No need to get up, really."

Moss surveyed the antagonistic faces ringed around him. "I just need a little information, guys, and then I'll be outta here faster than you can say search warrant."

No one said a word, but the hostility was palpable. Moss glanced at the broken furniture, the skin mags on the floor, the half-smoked joint burning on the top of a beer can.

"Let's reacquaint ourselves," Moss said, strolling around the room. "*I'm* Lieutenant Moss . . . and for those of you who've done too much dust and have *really* short attention spans, *you're* the Dead Romeos." He wasn't particularly surprised when no one laughed.

A burly youth spoke up. "Not us. You got the wrong guys, Lieutenant. We a reading group."

"No kidding?" Moss said genially. "Reading, huh? I hear you dabble in a little creative writing, too. You know, bad checks, ransom notes, forgeries, that kinda stuff."

"Say what?" said the burly youth.

"Oh," Moss pointed to the graffiti on the wall, "and by the way, there's only one k in suck." He came to a closed door. "So, let me guess, this must be the reading room, right? The place you keep all the books?"

He saw the faces tense up and knocked the door quickly open. Beyond it, just as he had suspected, was a smaller room filled with the gang's illegal cache. There were stolen TVs and VCRs stacked nearly up to the ceiling.

Moss turned to his audience, hoping no one was getting antsy enough to risk wasting a cop. "Gosh, fellas, these sure don't look like the classics to me."

"Shower gifts?" offered one of the guys feebly.

Moss shook his head in mock dismay. "And this is exactly why Johnny can't read . . . too much TV." His smile was thin. "You guys wanna graduate from school, get decent jobs."

"What, like bein' a shit-paid cop like you?" one of the kids snorted.

Moss ignored the insult. "Get decent jobs," he repeated, "maybe take a shot at white-collar crime—that's where the *real* money is."

"What you want, Moss?" the burly leader demanded, cutting through the banter.

"All right, bottom-line time—now we're talking," Moss said approvingly. His eyes swept the room. "Okay, class, time for a pop quiz. Answer correctly, and no one takes away your watching privileges."

Moss positioned himself to pace between them and the television. One kid still had hold of the remote control, and in an elaborate show of ignoring Moss, he clicked continually from channel to channel.

"There's a shooter out there using hollow-point safety slugs in a retooled .45," Moss informed them. "Beefed up gun barrel, laser sight . . . the kind of gun we took from you book lovers in a liquor store last month, remember?"

There was no answer, just a sullen silence filled by the sounds of a commercial for a Mita copier.

"Okay," Moss said. "Now I know and you know it takes a real specialist to modify a gun like that. Might be one or two people in this entire city who can do it." His eyes bored into theirs, one angry face at a time. "And I figure you've got a pretty good idea just who the expert might be."

Click! An ad for Continental Airlines filled the silence.

"Sorry, couldn't hear you over the TV. What was that name again?"

Click. Moss stiffened as he heard Nick Lang's now-familiar voice. "Well, Bryant," he was saying, "I think *Smoking Gunn II* is the kind of film that gives the public a little break from reality. And, frankly, I think we can all use a break once in a while, don't you?"

There was a sudden crash as Moss, without even thinking, smashed his plaster cast through the television screen. "Now," said Moss, "did anybody want to tell me anything?"

Still no answer. Moss shrugged. "You don't learn very fast, do you?" he asked. He stepped into the small cache room and casually swung his bat. "Target practice," he informed the gang, as the first of the televisions exploded into pieces.

Lang was bored. After all, framing shots was a director's job. He leaned into the car and pulled a bag phone from a piece of luggage. As he backed out, he bumped smack into the raggedy man again. He could smell the sour breath and body odor and instinctively shrunk back.

Then he remembered who he was, and what he was doing. "Look, buddy," he said, "just what do you want?"

He half expected the man to start talking about killing him again, but the bum just said, "Change, man. For some wine."

Lang reached impatiently into his pocket and came up with a twenty. "This is all I've got . . . ," he began.

The man snatched it from Lang's hand. "That's okay," he said. He smiled at the bill. "Think I'll get me a hearty cabernet."

Lang stared as the raggedy man wandered off down the street. Oh, well, he thought. He punched out a number on the phone and paced up and down the sidewalk.

"Get me Angie," he said. "It's me, Nick." After a moment, he heard his agent's voice. "Angie," he said excitedly, "you're not gonna believe where I am!" He paused. "No! Not the Russian Tea Room." He listened. "No . . . no . . . no! Forget about guessing, you'll never guess, this is too good." He paused for effect. "I'm in a *ghetto*!" He listened for a moment. "No," he said, "it's not a tour! I'm here with Moss on a *real* case! I mean, this is too much, Ange . . . I've been in town, what, two hours? And I'm already in the middle of a *murder* investigation, can you believe it?"

He listened impatiently as Angie lectured him on the value of his hide, and what the hell did he think he was doing endangering himself like that? What if the insurance company found out?

"It's no problem, Angie," Lang assured her. "I'm safe as a baby with Moss." He glanced nervously up at the tenement Moss had disappeared into. "And besides, I know I'm gonna get the part—I'm positively soaking up the reality of it all, Angie, the grit, the human drama, the crime! You can literally *feel* it, I'm telling you, it's like . . . all *around* you . . . "

And with a whoosh the phone was gone, ripped from Lang's hand.

"Hey!" he screamed at the car full of teenage boys, "Bring that back! Goddammit, bring it back! I need that phone, I'm in the middle of—"

He saw them holding the phone and waving derisively in his direction. "Fine!" Lang exploded angrily. "I'll just tell the cops! There's one right inside that building!"

The car suddenly screeched to a halt and started to back up. The crowd of young faces inside it stared at him in a distinctly unfriendly way.

"Oh . . . shit!" Lang yelped, as he made a mad dash for the tenement. From the relative shelter of the doorway, he screamed, "At least could you just hang it up, it's on my bill!" Then he ducked inside.

"Jesus!" Lang jumped a foot as a huge rat went scurrying by him. He looked around and shuddered. This place was definitely . . . creepy. He wondered where Moss was, and then he began to hear loud crashing sounds coming from somewhere upstairs. Lang glanced nervously out to the street, but the car full of kids was still there. He glanced up at the noise from above. Moss was *probably* there. Lang didn't really seem to have much choice.

He took the steps two at a time and, without thinking, burst through the door to the Dead Romeos' clubhouse. He stopped dead in his tracks as he saw Moss hold up a television and drop it casually to the floor. Lang did a double-take. The room looked as though Moss—or somebody—had just destroyed dozens of televisions and VCRs. Five or six gang members in colors stood around helplessly, watching Moss.

All eyes swiveled to Lang as he burst in. "Moss . . . ," he panted.

"What the hell are you doing here?" Moss snapped.

"Moss . . . ," Lang began again.

"Shut up and stand against that wall and don't *talk*," Moss ordered him.

"Now," Moss said, turning his attention to the gang again, "what could this be?" Moss took a baggie full of white powder, held it up, then bent over and pretended to find it in the rubble.

"That's bullshit!"

"We don't do that stuff!"

"Hey, shit . . . "

Moss held a finger to his lips, and the protests hushed. "Guys, guys . . . guys," he sighed. "Let's play pretend. Pretend you're watching 'Let's Make a Deal,' okay? Get it?"

Lang watched, fascinated by this real-life drama being played out right in front of him, as silent eye contact and signals among the gang members filled the sullen silence.

Finally, the burly one spoke. "Terranova . . . "

Moss's eyes bored into his. "Who?" he demanded.

"It's this dude name of Terranova," the kid repeated. "The gun man."

"Where?" Moss snapped. "Where can I find him?"

The kid shrugged. "*You* can't," he said pointedly. "He moves around a lot, works out of a van. He . . . makes guns. Whatever you want, special."

"Well, well," Moss said thoughtfully.

"Moss," Lang said, "if you're about done here, I've got a crime to report. A bunch of kids stole my bag phone."

"I told you to wait in the car!" Moss snapped.

"Hey," said one of the gang members, peering at Lang, "anybody ever tell you you look like that Nick Lang dude?"

"I know, I know," Lang said impatiently, "but shorter, right?"

"Yeah, man, and whiter!"

"Look, Moss, I'm sorry, it's just that these guys look like they might be a *gang*!"

"What gang?" demanded the burly kid.

Moss stared manically from Lang to the burly kid and back.

"Get down!" he shouted, as the room erupted in gunfire.

Moss threw himself bodily on top of Lang as the windows blew out, shattered by gunfire from the car full of kids who had stolen Lang's phone. Walls splintered, the Dead Romeos dove for cover, and Lang squirmed. Then the shooting was over as abruptly as it had started, and they heard the car screech away in the distance.

Moss got up and grabbed Lang, pulling him roughly to his feet. All around them, the Dead Romeos were surveying the damage and reaching for hidden weapons.

"We gotta go now, Moss," said the burly kid meaningfully.

Moss glanced at the armory of illegal weapons.

"You got what you came for," the leader reminded him.

Moss looked him in the eye and nodded. "Okay," he said. Then he yanked Lang unceremoniously out the door and into the hallway.

"Moss . . . " Lang was hanging back.

"What!"

Lang peered at him with one hazel eye and one brown one. "I think I lost a contact in there," he said.

"You little asshole!" Moss exploded, pulling Lang with him down the stairway, "you told them I was in there! You led them *right to* a rival gang, not to mention right to *me*! You could've gotten everyone in there *killed*!"

"Hey!" Lang snapped back, "I tried to warn you! I said it was a gang . . . " He paused and looked proud of himself. "That's great, I knew it was a gang!" He nodded. "Yup, I think I've got a knack for this stuff."

"Knack?" Moss seethed, pulling the actor along. "Good! Then tell me what the license plate of the car they drove was!" He stared challengingly at Lang.

Lang just looked blank. "License plate?"

"Not even a partial?" Moss sneered. "You want an education, Hollywood? Well, you just flunked Cop 101!"

Moss burst through the door, dragging Lang with him. The street was utterly deserted now. Not even the raggedy man lingered in the wake of the shooting.

Moss pointed across the street. "Notice anything different about the car?" he asked Lang, sarcasm dripping from his words.

"Oh, my God!" Lang gasped.

The car was stripped. Doors, trunk, and hood stood gaping open. The radio and hubcaps were gone. Getting closer, they could see that the seats were slashed and Lang's suitcases were gone, although a trail of clothing led across the street to the door of a seedy bar with a broken beer sign in its window.

"All my clothes were in that bag!" Lang yelped, outraged.

"At least they didn't get your rubber-ducky gun," Moss said, with a sharklike smile.

Lang narrowed his eyes. "They're in that bar, Moss," he said, pointing to the trail that led to the door of the dive. "You gotta go in there. You gotta get my things back."

Moss grinned, leaning against what was left of the car. "Gotta?" he repeated dubiously. "Nah, that's not procedure, Lang." He grinned at Lang. "This stuff takes *time*. First, you have to fill out the proper forms, then *maybe* I get assigned to the case. I ask some questions," he said, glancing down at his fingernails, "file a report, takes days. Weeks, sometimes . . . "

Lang stared, fuming. "Fine!" he snapped finally. "I know what you're doing. And if this is how you want to play hardball, no problem—I'll get them myself!" He started determinedly toward the seedy bar, calling over his shoulder, "You think I'm scared, you think this is some kind of *test* or something . . . well, Moss, we'll see who flunks *this* one!" And with that, he disappeared through the dark entryway to the bar.

Moss leaned against the car, pulled a cigarette out of his pocket, and, unlit, stuck it in his mouth. He wore just a trace of a smile on his face. Keeping his eyes on the dark bar, he counted softly, "One . . . two . . . three . . . four . . . "

On the count of six, Lang's body was hurled through a blacked-out plate glass window and landed in a pile of trash outside. Moss just stayed where he was, watching.

After a moment, Lang sat up, dazed but unhurt. He looked up at the shattered window, looked down at himself, then looked at Moss. He picked himself up and, with some attempt at dignity, started to brush the clinging garbage off his clothes.

"They said they didn't have them," he told Moss.

"No kidding," Moss replied.

NINE

MOSS CASUALLY PULLED THE CAR TO A STOP IN A No Parking zone in downtown Manhattan. He seemed to be oblivious to the emotion known as embarrassment, but Nick Lang, crouched down as low as possible in the passenger seat, wasn't. Lang cringed as he saw the stares the car elicited from even the most jaded passersby.

"Moss," Lang ventured mildly, "are you absolutely *sure* that impound didn't have something a little more, uh . . . low profile?"

It had taken them over two hours to get the mess with the trashed sedan straightened out. That included the time it took to stop the uniforms who had finally responded to their distress call from laughing too hard to get the wreck towed away, the actual time it took to get the battered sedan towed to the yard and fill out the paperwork needed for an explanation, and the time it took to be issued a new vehicle.

Lang could understand the hassle and the time spent— *that* was no problem—and he could understand the scarcity of decent-looking cars, but he was pretty sure he couldn't understand *this*, this . . . *thing* they were currently riding around in. It was a ten-year-old Lincoln, lowered nearly to the ground and painted three shades of electric blue. It was outfitted with every conceivable accoutrement that might cry out, "Pimpmobile!" From the tatty velour seat covers to the leopard-skin fake fur dashboard to the fuzzy dice hanging from the rearview mirror, this car was a rolling humiliation.

Moss didn't bother to respond to the question. Obviously, being the butt of the street's jokes was no problem for him. Instead, he climbed out from his side and headed for a nearby phone booth. Lang sighed and climbed out after him. It seemed that Moss was giving him the silent treatment once again. Or would that be still? Could you really count the few minutes of verbal outrage back at the Dead Romeos' hangout as "communication"? Lang wasn't sure.

Still, he trudged along. And he perked up as he listened to Moss, who tried—and failed—to keep his conversation a secret.

"Oh, hi, Bonnie," Lang heard him say nervously. Lang bit back a smile of glee. John Moss actually sounded nervous!

"I didn't expect to . . . No, this isn't Mr. Tibor, this is John Mo— . . . No, it isn't Frankie, either. No . . . this isn't Alphonse. What *is* this? Are these guys your mom works with or something?"

Lang smirked. Moss wasn't only nervous, he was jealous! It was nice to know that Moss had feelings, *any* feelings.

"Bonnie," Moss said, "let me get a word in here, okay? This is John Moss. Is your mom home? . . . No, no, I'll call back. Is twenty minutes enough ti— . . . Hello? Hello, Bonnie?" Moss hung up the phone in frustration, and Lang wiped the grin off his face.

Not that Moss seemed to notice. Preoccupied, he walked down the street to a hot dog vendor, Lang tagging along after him.

"Frog dog, Billy," Moss said to the vendor.

Lang watched curiously as the vendor handed Moss a hot dog and a paper envelope of french fries. Moss promptly poured the fries over the dog, then topped the mound off with a huge glob of mustard. Lang stared, studying every move, as Moss picked the entire thing up without spilling a single fry and, in one bite, devoured half the dog.

"Wow," Lang said. He turned to the vendor. "I'll have a frog dog, too."

Moss sank down on some steps nearby as the vendor handed Lang his dog and fries. "Thanks," said Lang. "Do you happen to have any Grey Poupon?"

"Wattaya?" The vendor glared at him. "From yuppie Pluto or somethin'?"

"Just kidding," Lang said hastily, taking the dog from the man's hand.

Lang turned his attention to the creation of his frog dog, trying to mimic Moss's every move. He poured the fries over the hot dog, but in his unpracticed hands, more than half of them ended up on the sidewalk. He didn't fare any better with the mustard, which seemed to land mostly on his hand, not on the dog. Finally, he picked up the mess he had created and attempted to shove it into his mouth, just as Moss had done. His chin, his shirt, and the ground got the bulk of it. Lang walked over and sat down on the steps by Moss, chewing thoughtfully on the small amount of dog that had actually managed to reach his mouth.

" . . . iss is good," he said through his food, glancing over at Moss. He shifted position, crossing one leg over the other, mimicking Moss precisely. Moss didn't reply; he merely stared at the sidewalk, preoccupied and glum.

"Girl problems, huh?" Lang ventured. This was something he knew about—maybe they could finally find a common ground.

Moss shot him an affronted look, and Lang indicated the phone booth. "Sorry, I couldn't help overhearing," he said. "Must've been the daughter. I could tell from the way you were talking to her," he continued pragmatically. "I know that route. Young girl, single mother, no dad—the kid doesn't trust men anyway, and especially the ones who hang around her mom. And you want to see more of the mother, but you can't catch a break from the kid, and you *know* mom is going to be ultrasensitive to the little girl's feelings, and you're gonna get stuck simmering on the back burner, right?"

Moss didn't answer, but Lang could tell from the surprised and grudging look on his lean face that he had nailed the situation exactly.

"Well, listen," Lang said. "I have an idea. Why don't you try asking her to bring her daughter along with you guys when you go out some night."

Lang had a feeling the suggestion had hit home, even though Moss was trying hard not to look as if it had.

Moss finished his last bite of dog, and Lang copied the action exactly, down to chewing on one side of the mouth. Well, he thought, looking at the new layer of fries and mustard which had just landed on and around him, maybe not *exactly*, but close.

Lang gulped. "So," he said conversationally, "you eat like this all the time?" Moss continued to stare straight ahead. "You know," Lang continued, "it's probably not the smartest thing, healthwise, that is. Hot dogs aren't absorbed by the body all that easily, and Jesus, you don't even want to *know* what goes into making them. Be good to your bowels, and they'll be good to you, right?"

"Don't tell me," Moss said, finally breaking his own silence, "you learned that from your nutritionist, right?"

Lang was pleased. At last, a response. "Would you like her number?" he asked.

Moss shot him a look.

"Wouldn't hurt," Lang shrugged.

He watched as Moss took out a cigarette and flipped it neatly into his mouth.

"May I?" Lang said, and Moss shrugged as Lang pulled a cigarette out of his pack. He attempted to flip it into his mouth exactly the way Moss had, but he missed his mouth and the cigarette bounced off his chin. Lang fumbled, grabbing it just before it could fall to the ground and take its place amidst the mustard and the fries. He thrust it casually into the corner of his mouth.

Moss jumped to his feet. "Knock that shit off," he said, irritated.

"What?" Lang said, jumping to his feet, too.

"All of it!" Moss snapped. "Quit doing everything I do just the way I do it! Jesus, it's like carrying a goddam mirror around with me, it's nerve-wracking!"

"Nerve-wracking?" Lang echoed, clearly puzzled.

Moss glared. "Don't sit like me, don't eat like me, don't *smoke* like me!" He yanked the cigarette out of his mouth and tossed it away. "I'm trying to quit anyway!"

Lang snatched his own cigarette out of his mouth and tossed it away. "Me, too," he said.

Moss looked as though he might reach over and strangle him.

"Look," Lang said patiently, "it's not personal. It's just that performance is about detail, and the smallest gesture, the tiniest quirk can enhance an actor's—"

"Lang!" Moss yelled.

"What?" said Lang, startled out of his speech.

"I don't care!"

"Oh," said Lang. Okay, he thought, Moss could have the last word; he was welcome to it. As long as there *were* words. This was good; he could sense it intuitively. Moss was beginning to come around, beginning to really respond. He fell briskly into stride with Moss as he returned to the car.

"So . . . ," Lang said, "let's talk about something else."

"Good idea," Moss muttered.

"Why don't you tell me about the Party Crasher?" Lang suggested.

Moss threw his hands up in disgust and kept walking.

But Lang wasn't about to be put off so easily. Not now that there was a chink showing in the communications armor. "Come on, Moss," he said earnestly, "tell me. I mean, this guy kills four, five people, right in front of you . . . What does it take to do something like that, to be someone like that?"

Moss shrugged impatiently. "He's crazy," he said.

"That's it?" Lang asked in disbelief.

Moss shrugged again. "I guess," he said.

"Come on," Lang said, "you work with loonies and murderers all the *time*, you've got to have more insight into it than that!"

"No," said Moss, shaking his head. "I don't. I leave that to the forensic shrinks. As far as I'm concerned, the guy just has too many birds on his antenna. Who knows? How the hell would *I* know what makes a guy like that tick? Besides," he added, "catching them doesn't exactly qualify as 'working with them.' "

"What about that theory that cops and criminals are just flip sides of the same coin?" Lang said curiously.

"It's bullshit," Moss replied succinctly.

Then Lang had a moment of inspiration. He knew it; he knew *exactly* why Moss was stonewalling him on this. "Hey, Moss?" he said.

"What?" Moss said irritably.

"You ever kill anyone?" Lang asked softly.

Moss turned his high-beam look on Lang. There was a heartbeat of silence between them. "Counting today?" he asked.

Without waiting for a reply, he turned to stalk off around to the driver's side of the Lincoln. Lang grabbed his arm and stopped him.

"Wait, Moss," he said. "This is serious, I need to know how it feels. My character kills someone, someone who was just an innocent bystander. I want to know what that's like, knowing you're responsible for something like that."

Moss looked thoughtfully at him. "You can't," he said finally. "Not by asking someone anyway."

"Then how?" Lang persisted. "What are you saying, that I have to kill someone to be able to figure out how that would feel?"

Moss shrugged. He obviously couldn't care less. Lang wondered if this guy ever went to the movies, if he had any idea how much work it took, how sensitive you had to be to achieve the right tone and emotion and nuance.

72

"Come on, Moss," Lang cajoled him. "Open up a little here. I'm just trying to be responsible."

Moss looked puzzled. "What are you talking about?" he asked.

"Reality!" Lang exclaimed.

"Reality?" Moss echoed, one eyebrow arching up.

"Getting it right for the camera!"

Moss gave him a disgusted look and shoved his hands in the pockets of his windbreaker.

Lang shoved his hands in the pockets of his leather jacket.

"Lang, goddammit!" Moss snapped.

"Okay, okay." Lang pulled his hands from his pockets and raised them in a placating gesture. "But listen, Moss, I really am trying to be responsible. I want my Tony DiBennedetti to be *real*, to be *you*! I wanna do this thing right, the way Olivier or Harrison Ford would!" He warmed to his topic. "I wanna know what it means, *really* means, to be a cop. I wanna get inside your skin . . . "

Moss got a peculiar look on his face, as if he had smelled something rotten. Then, with a swift motion, he ripped his hands from his pockets and shoved Nick Lang up against the side of the garish Lincoln. He didn't give a damn what the Captain would say, he was way past that point now.

"Listen, you little dirtwad!" he said, his face an inch from Lang's. Intensity rolled off him in waves. "I don't *want* you inside my skin. It's *private*! What's in there belongs to *me*, not you, not the director, not the audience! And you are not, I repeat *not* gonna learn what it means to be a cop by eating hot dogs and chewing unlit cigarettes and asking stupid questions! We *live* this job," he emphasized, his face sharp and hard. "It's something we *are*, not something we *do*! Every time a cop walks up to give someone a speeding ticket, for Christ's sake, he knows he might have to kill someone, or he might get killed himself—that's not something some Hollywood pretty boy steps into by strapping on a rubber gun and riding around in a patrol car for a couple of days! You'll go right back to your million-dollar beach house and your bimbos and your power breakfasts, and you'll get your seventeen takes that you need to get it right. But we only get *one* take, one take that lasts our whole lives! And if we mess it up, if we blow that one take . . . we're dead!"

Moss finally ran out of steam. He released Lang's shoulders and stepped back, taking a deep breath, trying to calm himself.

"Jesus, Moss," Lang said soberly. "That was great!"

Moss looked at him with amazement. "Great?" he echoed in disbelief.

"Great!" Lang assured him. He pulled his micro-recorder from his pocket. "I'm serious, I can use that." He held up the recorder so that Moss could talk into it. "Could you do it once more," he asked, "from the top?"

TEN

NICK LANG PRIDED HIMSELF ON A CERTAIN SPE-
cial character insight and sensitivity. Otherwise, he figured,
how could he be such a damned good actor? It all had to do
with paying attention to that inner voice, and right now, that
inner voice told him just to be quiet. He had been quick to
realize that John Moss wasn't in any mood to re-spew the
speech he had made. No, Lang thought, it wasn't a speech; it
was a spontaneous outburst of emotion that had clearly come
honestly and dramatically, right from the heart.

Besides, Lang told himself as they approached Moss's
apartment building, he didn't want to blow this new line
of communication. That outburst had been the single longest
string of words he'd heard from Moss since they had met. It
was a sign, a good sign; he was *sure* that Moss was finally
opening up to him.

Moss glowered sullenly as, temporarily resigned to his fate,
he picked up his mail, rode up the elevator, and stalked—
trailed by Nick Lang—toward his apartment door. Lang
followed, laden with the bags and bundles of replacement
clothing they had picked up on their way home. He had finally
admitted that his chances of getting the original clothing back
were slim at best.

Lang's voice came from behind the mound of packages.
John Moss hadn't offered to help carry anything for him,
but Lang wasn't going to hold it against him. Instead, he

said appeasingly, "Sorry it took so long, John . . . I'm not used to buying off the rack."

John Moss sighed as he put his key in the door. No, he thought, of course you're not. He turned as he heard the door to the apartment across the hall swing open and saw his landlady, Barbara Lu Keppler, emerge. Her iron curls were in slight disarray, and her round face appeared flushed.

"Oh, Lieutenant Moss . . . ," she said, embarrassed, "I was just, uh . . . returning their vacuum cleaner."

Moss peered over her shoulder. "Uh huh, Barbara Lu," he said genially, "you mean the one they keep in the liquor cabinet?"

Barbara Lu Keppler slammed the door shut and squared her shoulders. "Well, I never!" she said indignantly as she stalked off.

"Not much gets by you, does it?" Lang's voice, muffled by the pile of packages, queried.

"Not much," Moss agreed stonily and led the way into his apartment.

He flipped on the lights and crossed the room to the counter that separated his living space from his kitchen. Without so much as a glance in Lang's direction, he began to sort through his mail.

Lang dropped his packages on the gray tweed sofa and looked around the living room, more than a little surprised. The apartment was nicely coordinated, a masculine, understated sort of place with clean, dusted surfaces and contemporary furniture. There were surprisingly good prints framed on the wall, and well-cared-for books in a polished oak bookcase. This place had the look of being constantly looked after and was not at all what he had expected.

"How often does your housekeeper come?" Lang asked curiously.

Moss looked up from the mail, amazed. "My *what*?" he asked. He walked into the kitchen and opened the refrigerator. He grabbed a beer and popped it open, just as if Nick Lang wasn't there.

"Your housekeeper," Lang repeated. "You don't keep this place this way yourself, do you?"

Moss gave him a withering look. "You're a walking cliché, Lang," he said.

"What do you mean?" Nick Lang said defensively.

Moss shook his head in disgust. "You *really* think that all cops live in pigsties, just because it's like that in the movies?"

Lang reacted, trying to cover the fact that that was *precisely* what he had thought. "No, heck no!" he exclaimed. "Of course not! It's just that, well . . . you know, filth has a certain *reality*, a kind of edge to it."

"Oh, Christ," Moss said wearily, taking a long swallow of beer, "here we go with the Hollywood version of reality again."

"Well, all I meant was that it was nice that this doesn't have that rea—uh, edge," Nick Lang said. He paused and thought of all the tough cop films he had seen and worked on, all the detective novels that featured run-down office-apartments with whiskey stashed in the desk and three years' worth of dust on the filing cabinet. They couldn't *all* be wrong! "But some cops do, don't they?" he insisted. "Live in filth, I mean, at least a *little*? You know, rings on the coffee table, overflowing ashtrays, some dust bunnies under the couch?"

Moss just stared coldly at him.

Lang shrugged and looked around again at the clean, pleasant living room. "Hey!" he said, noticing a polished rosewood upright for the first time, "you play the *piano*?" He couldn't keep the amazement out of his voice.

Moss shrugged out of his jacket and hung it neatly in the small hallway closet. "My dad played," he said matter-of-factly, loosening his tie.

Lang shook his head in wonder. "See what I mean?" he said. "This is the real stuff, the character stuff. A cop's dad playing the piano, the son keeping the piano. It's so good, I love it! I mean, it has its own reali—uh, there's something so *authentic* about it."

"Authentic?" Moss echoed disdainfully. "I'm glad you think it's authentic. After all, it *is* my life."

Lang nodded thoughtfully, his mind on himself as Tony DiBennedetti. "Wish I could use it," he said. He noticed Moss staring balefully at him and added hastily, "But I won't, honest. No one would believe it anyway."

Moss shook his head. He crossed the room to the end table that held the phone machine and hit the replay button.

Nick Lang stared out the window, trying to pretend he wasn't listening to the string of messages—from the cleaners, a man who claimed he had some interesting information for Moss, from the dentist, confirming an appointment.

"Hey," Lang exclaimed, delighted, "look at that!" He pointed to his own bigger-than-life face. "They're putting my *Smoking Gunn II* billboard up right across from here!"

"Good," Moss replied genially, "then you'll be sleeping close to the one you love best."

Lang decided to ignore the jab—after all, at least Moss had acknowledged the fact that he was staying here. "So where's the guest room?" he asked.

Moss pointed to the couch beneath the pile of clothing bags. "Under your clothes," he replied.

"Oh." Lang looked down. "Huh?"

Moss stared at him, his dark eyes unrevealing. "It's called a sofabed, Hollywood," he said flatly.

"Oh, yeah, of course! A sofabed." Lang patted the arm. "No problem. I can deal with that."

"That's good to hear," Moss said sarcastically. "I was really worried about it."

Suddenly, Moss perked up as a woman's voice came through on the machine. This time, Lang didn't even pretend not to listen.

"So, John . . . ," said the woman.

"Oh, shit!" Moss exclaimed. "Susan!"

" . . . you forgot to call back again," the woman continued, with what sounded to Lang like amazing tolerance. "What is it this time, another murder?"

Moss groaned.

"Just kidding," she said with a little laugh. "Listen, I thought we'd go to Sal's, get some pizza, beer, keep it real casual, okay? Anyway, I hope you get this message, cause we said eight-ish, right . . . ?"

Moss looked at his watch. So did Lang. 7:40. "Damn!" Moss said, ripping off his tie and shirt as he headed for what Lang figured must be the bathroom. Sure enough, a moment later, he heard the sound of the shower running.

Lang fished his micro-recorder out of his pocket and turned it on. "John Moss," he said into it, speaking softly. "The private side."

He strolled over to the counter, thumbing nosily through the pile of mail. "Bill, bill, bill, occupant, bill . . . " He angled an envelope so he could read something inside. " . . . Looks like he's a little over on his MasterCard. Hmm, not much on the personal mail side. No surprise."

He strolled into the neat kitchen, continuing to pry and to dictate. "Let's see," he said, opening cabinets and drawers and rummaging around, "a few pots and pans, a couple of dishes . . . Either he doesn't eat at home much or the guy's fasting."

He opened the refrigerator and took stock of its contents. "Ketchup, mustard . . . two beers—domestic, ugh! Some kind of . . . Jesus, I don't know, mystery meat or some *really* old cheese. I don't think I wanna know." He shook his head. "Not a vitamin in sight, so he obviously lacks B, C, and E . . . Well, that helps explain that temper of his."

The kitchen was just plain bachelor-style dull, Lang decided. Nothing other than the fact that Moss didn't spend much time there was going to be revealed by searching it. Lang walked out of the kitchen and back into the living room, over to the oak case that held books, magazines, knickknacks. He cocked his head warily, but he could still hear the shower running, so he went back to his snooping.

Suddenly, he blinked, startled by what he found. "Six citations for heroism just stacked on a shelf, jeez!" He scanned the titles of the books. "Seems to read a lot, or likes to look like he does. No, scratch that—this guy doesn't go out of his way to impress anybody. Heavy into biographies and history." He fished a skin magazine from the bottom of a pile. "Not bad," he said, gazing wistfully at the half-naked girl in the foldout. He was used to a certain steady amount of cheerful, acquiescent female companionship, and he was pretty certain that *that* wasn't going to be part of this research trip.

"Okay," he said, continuing down the hall. He pulled open a closet door and surveyed the clothing hanging in it. "Four identical standard-issue suits," he spoke into the recorder. "One overcoat, not bad, but there's a lotta mileage on this baby. Four white shirts—jeez, this guy shops at J.C. Penney's!"

Lang shook his head in amazement, and then his eyes widened as he saw Moss's gun, hanging there in its holster. "Wow," he said, "Moss's gun." Without thinking, he pulled it from its leather holster, hefting the weight in his hand. "Wonder if it's loaded." He stood there, just feeling the heavy weapon in his hand, impressed by its density, its silent, implied power.

Lang was unable to contain himself. He walked quickly back into the living room, holding the gun carefully, and stood in front of a wall mirror. He whipped the gun up, two-handed, like Sonny Crockett in "Miami Vice." "Freeze, sucker!" he said, grimacing.

This was different from a prop gun, and Lang was a little awed by it. But the actor in him soon overcame that. He turned his back to the mirror and stood still for a moment. Then, suddenly, he whirled and pointed the gun, one-handed, at his reflection.

"Lookin' good," he assured his reflection.

He tried a few more positions—drawing from the hip, pulling the gun from his pocket. The last effort made him fumble, and he dropped the gun to the floor. Lang jumped back, unnerved, then recovered his aplomb and leaned over, picking the weapon up gingerly.

Brandishing the gun casually at his side, he went to work on his Tony DiBennedetti-from-John Moss act. He scowled into the mirror. "It's my life," he said forcefully. No, that wasn't quite right. He squinted and frowned. "It's *my* life," he said. That sounded petulant, not tough. "No shit, punk," he growled, "it's my *life!*" That was a little better. But not perfect. Lang posed and turned, trying several other expressions.

"What's wrong, got a split end?"

Lang jumped a foot when he heard Moss's voice. He hadn't even heard the shower being turned off. Quickly, he hid the gun inside his waistband, as Moss hurried out of the bedroom to tie his tie in the same mirror Lang had been using.

Lang strolled casually over to Moss's lifecycle and hopped on. He couldn't reach the pedals. "I've been counting," Lang informed him. "You've got seven expressions, you know that?" Off Moss's blank look, he explained, "Seven facial expressions."

Moss ignored him.

Okay, Lang thought, time to change the subject. "So . . . ," he said, "a date, huh? You know, it would be a real education to see what you're like with a woman." He warmed to the idea. "A situation fraught with sexual tension, innuendo, unspoken desire . . . Don't suppose you'd like to make it a threesome, would you?"

From the expression on Moss's face, Lang revised his earlier numbers. "I was wrong," he said, "you've got *eight* facial expressions! Okay," he added, seeing a murderous glint come into Moss's eyes, "I'll just stay here tonight, kick back, find something to do. What *is* there to do, anyway, any suggestions?"

Moss shrugged. "Do what you do in Hollywood. You know, hang out in fern bars, drink some rum drinks with little umbrellas in them, watch a couple of dancing transvestites get into a fight over Judy Garland's pinafore . . . "

"Why, Moss!" Lang said in surprise. "You've got a sense of humor."

81

"Don't count on it," Moss said, heading for the door. "Hey, Lang?" He turned back for a second.

"Huh?"

"Take my gun out of your pants before you shoot your dick off."

And he was gone with the slam of the door, leaving Nick Lang feeling like a fifteen-year-old busted for keeping *Playboy* under his bed. He pitied John Moss's date, whoever she was.

ELEVEN

MOSS COULDN'T BELIEVE HE HAD FORGOTTEN TO call. Again. He couldn't believe he was late. He swore softly under his breath as he screeched into a No Parking zone near Susan's apartment. Well, no wonder he was distracted, he thought, getting stuck with a baby-sitting job for that little dipshit actor, who did absolutely nothing but be a major pain in the ass and get in the way of everything. Still, Moss found himself almost smiling when he thought about Lang being tossed out right on his butt from that gang bar. After all, it *had* been pretty funny, and Lang had taken it with a certain amount of, well, to say dignity would be going too far. But at least he hadn't started whining.

Moss hurriedly checked his reflection in the mirror. Yup, it was him, all right—cropped hair, angular face, crooked smile, *when* he smiled. He thought for a moment that if he had to describe himself in one word, it would be jagged.

Moss climbed out of the car, taking care not to bump his cast and feeling a twinge in his ribs. He wondered briefly where on earth that thought about how he would describe himself had come from. I must be spending too much time with Hollywood, he thought, beginning to worry about how I look. Really!

Mentally, he tried to steel himself for his forthcoming date—not that a date with Susan was bad, quite the contrary. It was just that the entire concept and practice of dating were so damned alien. Uncomfortable. He wondered about people who thrived on this kind of social life. For Moss, it had all been just plain weird, ever since the divorce. Women, those strange creatures, and their demands and needs; he never seemed to guess right about what they were. But, he reflected with unusual optimism, maybe things would be different this time. Susan was . . . special.

His first surprise greeted him at Susan's front door when, instead of Susan, it was her eleven-year-old daughter, Bonnie, who answered his knock. Taken aback, Moss felt even more nervous. He had absolutely no idea what to do with children, and less desire to learn. And this one, with her world-weary air and seeming sophistication, just confused him more.

"Oh. Hi, Bonnie," he said weakly. "It's good to see—"

The rest of his greeting was cut short as Bonnie, jaded, unenthused, and rude, interrupted him. "Mom," she yelled, "he made it."

Susan walked into the foyer, looking wonderful, warm, and happy to see him. "Nice mouth on you," she said to her daughter reprovingly, then smiled at Moss. "Well," she said, "you actually *did* make it."

"Uh, yeah, well . . . " Moss heard himself stuttering. "I, uh . . . " He thrust a bouquet of flowers at Susan. "I picked these up on my way."

"Oh." Susan smiled again, bending to sniff them. "John, how nice."

"On the way is right," Bonnie said snidely. "From Mrs. Nussbaum's flowerbox, I'll bet."

Moss froze, stricken with guilt.

Susan saw his reaction and covered politely. "Bonnie," she said firmly, "it's time to go over to Mrs. Osbourne's place."

"Oh, Mom . . . ," Bonnie said plaintively.

Something Lang had said suddenly surfaced in John Moss's mind and emerged as words before he had a chance to check them. "Wait, Bonnie," he said impulsively, "you don't have to go."

"I don't?" she asked, surprised.

"She doesn't?" Susan echoed.

"No," Moss said, taking a deep breath. It was too late to undo the damage now. "I was thinking . . . I mean, if she wants, Bonnie could get a pizza with us. You know," he added, "the three of us."

Susan looked at him with pleased surprise, and Moss thought maybe it really was the right thing to do. "John, how sweet!" she said. "Bonnie," she said, turning to her daughter, "what do you think?"

Bonnie regarded him with dark suspicion. "Sure," she said succinctly. But John Moss had the feeling that he would *really* have to watch his step now.

The ride to Sal's pizza place was just as uncomfortable as the greeting had been. Bonnie couldn't stop talking about the car—how totally weird it was, how gross, how atomically embarrassed she would be if anyone from school saw her in such a pimpmobile.

"Pimpmobile?" Susan echoed in a near yelp. "Where the hell did you learn that word?"

"Oh, Mom," Bonnie said wearily. "Grow up."

Moss groaned silently to himself, revising his opinion that this was maybe a good idea, damning Lang for giving his advice, damning himself for taking it.

But as he pulled up to Sal's, he perked up a bit. He liked this place and was pleased that Susan had suggested it: it meant they had something in common. It was cheerfully loud, but not too loud to talk. It was crowded and bustling, and it was just plain fun. Even a kid would have to like Sal's.

Fifteen minutes later, after a near-silent wait for their table, punctuated only by Susan's attempts to get a conversation going and Bonnie's criticism of everything around them—the checked tablecloths, the oldies music, the dumb candles stuck in dumb Chianti bottles—they were seated and staring at their menus, not saying a word. Moss felt his optimism slipping away. Once again, he was beginning to feel that this was all a horrible mistake, that he shouldn't be dating, that he might as well just join a monastery or something. All around them, people were laughing, talking, obviously having a good time. Not at their table.

Finally, Susan broke the silence. "So," she said too brightly, "what looks good to anybody?"

Moss took a breath and plunged in. "What do you think about an extra large with . . . everything on it?"

"Everything?" Bonnie echoed.

"Everything," Moss assured her. A kid had to like that, right?

"You mean . . . like anchovies?" she said.

"Oh, yeah," Moss replied happily. "I love 'em; they're my favorite part."

Bonnie fixed him with a cold eye. "I hate them," she said flatly.

Susan jumped in to mediate. "We could get half with anchovies," she suggested, "and half without."

Bonnie looked sullen. "But sometimes they slide over to the other side," she said.

"Only when the cook forgets to kill 'em," Moss joked.

It didn't work.

"Gross," Bonnie muttered, frowning. Then she looked down at her menu again.

Susan spoke into the dead silence. "John, how's your arm?"

Moss shrugged evasively.

"John," Susan said firmly, "this is our second date. It's *okay* to talk about yourself. Really!" She grinned at him, trying to lighten up the atmosphere. "Most guys don't talk about anything *but* themselves . . . " When Moss didn't respond, she sighed. "Okay," she announced, "here's the deal. We're not going to order anything to eat until you tell us something personal about yourself. *Anything*," she emphasized. "It can be something you love, something you hate."

Jesus, Moss thought, feeling like a butterfly, pinned and formaldehyded, what was he supposed to do now? Just at that crucially uncomfortable moment, a disturbingly familiar voice piped brightly into the conversation.

"John? Is that really you?"

Moss felt his spine stiffen. He swiveled slowly in his chair and fixed Nick Lang with a stare cold enough to freeze hell.

Lang was oblivious. Or pretended to be. "Wow!" he exclaimed, all smiles and charm and utter adorableness. "Can you believe this? I mean, you, me, same place, same night? What are the odds on that?"

"Even money," Moss said through clenched teeth.

Lang's hazel eyes were twinkling. Somewhere along the way, Moss noted irrelevantly, he had ditched the other brown contact lens.

Lang grinned heartily. "And they say New York is a big town . . ."

"Not big enough," Moss muttered.

"You know," Lang said conversationally, glancing over Bonnie's shoulder at her menu, "I heard somewhere Sal's had fantastic pizza, and I thought I'd give it a try. It was either this or a sushi bar." He turned the full amp power of his grin on Bonnie. "I picked here . . . I hate all those drunk sushis, don't you?"

Bonnie giggled. Moss fumed. Great, he worked like a dog to get the kid to do more than throw an occasional sullen insult in his direction, and all Lang had to do was show up and smile!

Lang continued twinkling. "You've got to be Bonnie, right?"

Bonnie nodded, charmed and intrigued.

"Moss told me you had a great laugh," he said, winking at her. "And Susan," he turned the wattage in her direction. "I'm Ray Cazenov, John's new partner. God, it's *great* to finally meet the woman who managed to turn this guy's head."

Moss wanted to bury his head in the sand. Better, bury Lang's head in the wall.

"Well . . . thank you," Susan smiled back at Lang. "Better than turning his stomach." She giggled at her own joke, and so did Lang.

Well, Moss thought, like mother, like daughter. Women. Actors. How did this happen to him?

Bonnie had been staring hard at Lang. "You know something," she said quizically, "you look just like Nick Lang, the actor."

Moss wanted to add, "Yeah, but shorter and whiter," but he refrained.

"You think so?" Lang said.

"Uh huh," Bonnie said.

Moss could practically *see* Lang's ego fighting and losing a battle with itself.

Lang said, "Do you like Nick Lang?"

"Funny you should ask that," Moss remarked. No one paid any attention.

"I used to," said Bonnie matter-of-factly, "when I was a little girl."

"A little girl?" Lang echoed, stunned.

"Uh huh," Bonnie nodded. "Now I like Mel Gibson."

Okay, Bonnie, Moss cheered silently, one for my side! And now it was definitely time to say good-bye. "Well, *Ray*," Moss said heartily, "it's great seein' ya, but we're getting real hungry and it's time to order. Don't be a stranger, now."

"Why don't you eat with us?" Bonnie piped up.

"No!" exclaimed Moss. "I mean," he said, softening his tone, "Ray is probably busy. *Aren't* you, Ray?" he said meaningfully.

"Well, not really," Lang said. "But I think John's probably seen enough of me, Bonnie," he told the little girl. "We work together, I'm staying at his place . . . " He turned his glance apologetically in Moss's direction. "By the way, I'm really sorry about the trash compactor—I honestly thought it was the dishwasher. But hey, I'm good for a new one."

Before Moss could say anything, Susan turned to him. "John, Ray is staying with you? But you never even mentioned him."

Once again, Moss didn't have time to open his mouth.

Lang's expression became doleful. "That's, uh, because I

88

didn't want him to, Susan." He turned sad hazel eyes on her. "I've been having some . . . well, problems. I didn't really want people knowing."

Moss shot him a look of fury. How the hell did Lang figure out Susan was a psychologist? How did he instinctively seem to know exactly how to appeal to her?

"It's a little painful for me," Lang continued, looking down at the table shyly. "It's not easy to talk about."

What a perfect thing to say to a shrink, Moss thought snidely.

"You don't have to talk," Susan said soothingly, "but Ray?"

"Yes?" Lang looked up, just a hint of hope in his eyes.

"It might help," Susan told him softly.

Lang took a breath. "Well," he said, "I used to work midnights. Every morning I'd take my old partner by the house for coffee. My wife would get up and make it for us. It was like a ritual; it was a family thing, you know?"

Susan nodded encouragingly.

Moss wanted to gag.

"Well," Lang said again. He sighed. "This is so hard for me. One night my partner calls in sick; I don't think anything about it. But in the morning, when I get home . . . " He stopped, seemingly fraught with emotional stress, unable to go on.

"It's okay, Ray," Susan encouraged him.

I'm gonna kill you, Lang, Moss thought.

"I'm . . . sorry," Lang said, choking up. "The thing is, I got home and everything was gone. Her clothes, her jewelry . . . the toaster oven." He turned his wounded eyes on Susan, full power. "It's such a cliché, I know you've probably guessed it already . . . my wife and my partner . . ." —he cast a sidelong, circumspect glance at Bonnie— "uh . . . moved in together. And I lost the two people I was closest to in the world, all in one night."

"Oh, Ray," Susan said, filled with empathic emotion, "I'm so sorry."

"So, you see, I just couldn't bring myself to go back there, to live in the place where the three of us . . . " Lang let the words trail off. "And John offered."

Moss shook his head, incredulous at this spur-of-the-moment performance.

"John, that is so sweet of you!" Susan exclaimed.

Moss stared meaningfully at Lang. "*Ray*," he said grimly, "ol' buddy. Isn't it about time for you to take your Thorazine? It's in the medicine cabinet," he said pointedly, "*back at the apartment*."

Lang grinned wistfully, first at Moss, then at Susan. "Isn't it great?" he asked her. "I mean, what a kidder. This guy," he punched Moss lightly on the arm, "he really tries to keep my spirits up."

Their harried waitress chose that moment to appear at the table. "Ready to order?" she asked, pencil poised over her order pad.

Bonnie tugged at Lang's sleeve. "You should stay and eat with us," she said. "*Please?*"

"Well . . . ," Lang said tentatively. "I hate to intrude."

Moss felt himself freeze in place.

Susan looked over at him. "Is it okay, John?" she said softly.

Moss looked from Bonnie to Susan. Right, he thought, like I really have a choice here.

Lang took his silence as a yes and cheerfully pulled up a chair. "Okay," he said, "this is great!" He beamed at all of them and clapped his hands together. "But one condition . . . I'm buying!" He smiled up at the waitress. "We'll have two extra-large pizzas, double cheese, with everything on them. Oh," he added, "except anchovies. If we spot so much as *one* anchovy"— he flashed his phony badge— "you're busted!"

The waitress smiled, Bonnie giggled, and Susan looked on approvingly. Moss wondered if steam was coming out of his ears.

TWELVE

HE ALWAYS KEPT THE APARTMENT DARK. DURING the day, the drapes remained drawn. At night, few lights except those needed for his essential reading were ever turned on. The location was surprisingly elegant—high at the top of a building that rented to the wealthy and near-wealthy. Most of the apartments here were designed and cared for by an army of servants. Not this one. No one ever came here.

The furnishings were minimal, functional; the place had a spartan feel to it. The only thing that contradicted this feeling, the only thing that saved the place from seeming eerily empty, was what dominated the apartment: books. Stacks and stacks of them, bookshelf upon bookshelf, each shelf heaped and crammed to overflowing with leatherbound books, paperbacks, old cloth books, bright new titles, slick little pamphlets.

And if you got close enough to examine them, all the titles carried a theme. *Mein Kampf*, *Aryan Brotherhood*, *The Supreme Race*, *Tactical Weapons and Their Applications*, and so on. Every book that lined these shelves had to do with white supremacy, with self-defense, with death. And how to cause it.

Tonight, only the flickering light from a tape running on the VCR, and the music that emanated thinly from it, gave away the presence of anyone at all. On the television screen, Gary Cooper, standing tall, was preparing to battle it out with his evil adversaries, the men who would take the town from him, take it from law and order, take it into chaos. Only he could do something; only he could stop them. Cooper prepared for battle. The theme from *High Noon* was the only sound in the room.

Outside, on the balcony, the view was spectacular, a fitting setting for the music, a fitting setting for a hero. The Party Crasher surveyed the land below him. His land, he thought, his town. He stood as tall as Cooper, he thought, and, with his own personal mission in the city, was probably more heroic. Cooper had had to be talked into his responsibility; the Party Crasher knew instinctively what his was. He didn't shirk; he didn't hesitate. The evil forces in this city were too widespread for that, too powerful. If he hesitated, he would be . . . lost. He stared down into the nighttime cavern of Manhattan, spread out below him like a child's puzzle.

He smiled to himself. He knew there wasn't anything he couldn't do, if he just set his mind to it. Then his smile faded. Perhaps calling those ineffectual police hadn't been the best idea. He had believed his warnings would serve as taunts, as reminders that, despite their uniforms, their rules, their legally carried weapons, they were really helpless, inept, and impotent against the wave of violence, the blood-borne corruption and evil that faced them. Against a plague of drugs spread by dark-skinned cockroaches, against a plague of the blood spread by weak, vicious junkies and whores, against a plague of violence spread by unwanted, unschooled children, throwaways living out the violent fantasies of their small-screen minds.

But it hadn't worked that way at all. Instead of the respect, the admiration, the *adulation* he should have received from the police, instead of receiving acknowledgment for his heroic deeds, he was . . . vilified. He was hunted down, like one of his own prey. The thought of it made him furious. Why couldn't they see that he was a hero, not a villain? Why couldn't they understand that he alone could save this city?

He pictured the face of the man behind it all, the man who was trying to hunt him down and bring him in, the man who had the audacity to want to stop him. He pictured the man he blamed for this terrible misconception about him, and saw the face of John Moss. It was imprinted clearly on the killer's mind. Clearly from that battle they had fought down the streets of the city. Clearly, too, from the news coverage, the media scum-mongers being only too eager to play and replay, ad nauseam, the inarticulate, distraught interview with John Moss. Moss's angry face, lean and haunting, was everywhere. And Moss made no secret of the fact that the Party Crasher was his quarry.

It was all wrong, the killer thought. He would have to take care of this problem before it got out of hand. And there was only one way to do that.

"Too bad, Moss," the Party Crasher said softly. "Too bad for you."

He stared out dispassionately at his dark kingdom. What had to be done would be done. No one would get in his way. No one.

"This town isn't big enough for the both of us, Moss," he said, and mimed drawing a gun. Silently he pointed it out at the city, at the imaginary face of his adversary, John Moss.

"Bang," said the killer softly. "You're dead."

THIRTEEN

MOSS STARED SULLENLY ACROSS THE TABLE, WATCH-ing Lang, Susan, and Bonnie, huddled cozily together, making an absolute mess out of an already whine-filled Beatles tune. He refused to join in, shaking his head firmly no when Susan tried to get him to sing. No, he thought, he would rather just sit here in miserable silence and let them enjoy themselves.

They had been at Sal's for nearly two hours now. The extra-large pizzas—"*without* anchovies," Moss mimicked Lang in his head—had been done away with; all that remained on the table were a few crusts and some wadded-up napkins. Whose brilliant idea the jukebox sing-along had been was anybody's guess. Lang had held the table—at least, the female portion of the table—so completely enthralled with his boyish charm that John Moss had practically given up even trying to engage in conversation, let alone get some kind of personal connection going with Susan.

So this was his reward, Moss thought resentfully, when he had actually taken that little shit's advice and brought along . . . the *daughter*. Well, he would be a hell of a lot more careful from now on. From now on, whatever Lang suggested, he would do the opposite.

"Come on, John!" Lang shouted over the noise, "let's hear you sing!"

Moss just shook his head again, wincing as the happy

threesome, grooving and moving to the music, put their heads together for one last blast, a truly atonal "Ooooooo . . . "

And then, thankfully, it was finally over.

"God, that was so much fun!" Susan said, her face flushed and happy.

"Really fun!" Bonnie echoed, without a trace of her former snottiness.

Obviously the fun began with, emanated from, and finished with Lang. Bet he's good with dogs, too, Moss thought resentfully, aiming a laser look at the actor. Lang, naturally didn't seem to notice.

"Yeah, maybe we should try recording together. What do you think?" Lang joked. He nudged John in the ribs, and John winced.

"What's the matter with you, John, did you forget the words?"

"I tried," Moss said.

"Oh, you're such a kidder!" Lang winked at him. "You should open up a little bit!" Then he turned to Susan and Bonnie, his face excited. "Say, John probably never talks about it—he's so modest—but did you guys know that we have an honest-to-God hero at this table?"

He threw a friendly arm around Moss's shoulders. Moss shrank back, but Lang kept a firm grip on him.

"Hero?" Bonnie echoed in surprise. "What do you mean?"

"You bet he is!" Lang assured her. "Why, only two days ago, this man was swinging from the open door of a tow truck going sixty miles an hour."

"What?" Susan exclaimed, horrified.

"Oh, really," Moss said, shrugging, "it wasn't that—"

"—eye to eye with," Lang interrupted him, then paused for dramatic effect, " . . . the Party Crasher!"

"The killer?" Bonnie squeaked. "The one on the news?"

"John!" Susan said. "Is he serious?"

"Am I serious?" Lang repeated. "Come on, Suze, would I make this up? *Could* I make this up? This is so crazy it *has* to be real! Of course I'm serious!"

"Ray," Moss said crossly, "could you please just cool it?"

No, Ray couldn't. "We're talkin' tough guy, here," Ray said, completely ignoring Moss's plea. "I mean, the Party Crasher is beating John up with a tire iron, and this guy *still* won't let go!"

"What happened?" Bonnie asked, breathless. "Did you kill him?"

Oh, great, Moss thought, so this is what the kid likes! A little violence, a little bloodshed.

"He would've," Lang said loyally, "except . . . "—he eyed Moss a little sheepishly— "he, uh . . . crashed through a billboard."

"John! Is that true?" Susan looked worried, which John figured was a good sign.

"Well, yeah," he said. He smiled thinly at Lang. "Actually," he continued thoughtfully, "the billboard was the worst part of it."

"So *that's* how you broke your arm," Susan said. "I can't believe you never mentioned it . . . Not," she added thoughtfully, "that you ever really talk about what you do."

"Look," Moss snapped, "I don't like talking about work, okay?"

He saw both Susan and Bonnie look at him strangely, startled by his vehemence. But it was true, he *didn't* like talking about work, and he certainly didn't like this kind of silly macho bragging about daring police exploits, which was what Lang was obviously trying to turn this conversation into.

"Come on, John," Lang said, getting up and pulling on Moss's arm, "we're gonna go pick the next song on the jukebox."

Moss allowed himself to be dragged across the room, fuming.

"Way to go, Moss," Lang said reprovingly when they were out of earshot. "I was just trying to smooth things out for you. Susan's all right."

"I can smooth things out for myself!" Moss snapped. "I don't need any help from you!"

"Right," agreed Lang, sarcastically. "I can definitely see that." He pointed to the jukebox. "Pick a song."

Moss shrugged and punched the first button he touched. He cringed when "Johnny Angel" began. Lang smirked.

"Oh, shut up," muttered Moss as he headed back toward the table.

As he took his seat again, he noticed that the table next to them, full of drunk investment banker types, was getting louder. The more beer they consumed, the greater their volume became. And the level of conversation was definitely getting cruder.

A well-fed suit wearing a loosened duck tie was holding forth. "So she's right there, and she flashes a little leg—well, more than a little—I mean we're talkin' this is a chick who wears stockings and garter belts to work, and I could see where they came together! Wow, I mean, I wanted to throw her down on her desk and bone her right there in her office."

One of his companions chimed in. "Are you talking about the one with the mega-jugs, the blonde down in payroll?"

Moss, already steaming, had had it. He turned and tried to stare the bankers down. With Moss's eyes, that kind of thing generally worked, but they were too far into their cups and their bragging to pay him any attention.

"Oh, yeah," his buddy replied, "and I wish she was down on me!"

"Hey . . . ," said Moss, trying to get their attention. "Hey, guys."

No one gave him so much as a glance. "I get a world-class woody every time I go near payroll!" said a third member of the party.

"Hey!" Moss said sharply. "Guys. Do you think you could cool it a little? We got some ladies here."

The first banker looked at him and grinned nastily. "Bet that's a first."

His table of cronies howled.

Susan reached over and put her hand on Moss's. "John," she said softly, "it's okay."

98

Moss looked at her. "No," he said evenly, "it's not okay. Your daughter's here."

"It's all right," Bonnie assured him. "I know what a woody is."

"What?" Susan said.

The first banker continued on, not bothering to turn down the volume. "So then I hear that Jay had her already, in the computer room."

"He just punched the 'enter' key!" smirked one of the others.

"And the secretary gave the boss a raise!"

The men howled in appreciation.

Moss had reached his tolerance limit. He started to get up and was restrained by Lang, who put his hands on Moss's arm.

"John," he said in a warning tone, "maybe we should just get another table."

Meanwhile, one of the bankers finally noticed Moss's attitude. "You got a problem, buddy?" he yelled belligerently.

"I asked you to keep it down," Moss said, trying to keep his own voice calm and level.

"Hey," said the banker, raising his middle finger, "sit on this!"

Moss jerked out of Lang's grasp and straightened up. "What did you say?" he asked softly.

Lang thought it would be difficult to miss the promised menace in John Moss's voice, but the bankers were either really stupid, too drunk to care, or simply unable to conceive of one man taking on all of them. The banker kept his finger stiffly in the air and repeated his invitation. "You heard me," he said with a smirk.

Moss started toward the table.

"John, really," Susan said, "just let it go."

The second banker was suddenly diverted when he spotted someone they knew across the room. "There's Jay!" he said excitedly. "Hey, Jay-bird!" he screamed. "Hey, Jay, you homo . . . Yeah, you, the one with the flowers on your tie, get over here, fag-bait!"

The pudgy banker in the duck tie decided this was the perfect moment to let forth with a huge belch. Then, apparently trying to top his buddy in the crudeness department, the banker who had just been screaming got up, pulled down his pants, and mooned their friend across the room.

"That's it!" Moss announced furiously.

With two strides, he was at the bankers' table, and before they even knew what hit them, Moss had the pudgy banker slammed up against the wall, one of his hands twisted painfully behind his back.

"Ouch, you mother-fucker . . . ," yelped the pudge, as his buddies rushed drunkenly to the rescue.

Moss heard Susan scream just as one of the bankers clubbed him cheaply behind the ear. Moss felt himself stagger momentarily, but his training and strength asserted themselves, despite his injuries. As the banker who'd dropped his pants rushed him, he kicked out with a steel-toed boot, catching the man in the groin. He whirled just in time to fend off the one who'd clubbed him; Moss smacked him across the nose with his cast.

The banker retreated, clutching his bloody nose and screaming, while the pudgy one, now free from his up-against-the-wall position, came at Moss, swinging. Moss kneed him in his soft gut and sent the man doubling over, moaning.

"John, don't!" Susan kept saying over the racket.

"Break his face, yeah, John! That's the way!" he heard Bonnie scream. "Kill him!"

Meanwhile, Nick Lang didn't make a move to enter into the fracas. Instead, he positioned himself protectively in front of Susan and Bonnie, who both kept trying to get around him for a better look at the action.

Moss managed the brutal fight single-handedly. As the banker with the bloody nose, temporarily recovered, leapt at Moss, Moss grabbed a nearby chair and busted it over his head, sending the man spinning into oblivion. The pudge wound up thrown over the bar. The third man found himself handcuffed to the immovable leg of a booth. And it was all over.

"Wow!" said Bonnie.

Moss finally took a breath, and saw the crowd of curious and alarmed faces ringed around him. With his good arm, he fished his badge out and flashed it at them.

"Sorry, folks," he said and looked at the proprietor of the restaurant. "I'm a cop."

Moss heard the handcuffed banker groan in dismay.

Moss looked at Nick Lang, still carefully positioned in front of Bonnie and Susan. "Call Midtown," he told him. "Tell them it's a code 40; we need a blue-and-white. No," he said, "make that *two* blue-and-whites."

Lang nodded and headed for the pay phone at the back of the restaurant.

"John," Susan said quietly, "can we get out of here now? Let's go back to my place. I really think that Bonnie has seen more than enough for one night."

"Mom . . . ," Bonnie protested.

Moss sighed. "I'm sorry, Susan," he said, "I can't. I'm going to have to go to the precinct and explain this, and then I've got to do the paperwork."

A brief look of disappointment crossed Susan's face, and then she nodded toward Lang, who was making his way back to them through the dispersing crowd of onlookers.

"Can't Ray do that?" she asked.

Moss opened his mouth to say that Ray wasn't Ray and he couldn't do diddley. Then he closed it again. "No," he said flatly, without attempting any further explanation. "He can't."

Susan stared at him for a moment, a look of disappointment mixed with incomprehension and, perhaps, just a little anger.

"Okay," she said shortly, "then maybe Ray can see us home."

"Sure," said Lang, who had moved into earshot, "I can do that. Okay, John?" He looked apologetically at Moss.

"Okay," said Moss tightly. What choice did he have?

As they turned to go, Bonnie looked back at him. "That was better than Dick Tracy," she said solemnly. " 'Cause you did it with only one arm."

And then they were gone, leaving Moss to stare at the mess he had caused. Amazing, he thought, what a little physical battle could do for you in an eleven-year-old's eyes. Great, he thought ruefully, so Bonnie's now a fan. That was all fine, but he still had to wonder if Susan would ever want to see him again.

FOURTEEN

MOSS WAS WELL INTO HIS SECOND DOUBLE SCOTCH, but he didn't seem to be feeling the effect. He downed the rest of the contents of his glass and motioned the bartender to do him again. He pushed a few bills across the dark mahogany bar, feeling bruised, sore, and slightly sorry for himself. His mood didn't undergo any perceptible change for the better when Nick Lang walked through the door and perched beside him on a bar stool.

"I, uh, went by the station, after I dropped Susan and Bonnie off," Lang said quietly. "You were already gone, but one of the guys said he thought you might be here."

"And here I am," said Moss, staring down at his fresh drink.

"Look, John," Lang said, "I didn't mean for things to turn out like they did. I didn't know they'd ask me to stay . . . I just came by Sal's for a quick look, and things just sort of . . . got out of hand, I guess." There was no response. "Well, anyway," Lang continued, "they got home safely."

Moss nodded.

"She's nice, Susan," Lang said. "So's Bonnie." He smiled as he remembered his advice to Moss earlier. "So, you decided to take her along, after all, huh?"

Moss took a sip of his drink. "She hates me," he said.

"Oh, well," Lang shrugged, "it's that age, it's very Freud-

103

ian. I wouldn't worry about it. Maybe you should buy her a horse or something."

Moss finally looked at Lang. "I'm talking about Susan," he said.

"Oh." Lang thought for a moment. "No," he said, "she doesn't hate you. She's just trying to get to know you, which, let's face it, isn't the world's easiest thing to do."

"Hmmph," said Moss.

"If I could just offer you a little piece of advice . . . ," Lang began.

"No," Moss said firmly. "I took your last piece of advice, and look what happened."

Lang paused, brow furrowed, trying to regroup his thoughts. It was perfectly obvious that John Moss needed some serious counseling on his behavior with the opposite sex. And Nick Lang, an expert on the matter, wasn't about to just sit by and let nature run its course. He couldn't, not in this case, he thought. Nature wouldn't stand a chance.

"Look, Moss," he said, just as firmly as Moss had said no, "you may not want to hear this, but I really do know people, and you *have* to listen to me about this."

Moss groaned and put his head in his hands. "Can't you just go away?" he asked.

Lang ignored the question. "I know what makes people tick," he said, "what makes them cry, what touches them. Especially women."

Moss shot him a look, and Lang shrugged.

"It's what I do for a living," Lang continued. "You may not want to hear this from me, but I'm going to say it anyway."

"What a surprise," commented Moss.

Lang ignored the jab. "It's pretty obvious," he said, "that your main problem with Susan is plain old communication. You're just not opening yourself up to this woman."

"It was our second date!" Moss exclaimed.

"But women want that kind of stuff right away!" Lang said earnestly. "You've got to let her inside, Moss, you have to give her a look at what's under the surface, bare your soul a little."

"California crap!" Moss said. "The home of sprouts, tofu, earthquakes, and self-realization!" He downed the rest of his drink and motioned for another.

Lang was amazed; Moss didn't appear to even *feel* the liquor he was knocking back. "Look," he said, "whether you like it or not, what I'm telling you is true. If you want to have any kind of meaningful relationship . . . "

"Please," Moss groaned, "spare me."

" . . . it just takes a little practice," Lang continued firmly, as if there hadn't been any interruption at all. "I'm serious, Moss. Pretend I'm Susan."

Moss glanced over at him, one eyebrow raised. "What?" he said.

"Oh, come on, Moss," Lang said. "You can do it. I spend half my *life* pretending I'm someone else. It's easy!"

"That's because you're an actor," Moss said sullenly.

At least he was responding, sort of, Lang thought. "Try to let your hair down a little, you might learn something," Lang urged him.

"Like what?" muttered Moss. "Like all that touchy feely psycho-babble?"

"Come on, just do it," Lang urged him. "I'm Susan, and you're John."

Moss shot him a horrified look. "No," he said, "you're sick, and I'm thirsty."

To Lang's amazement, Moss signaled for yet another drink. Well, he thought, if the booze is what it takes to loosen him up, why stop him? He sat in silence for a few moments, watching Moss consume the liquor, gauging when to move in for the kill.

Finally, he said, "Okay. I'll get it started."

Moss shrugged as if he didn't care, and Lang decided to take that as his cue. He pulled into himself, the way he had been taught in countless acting classes, and concentrated on

105

Susan, who she was, what she was like. He crossed and recrossed his legs, getting comfortable. He could feel his facial expression change as he "became" female.

Lang tossed his head back flirtatiously. "Well?" he said to Moss.

"Well, what?" Moss responded blankly.

"Talk to me, John," said Lang, his voice throaty, seductive.

Moss stared over at him, puzzled. "What the hell are you doing?" he asked.

"Come on, John," Lang said, getting deeper into character, "talk to me. Say what I need to hear."

"What you need to . . ." Moss looked at him with growing comprehension and horror. "Get away from me!" he exclaimed. "I'm not going to do this—it's too damned weird!" He turned resolutely away from Lang, facing the other end of the bar.

"You see?" Lang demanded. "This is the problem, right here in front of us. You *never* talk to me!"

"Would you please stop this?" Moss hissed, still looking away.

"No!" Lang said petulantly. "You always keep me at a distance, you treat me like . . . like some princess that you can't even touch!"

Moss cringed.

"Well, maybe I want to be touched, John!" Lang continued, oblivious. He was really getting into his part. "Maybe I want to be treated like a woman, not a saint!"

Moss searched the room fruitlessly, hoping to spot a place to take his drink and perch, somewhere out of this lunatic actor's vocal range. The man on his other side was eyeing him peculiarly.

Lang sailed on, being Susan. "But not you! No, you just sit there like, like . . . Jimmy Stewart or someone, all tongue-tied, sputtering . . . like you think it's attractive!"

The man on Moss's left was now craning his head to look at Lang.

"Well, John," Lang said suggestively, "I don't know what your problem is—*other* men don't seem to have any trouble talking to me!"

"What?" Moss spun around on his bar stool to face Lang, forgetting all about his audience. Lang's words had hit emotional pay dirt. "What other men?" he demanded. "Did she tell you she's seeing other men?"

"Oh," Lang said coyly, "*now* he wants to talk. Now that the old green-eyed monster has raised its ugly little head."

"Listen, Lang . . . ," Moss began.

"Susan," Lang corrected him calmly.

"Lang!" Moss's eyes narrowed down to slits.

"Susan!" Lang insisted.

"Whoever!" Lang exploded. "Just tell me, did she say that she was going out with other men? Frankie? Alphonse? Who?"

Lang stared straight ahead, his expression miffed. He turned his nose up in the air and kept quiet.

A few more bar patrons were watching them with open interest. Moss was torn between utter humiliation and burning curiosity. After a few minutes of thick silence, he realized unhappily that curiosity had won out. He closed his eyes, praying no one he knew was around to see this and report on it.

"Okay," he said through gritted teeth, "Susan." There, it was out.

"Yes, John." Lang replied pleasantly.

Moss tried to contain his fury at having to go through this mortifying charade. "Is she . . . " He saw Lang toss a warning look at him and corrected himself. "Are you seeing other men?"

Lang looked at Moss with pure longing in his eyes. Moss wanted to die as he heard the man on his left bite back a snicker.

"No, John," said Lang, casting his eyes modestly downward. "There's only you, and that's why it's so hard. Any woman can see that you're strong, forceful . . . "

107

"Jesus," Moss muttered, putting his head down on the bar. "Tell me this isn't happening."

" . . . and I have eyes, John, I can see it, too!" Lang said, tossing his head. "But you always hold back around me."

"Bartender!" Moss yelled, looking up again. He reached nervously for a pack of cigarettes on the bar and pulled one out.

"I thought you were quitting for me," Lang said, disappointed.

Moss tossed the unlit cigarette into an ashtray. "This is too damned strange," he muttered.

"No," Lang said, "I'll tell you what's strange . . . what's really strange is that a cop who's so tough, who's so in charge, really isn't confident at all about who he is. Outside of his job, that is."

"That's bullshit!" Moss said sharply.

But Lang's words had touched a raw nerve in Moss. Even through his drunken haze, he knew that what Lang had said was somehow . . . *right*! He tried to collect his fuzzy thoughts.

"Look," said Moss, finally. "Okay, maybe you have a point."

"Now we're getting somewhere," Lang said smugly. "So . . . talk, John."

Moss took a deep breath, then plunged in. "Ever since my . . . divorce," he said, "I've been having a kind of rough time. I mean, every time I start to, uh, get serious about a woman, I get . . . scared." There, he thought, the ugly truth was now public knowledge. The man on his left had stopped laughing and was nodding in sympathy.

"What do you mean, every time?" Lang queried.

"What do you mean, what do I mean?" Moss replied, confused.

"Exactly how many women have you been serious about, John?" Lang-as-Susan managed to imbue the question with the perfect combination of professional psychiatric caring and pure female accusation. "Three? Five? Twenty?"

108

"None!" Moss said, thoroughly flustered now.

"None?" Lang repeated archly.

"Well, not . . . I meant, none besides my wife, that is, my ex-wife."

"What about me?"

"Well, yeah, and you . . . ," Moss said, then backtracked hastily, "I mean *her*, Susan!"

"Uh huh," Lang nodded judiciously. "That's it?"

"Yes!" Moss said. "That's it. They're . . . you're . . . the only ones!"

"That makes two, right?"

"Huh?" Moss said, squinting into his glass.

"Two." Lang smiled. "Not ten, not twenty, *two*. So how would you even know that you get scared 'every time'?"

It seemed to Moss, through his drunken haze, that Lang-as-Susan had just scored a victory in the communications battle between the sexes. The last thing he wanted was to have to reexamine himself psychologically, emotionally. But he had to admit, somewhere down deep inside him, that Lang had a point. He *was* scared, and he was scared to admit it as well. Oh, no, Moss told himself, there was absolutely no way he was dealing with this, making any admissions, doing anything, not right . . . now.

He peered over at Lang, who was looking far too proud of himself. "Dammit," Moss said, "that's it! I don't want to talk about this anymore!"

"Okay, John," said Lang with a smile.

"Isn't that just like a woman?" Moss nudged the man on his left. "To turn it around, stick you with it, and then give it the old twist . . . just . . . like . . . a knife."

And, with his last word, Moss's head fell forward, and he passed out on the bar.

Lang looked around. There were people staring at them, people who had obviously overheard the entire exchange. Lang shrugged his shoulders eloquently.

"Men," he said.

FIFTEEN

LANG OPENED HIS EYES SLOWLY, FEELING A LIT-
tle disoriented. Everything around him seemed so unfamiliar.
Then, through the slatted window blinds, he spotted his own
face, much, *much* larger than life. The *Smoking Gunn II* billboard was finally up, and all the mechanics were working. In
his sleepy state, Lang observed the huge cigarette regularly
puffing out a plume of smoke. Oh, right, he thought, I'm in
New York, I'm staying with John Moss. And I'm waking up
in his sofabed. Right. He yawned as Joe Gunn sent another
make-believe plume of smoke up into the atmosphere.

Lang watched lazily and made a mental note to talk to
the producers about changing that, if and when he ever
did another in the successful series of films. After all, he
mused, a smoking hero sent the wrong message to the youth
of America. Perhaps Joe Gunn could adopt John's habit of
keeping an unlit cigarette in his mouth. Pleased, Lang smiled
at the thought of utilizing one of John Moss's real-life habits
in yet *another* screen character. He liked it; it would drive
the cop wild.

Lang thought about the night before. He sensed that he had
really broken the ice with Moss, that this was the beginning
of, well, maybe not a beautiful friendship, but at least a kind
of communication and understanding between them. Moss
might have been drunk as a skunk—getting him home had
been no simple chore—but he *had* finally let down his guard.

111

And now Lang knew that under that tough cop exterior lay a man who was human, a man who had foibles and fears, who, for God's sake, had insecurities about *women*! It was a nice irony, Lang mused, such a tough exterior, such a sensitive inside. It added complexity; it gave yet another dimension to the character he was building.

Well, he thought, time to be up and about, putting more detail on Tony DiBennedetti. *God*, he was going to be good! He was going to knock their socks off with his test for the part, and he was going to *get* it. Lang could feel himself pumping up for the challenge; it was almost a physical sensation. This could be it, he thought. This could be the chance to be taken seriously, for once, to get rave reviews from critics who had categorized him as a cute lightweight, to earn . . . an Oscar nomination, maybe ultimately to actually cop the golden statue and, with it, the permanent respect of his dramatic peers. And, he told himself magnanimously, he wouldn't stint on credit where credit was due. In his acceptance speech, he was definitely going to mention the debt he owed to John Moss for helping create the character.

Great, he thought excitedly, this is great. It was time to get rolling! He wondered if Moss had made coffee. Lang reached up to scratch his chin, but his hand wouldn't oblige.

"What the . . . " He twisted around to see what was stopping him from moving, what was making that funny clanking sound, and yelped in horror. His right wrist was handcuffed to the metal frame of the sofabed.

"Moss!" he yelled. "Moss, get in here!" If this was Moss's idea of a practical joke, the sooner he had his laugh, the better. "Moss!"

But there was no answer. The apartment just wasn't that big. Moss had to have left, Lang realized with a feeling of panic. He yanked on his right arm again. Nothing. Then his eyes lit on a note propped up against the lamp by the sofabed.

In huge block letters, Moss had written, "STAY."

"You son of a *bitch*!" Lang screamed.

Okay, he told himself, don't panic. There's a way to get out of this. He wrenched himself torturously around and managed to get out of bed, his body twisted and bent at completely unnatural angles. Lang stared furiously at the metal cuff. Then, with an anger-fueled energy, he jerked his chained arm up, lifting one entire side of the sofabed, and slammed it down, hoping to break the chain. But his action had no effect other than to make a huge, crashing noise and to pull Lang, clad only in his bikini underwear, completely off balance.

Grimly, he repeated the action. And again. The sound of the heavy sofabed hitting the floor was satisfying to his enraged soul, but it had absolutely no effect on the cuff.

"Moss, you bastard!" Lang shouted, thumping and pulling and crashing manically. Someone would have to hear this, he told himself, someone would have to show up. But, in the meantime, he appeared to be . . . stuck. And that wasn't the only problem.

"I can't even go to the *bathroom*!" he howled.

With that realization, he began to look around. There had to be a way out of this predicament. If he could lift this damned thing and send it crashing to the floor, he could . . . *drag* it, he realized. The door to the bathroom beckoned enticingly. Lang strained, his muscles bulging, as he slowly managed to pull the heavy piece of furniture across the room. The going was slow—the thing weighed a ton, he thought furiously—but he crashed his way along, scrunching up throw rugs, knocking over chairs. The ruckus he sent up was amazing; it sounded as if a couple of bull moose were battling it out in the apartment.

At least he was making progress, he thought grimly. A destruction-derby kind of progress, but progress nonetheless. Then, just as he reached the door to the bathroom, the phone began to ring.

"Oh, no," Lang groaned. There was no way he could let a ringing phone just keep ringing: it had to be Moss, calling from a corner pay phone, saying the joke was over and telling him where he could find the key to the handcuffs.

Lang headed back toward the phone, dragging the sofabed noisily in the opposite direction. This time, he managed to scrape the wall with the frame, leaving a huge black mark along it. Serves you right, Moss, he thought as he snatched up the receiver.

"Moss, goddammit!" he snapped. "You've got some weird kind of humor!"

"What?" said a familiar female voice. "Is that you, Nickie?"

"Oh, Angie," Lang said, disappointed. For once, a call from his agent wasn't what he wanted. He listened impatiently to her as she demanded to know what was going on, why he sounded so perturbed. "Angie," Lang interrupted the nonstop flow of questions, "I'm fine . . . Angry? No, don't be silly, why would I be angry?" He sighed. "Things are great," he insisted, hopping up and down to provide a distraction from his full bladder. "Couldn't be better. Moss and I are . . . ," he said, looking down at the cuff, "bonded, I think you'd say. One day and the guy is treating me like a brother. Didn't have a second thought about leaving me alone in his apartment." He looked at the cuffs again. "He's even letting me use some of his personal things."

"Uh huh," he said, as Angie prattled on about the opening of *Smoking Gunn II*. "I heard you, eight million opening night—that's terrific." He yanked furiously on the sofabed and sent a lamp flying. He managed to catch it with his free hand. "Uh huh, box office record. What do you mean, I sound preoccupied? I'm a little tied up, that's all." He listened for a moment. "No," he said, "I don't want to talk about the sequel, not now. You know I'm preparing for . . . *What?* You promised I'd have *two* weeks! No, no, he's the director; if he wants to see me in a week, I'll be ready. Listen, Ange, I'd really love to chat, but I gotta go."

Lang hung up the phone, then looked at the lamp he held in his free hand. He shrugged and tossed it to the floor, where it shattered into fragments. Lang surveyed the breakage with a certain amount of retributive satisfaction. Then he started to drag the sofabed across the floor again. If he didn't get to the bathroom soon . . .

The phone rang.

"Goddammit!" Lang yelled, changing direction again. This time, a small bookcase crashed to the floor as he dragged the sofabed by it. At this rate, he thought, Moss won't have any furniture left to come home to. But he had only himself to blame.

"Moss, that better be you!" Lang shouted into the receiver. "Oh, Susan, hi!" He sighed, trying to keep the tension he was feeling out of his voice. But if he didn't get to the bathroom soon . . .

"No," he said, "John's not here . . . Me? Yeah, sure, I have a minute. Of course." He listened to Susan and nodded, squirming. "Lunch, sure, why not? No, no plans at all. Uh huh, see you there at one." And he hung up the phone. "Unless," he muttered, "I'm still handcuffed to the goddam sofabed!"

An idea struck: if he could break a piece off the frame, then he'd only be dragging around part of a sofabed; it would make movement so much easier. Lang climbed awkwardly on top of the bed and, bent uncomfortably over, began to jump up and down, trying frantically to bend, break, or mutilate the steel frame. It was difficult, he thought, panting from exertion, but it wasn't impossible.

There was a brisk knock at the door, and Mrs. Keppler marched in. "Mr. Moss . . . ," she began. Her jaw dropped, and she stopped speaking when she saw that it was Lang, not John Moss. Her eyes widened in disbelief when she spotted the cuff.

"My God!" she exclaimed, horrified.

"Oh, hi!" Lang said, smiling his best Hollywood smile. "Boy am I ever glad to see you!" He indicated the cuff that linked him to the bed frame. "I could really use a little help here, a key, a file, a—"

"I don't even want to know!" she said, and with a slam, Mrs. Keppler was out the door. The sight of a nearly naked man handcuffed to a sofabed seemed to have stunned her beyond words or action.

"Oh, for Christ's sake!" he yelled after her, frustrated. "Come back here and help me! It's not what it looks like!"

But Mrs. Keppler was gone.

"Okay," he muttered to himself. "So there isn't going to be a cavalry arriving. Just think clearly."

With what felt like superhuman effort, he dragged the sofabed across the room again. He didn't care if the phone rang, if a fire alarm sounded, if the roof caved in. He was going to get to the bathroom. He reached the door and, pulling the bed up behind him, managed to wedge himself partway into the bathroom. He stared dubiously at the toilet, which seemed very far away. Then, with a shrug, he pulled down his briefs and let fly.

Now *this*, Lang thought, staring glumly down, is a *real* pissing contest.

Dressed in an off-duty sweatshirt and jeans, Moss hurried through the squad room toward his desk, trying to remain as inconspicuous as possible. He clutched a file in one hand, and as soon as he he sank into his desk chair, he opened it and began to leaf quickly through the pages, looking for something in particular.

As he glanced at the pages, the entire squad working on the Party Crasher case came in.

"John," China said, startled to see him, "what are you doing here?"

Moss shrugged elaborately and watched out of the corner of his eyes as a knowing look passed from China to Billy, from Skate Cain to Grainy.

"Right," said China calmly, "we've got it."

"What'd you do with the new partner?" Billy asked with a sly grin. "Put him under lock and key somewhere?"

Moss gave him a thoughtful look. "I guess you could say that," he replied. "He's waiting for me in the garage, and I told him to just . . . stay there."

"You left that little dufus without supervision?" Grainy asked, surprised.

"Really, Moss," Cain chimed in, "a good nanny never leaves his post."

Moss pretended to take their good-natured ribbing just the way it was intended and smiled placidly at them. "There's really nothing to worry about," he assured Cain. "I child-proofed the car and took out the cigarette lighter. I think of everything!"

Billy peered over Moss's shoulder, reading from the file he had opened. "Terranova," he said, "gunsmith . . . parole, three years for conspiracy. Interesting."

"Mmm hmm," Moss said noncommittally.

"I'll say," Cain remarked. "Interesting, too, that you happen to have that particular file in your hot little hand, John. I mean, aren't you supposed to be down at Bloomie's, busting kids for stealing makeup?"

Moss closed the file with a shrug. "Cazenov just wanted to see a file, check out our procedure. I grabbed the first one from the top of the stack."

"Uh huh," Grainy said, skepticism dripping from his words.

"Really," Billy said earnestly, "because we'd hate to think this had anything to do with a real case, say, getting some information on the Party Crasher . . . "

"Such *suspicious* minds you all have," Moss chided, shaking his head.

" . . . and that you might not share said information with your friends and colleagues," China added. "Your colleagues who are still officially working the case . . . " She let the sentence trail off.

"Guys, please." Moss looked pained. "That would be wrong! I wouldn't do anything wrong; you know me better than that."

"Moss wouldn't do anything wrong," China assured Billy seriously.

"No, no, of course not," Billy agreed.

"And *we* wouldn't be pissed off if he somehow got ahold of some important information and decided to work on his own, just because he wasn't supposed to be on the case anymore." Cain nodded at his partner. "Right, Moss?"

"Absolutely," Moss agreed solemnly.

"So, about that file . . . ," Grainy said, leaving the sentence unfinished and the implication clear and unstated.

"What? Oh, this!" Moss tossed the file to Grainy and smiled. "It's all yours. Listen, mouseketeers, I'm off to kindergarten duties. But," he said, eyeing them seriously, "if I should *happen* to come across any, uh, leads or have a, uh, *brainstorm* about the case—while I'm guarding the mascara, that is—you'll be the first to know."

He got up, saluted them with his good arm, and walked out, smiling to himself.

SIXTEEN

MOSS FINISHED PENCILING IN AN UNKEMPT MUS-tache on a small poster of Nick Lang preening himself as Joe Gunn. He stepped back and surveyed his work—a construction wall featuring an entire row of Joe Gunns, defaced with silly mustaches—and thought he probably shouldn't take so much pride in such childish behavior. But it was difficult not to feel a *little* gleeful.

First, he had left the odious little egomaniac handcuffed to the bed frame—and he was absolutely certain there was no way Nick Lang was going to Houdini his way out of *that* one—next, he had managed to finagle a revealing peek at the investigation of the Party Crasher; and now, even as he waited to meet the mysterious Terranova, he'd had an added, unexpected chance to make Nick Lang look like a fool, poster-boy style. All in all, it wasn't turning out to be such a bad day.

Moss checked his watch. Terranova should be here by now, he thought, but weapons dealers were by nature careful, and Moss was certain that Terranova would do a very thorough sweep of the environs before showing his face to a stranger—even a stranger who came with the alleged stamp of the Dead Romeos' approval. He strolled into the small, green park, where the meet had been set up, and looked around. No obvious candidate among the adults; they were mainly mothers and nannies with strollers, keeping a close watch on their young charges. At the play area near the jungle gym, there was some sort of commotion, and it attracted Moss's attention. He walked over and saw two little boys, about seven years old, rolling around in the dirt, punching each other as the gathered crowd of kids cheered them on.

Moss waded into the fracas and managed to separate the two, as they continued to scream and kick.

"Hey!" Moss said sharply. "Come on, guys, let's calm down here, okay?"

The two boys stared up at him mutely. Moss couldn't tell if that meant they were with him or against him, but he decided to risk it. He nodded judiciously and let go of their collars, then squatted down to be on their level.

"You guys don't really have to fight, do you?" He looked for response from either kid, but got none. "Okay, let's do it the grown-up way," Moss continued patiently. "Let's talk about it, then we'll shake hands, and we'll be friends. What do you say?"

"Get real!" said one of the kids.

Moss yelped as the other one reached over and popped him in the ear with a solid right. He sprang to his feet, clutching his ear and watching in amazement as the two ran off—probably, he reflected ruefully, to continue the fistfight out of the prying reach of adults.

"Boys will be boys, won't they?"

Moss turned toward the source of the comment and found himself face to face with an innocuous-looking young man, dressed in tasteful, expensive clothing.

"They think fighting is the only way," the young man continued. "And when they grow up . . . ," he said, shrugging, "it still don't change."

"You're Terranova," Moss hazarded.

The man just stared.

Moss looked around the park. "Some office you got yourself, here," he remarked.

Terranova pointed to the swing sets, where a pretty little girl, about eight years old, was kicking her heels high into the air.

"That's my daughter," Terranova said with pride. A look of sadness passed briefly over his face. "I get to see her exactly one Saturday a month." He glanced over at Moss. "She likes to come here, so we do. And I do a little business at the same time."

"Interesting combination," said Moss.

Terranova shrugged. "She doesn't know," he said. "She's happy—that's the good thing about girls; they're happy with things like swings." He turned and stared at Moss, gauging him. "So . . . talking of business . . . " He let the words hang in the air.

"Right," said Moss. "Business. Like I told your . . . friend on the phone, I need something special."

Terranova nodded. "Special," he repeated. "Okay. What did you have in mind?"

"I need a bored-out .45 that can't be traced." He stared at Terranova, trying to read the mind of a man who would conduct this kind of business with his little girl a few yards away. "Something that won't blow up in my hand," he added.

Terranova didn't say a word; he just stared at him. Then, he motioned to someone standing behind Moss, and Moss found himself slammed abruptly up against the fence full of Nick Lang posters, face-first. Moss knew better than to try anything. This was some sort of test.

"Jesus," he muttered, "I guess you're not exactly in the market for repeat customers, are you?"

He felt expert hands go to work on him, patting him down for traces of a wire or a weapon. The hands moved professionally down his back, then his front, to his ankles, up to his crotch.

"Oh, wow," said Moss, "I think I'm getting a hard-on."

The hands spun him roughly around, and Moss got a look at the man. He was huge, not just tall and fat, but enormous, imposing, like a mountain. He reminded Moss of those sumo wrestlers he had seen on television.

Moss knew he couldn't let anything except misplaced courage show. He stared at the huge man. "You might wanna

121

consider maybe skipping a meal now and then, buddy," he said. "Somewhere, you know, a small country is going hungry because of you."

The fat man didn't reply. He didn't blink or acknowledge Moss's comments in any way at all. He merely finished his frisk and moved silently away, standing close enough to help, should his boss want some help.

Moss looked over at Terranova, who stood watching impassively. "Not real talkative, is he?" Moss remarked. "Cat got his tongue?"

Terranova studied him calmly. "Actually, we don't know *who* has it," he said. "It got bitten off in a street fight last year."

Moss tried to hide his shock.

Terranova smiled thinly. "But that didn't change things. He won anyway," he said.

"So . . . do we do business?" Moss said with false bravado. He wanted Terranova to think he was more than just a street punk.

Terranova studied him for a few more moments. Finally, he shook his head. "No," he said. "I can't help you."

"What do you mean?" Moss demanded. "The Dead Romeos told me—"

Terranova shrugged. "I think you've got the wrong guy," he said. "I don't know from Dead Romeos, and I don't know from guns." He paused, and his eyes turned icy. "And besides, you talk like a cop."

"Cop?" Moss said indignantly. "That's crazy! What, just because I don't get my rocks off being fondled in public by some El Gordo with a crush on me?"

Terranova didn't seem to be impressed. He turned on his heel and started to walk away, the fat man following in his wake, like an ocean liner after a tugboat.

Moss had to think quickly. "Hey!" he called after Terranova. "Wait a second!"

There was no indication that Terranova even heard him. Moss jogged quickly beside him, playing for time. "Hey," he said desperately, "wait a second. I've got money, whatever it takes."

Terranova just kept on walking. He was going to collect his daughter, Moss figured, and stroll right on out of the park, and Moss's entire operation would be screwed. Just at that moment, his eye was caught by the row of defaced Nick Lang posters. Moss had a sudden inspiration.

"Listen," he said, putting a hand on Terranova's arm. "Look, Mr. Terranova, you don't understand, I'm completely at my wit's end. I don't know what else to do, where else I can turn!"

Something in Moss's urgent tone made Terranova stop and look. "What do you mean?" he asked.

Moss glanced briefly at Nick Lang's face. "It's this guy, he's . . . he's all *over* me, it's a nightmare! He's a frigging psycho. He forced his way into my life. He actually says right to my face he wants to *be me!*" Moss began to get into it.

"Be you?" Terranova repeated, his curiosity now obviously piqued.

Moss nodded frantically. "Swear to God, it's insane, man!" He held up his hands in a gesture of helplessness. "He moves into my apartment, moves in on my job, for Christ's sake! For all I know, my old lady is his next target!"

"So what do you want me to do about it?" Terranova asked.

"Just hear me out, man," Moss pleaded. "It's getting me *crazy*, I mean, everywhere I look, this guy's smiling at me. I turn on the TV, I hear his voice. You gotta help me, man. I'll pay anything you want; I just gotta get *rid* of this guy!" Moss was really getting into this—probably, he thought for a moment, because he really *did* feel that way about Lang.

Terranova seemed to size him up again, considering his desperate plea. Finally, he shrugged. His cold dark eyes fixed Moss's. "Passionate man," he remarked. He looked over at the fat bodyguard. "Watch Julie," he said.

"Well?" Moss queried.

"Come on," Terranova began to walk again. "I don't do business right out in the open."

He led Moss to a nondescript van parked halfway down the block and unlocked the back door. He motioned Moss inside and climbed in after him.

Moss had a moment of trepidation about waltzing unarmed into an enclosed space with this fully loaded stranger, cut off from view. Under normal circumstances, he would have had plenty of backup watching his every move, but this wasn't normal, and there was no one here to see if he walked out of the van alive or not.

Still, he was so close . . . His cop's instinct told him to just go with the program, to play it out. He looked around the inside of the van and noticed a couple of bumper stickers adorning the walls. "An Armed America is a Ready America" was one. Right on, thought Moss. "Gun Control Means Using Both Hands," read another. Uh huh, thought Moss.

Now all business, Terranova began opening cases and showing Moss the weapons he had for sale. "I have to be careful about who I deal with these days," he said. "You understand."

"Of course," Moss agreed, watching Terranova cock a revolver barrel into place.

"The police tend to frown on the guns I make." He flashed that cold smile at Moss.

"I'll bet," Moss agreed cryptically.

"You must understand. I mean, think about how you got to me. Through the Dead Romeos, and they aren't exactly candidates for upstanding citizen awards, right?"

"Got that right," Moss agreed. "They certainly aren't."

"I figure, let the scum shoot each other, so who cares?"

Moss had heard the line of reasoning before, and he merely nodded noncommitally.

"The thing is," Terranova said, picking out another weapon and demonstrating it to Moss, "I just make the guns. It's not my fault if people who purchase these weapons have occasionally used them for what you might call socially irresponsible acts."

Moss nodded again, thinking this line of reasoning was

124

actually another variation on the famous Nazi anthem, "I was just following orders." The responsibility buck definitely did not stop here, even if the greenback did.

"That is a beauty," Moss remarked, looking over at the gun Terranova was showing him. "This could be exactly the ticket for what I want to do."

"It's yours," Terranova said. Then he named a price.

Moss pretended to mull it over. He countered with a lower offer, just to make this seem real.

Terranova shook his head. "No way."

Finally, Moss sighed, nodded, and pulled a wad of cash out of his pocket. He handed it to Terranova. Terranova, in turn, handed him the gun.

Moss looked it over carefully, checking the clip, the barrel, sighting down it. "Very nice," he said. "Thanks. Now I'm sure of it—this is exactly what I need." He loaded the clip. "By the way," he said casually, "remember when I implied I wasn't a cop?"

Terranova nodded.

Moss pointed the gun at him. "I was acting."

The color drained from Terranova's face.

"I was pretty convincing, wasn't I?" Moss continued, keeping the gun pointed at Terranova. "Just one day, hanging around with this actor I know—can you believe people actually get paid for this?" He kept his tone genial, and the gun pointed straight at Terranova's forehead.

"You're shitting me," Terranova whispered.

Moss shook his head regretfully. " 'Fraid not," he said. "So, Terranova, what I need from you is a little bit of information."

"Wha-what?" Terranova stammered.

"You made a gun like this with a laser sight for someone else recently."

"No way," Terranova said firmly.

"Think about it," Moss suggested. "Tall guy? Strong build, dark hair . . . remember?"

"Uh . . . "

"Sure you do," Moss said cheerfully. "And now you're gonna help me find him."

Terranova's eyes darted to the side, and Moss figured the weapons dealer was trying to gauge just how he could get past him, out the door of the van, and get a signal to his bodyguard before Moss shot him.

"Hey," Moss said, "do I look stupid to you? Park's surrounded."

Terranova sagged.

"And you're on parole," Moss reminded him. "I bust you for selling these, you get stuck with accessory to murder, we're talking about a whole lot of years fighting off really big guys who find you attractive. And," he added, "you probably don't get to see that pretty little girl of yours take her first communion, either."

"Accessory to murder?" Terranova echoed blankly. "Who'd this guy do? The *Mayor*?"

"It's more than one who," Moss said. "This guy's blowing holes in people all over the city. You ever read the newspaper?"

Terranova looked stunned. "The Party Crasher?" he said in a whisper.

"None other," Moss assured him. "So, so much for your social responsibility theory, huh, Terranova? You look as though you feel just a little bit *culpable*."

"I didn't know," Terranova said feebly.

Moss waved the excuse away. "Where is he?"

Terranova just shook his head. "I don't know, man. Honest. He meets me, he gives me some design specs, that's it. I go, he goes, I do 'em, he gets 'em."

"You never asked why, huh?" Moss said curiously.

"No," Terranova said softly. "I just figured him for a nut case, a gun fanatic, one of those weekend warriors." He shrugged.

"Just another Bernhard Goetz loose in the subways?" Moss asked.

"What do I do to get out of this?" Terranova asked. The

ex-con wheels were beginning to turn in his head.

"Well, isn't that funny? I was just thinking about the same thing."

"I can't go back to the joint, man," Terranova said urgently. "I can't!"

"I can understand that, Terranova," Moss said seriously. "I really can. So. Let's talk about what you have that I might want," Moss suggested. "For instance, you say you don't have this guy's address, his name, anything . . . right?"

"Right," Terranova nodded. "But I have a gun," he said eagerly, "a gun I made for him. He's waiting for it."

"And you expect to hear from him, right?"

Terranova nodded again.

"When?"

"Tonight," Terranova whispered.

Moss felt a cold chill do an arpeggio down his spine. "That's good," he said. "I'll be ready tonight."

SEVENTEEN

THE RESTAURANT SUSAN HAD PICKED FOR LUNCH was centrally located. It was also crowded, bright, and very noisy. And, Lang thought ruefully, slinking through the door in his ill-fitting off-the-rack clothes, it was too darned *light*. A dim eatery with secluded booths would have been his preference, given the . . . current state of affairs. But there was nothing he could do now. Hell, he thought, as he saw Susan waving to him from a table across the room, he was lucky he'd managed to actually make it here without dragging the sofabed with him.

As Lang maneuvered his way across the large, busy room, he kept his right hand buried self-consciously in his pocket. He pulled the chair out with his left and scooted into it.

"Hi," he said, as cheerfully as possible, "I'm sorry I'm late . . . "

"Oh, that's okay. I just got here a couple of minutes ago myself," Susan said, smiling.

Lang shrugged. "It's been one of those totally crazy mornings," he said.

"Couldn't get yourself out of bed?" Susan asked innocently.

Lang blinked. "Uh . . . not exactly. It was just, uh, stuff, you know. Stuff at the office, lotta paperwork." He wanted to get off the subject of work as quickly as possible—there was no way he could keep up the bluff for very long, and if Susan decided to ask him what case he was on or how long he'd been on the force, he was sunk. "So," he said, "you already order?"

Susan nodded. "I hope you don't mind, it's just with your schedule and all, I didn't know if . . . "

Lang dismissed her explanation with his free left hand. "No, that's okay, really. I'll just find something here real quick . . . " He perused the unappetizing menu, then lifted his right hand to flag the harried waitress, forgetting all about the pair of handcuffs that still dangled from his wrist.

Susan stared at the cuffs blankly. "Uh, Ray . . . ," she said hesitantly, "did you know that you have a pair of handcuffs on your wrist?"

"What? Oh, you mean *these*?" Lang gestured innocently at the cuffs, then faked a surprised laugh. "You know, forgot all about them. I, uh . . . I hadda take a perp in this morning and . . ."— he thought quickly— "I . . . lost the key, that's right, I actually lost it . . . down a drain. After, you know, I had uncuffed him." Lang tried for a hearty laugh, but what came out was more like a squeak. Still, Susan seemed to buy it, and that was the most important thing.

What had *really* happened was quite a different matter. After Lang had gotten out of the bathroom—well, technically, out of the *doorway* to the bathroom—he had dragged the sofabed to the archway that led to the kitchen. A hasty search through the drawers he could manage to reach had yielded a couple of hammers, a screwdriver, and a pair of pliers, and Lang had promptly set to work dismantling the entire bed frame. It was tricky, trying to reach parts of the frame in his manacled state, but he had finally managed to do it. Then Lang had simply slipped the empty cuff off of the rods it was around. The sofabed now lay in pieces scattered about John Moss's living room. But the cuffs were a different story. Until he got ahold of Moss in the flesh, it looked as though they were here to stay.

"Nice jewelry," the waitress remarked, staring at the cuffs. "What can I get you?"

Lang ignored the jibe and glanced down at the menu again. "I'll have the number six with romaine, not iceberg lettuce, sprouts if they're fresh, and the dressing on the side."

"No."

Lang looked up, startled. Had he really heard the waitress just say no? Her return stare was flat and belligerent, so apparently he had heard correctly. "Well . . . ," he said.

"You *can* have exactly what's on the menu, though," she said.

Moss looked down again. No way. "I'll just have an Evian. With lemon."

The waitress snorted. "I got tap water," she said, "with ice."

"That's fine," Lang said meekly. Why fight City Hall, right? Too bad he wasn't preparing for that famous scene from *Five Easy Pieces*.

"Good," said the waitress, grabbing the menu from him. "Big spender. Fresh sprouts." She snorted in derision again. "What're you, from California or something?" And she was gone.

There was an awkward silence when she had left, and Lang busied himself buttering a roll. But the cuffs jangled and kept getting in the way, and he finally gave up.

"So, Susan," he said, turning on his high-wattage smile, "here we are."

"Yes," she agreed, "here we are."

Silence descended again.

Finally, Susan spoke. She seemed a little embarrassed. "Ray," she said hesitantly, "one of the reasons I asked you to meet me here is that, well . . . it's about John. I don't want to put you in an awkward position or anything, but I really need to talk to somebody."

Lang nodded encouragingly.

"I mean, you two are pretty close, aren't you?" asked Susan.

"More than close, Susan," Lang said sincerely. "You might say that John Moss has been a kind of . . . mentor, a role model for me."

131

Susan sighed, crumbling a roll into bits. "I don't know what it is about him," she said. "I can't figure him out."

"I know exactly what you mean," Lang assured her quite honestly.

"You know," Susan said, frowning down at the pile of crumbs she was making, "when we met each other, a couple of weeks ago, I really thought I had him pegged right off the bat."

"You're kidding!" The words emerged before Lang had a chance to censor them. "I mean," he added hastily, "he's kind of . . . complex, don't you think?"

"Well, yes, of course," Susan said thoughtfully. "But he seemed so solid, so . . . confident. A sensitive kind of man."

Sensitive? Lang thought. Hah!

"And . . . ," Susan said as she blushed a little, "we really had some sparks going between us, right away. I mean, he asked me for my number five minutes after we met!"

"He did?" Lang asked, amazed. Were they talking about the same man? Was that neurotic bundle of romantic insecurity who'd been drinking himself into a stupor at the bar the night before, the one who knew nothing about women, the *same* John Moss she was talking about?

"Well," Susan amended, a little embarrassed, "no. Not exactly, that is. I mean, I kind of hinted that I was . . . listed in the book, and that I'd be home that night, after six."

"Waiting for his call?" Lang suggested with a smile.

Susan shrugged. "Yes, waiting for his call. Well, you know how it is," she added, "sometimes a guy needs a little push in the right direction."

"Oh, of course," Lang agreed sincerely. He didn't think Moss needed a little push; he thought a bulldozer headed in his direction might be more like it. "And besides, it never hurts to find out if a prospective partner is able to pick up hints and figure out what you want, does it?"

Susan smiled coyly. "No," she agreed, "it doesn't hurt at all."

"So . . . " Lang urged her on.

"So . . . he called, and we went out, and it was terrific. Well," she said, "actually, it was a little tense. But nothing major. I mean, it was just kind of awkward, you know, first date stuff, I figured. I thought we were really on the same wavelength, you know? Because after that, he came to give a talk where I work—I don't know if I told you this; I'm a counselor at a youth center. You know, kids who've had a little trouble, that kind of thing."

"John Moss could relate to them?" Lang was surprised.

"Relate?" Susan's eyes were bright. "He was great! I mean, I was really impressed how he connected with these kids; he had them in the palm of his hand."

"Hmmm," Lang said.

"But . . . ," Susan said, her bright face sobering, "when it's just the two of us, or—like last night—with Bonnie along, too, I'm not certain what it is, but it's not the same. I can't tell what he thinks about, what he cares about. He just goes . . . quiet."

"Yeah," Lang said thoughtfully, "I noticed."

"At first, you know," Susan said, toying with the salad in front of her, "I wondered if he was just . . . shy or something, just around me. But after last night . . . " She shrugged helplessly. "You saw how tense he was. And then that fight and everything." She bit her lip and stared down at her plate. "Maybe I read him all wrong. Maybe he's just cooling on the whole thing."

Moss, you first-class schmuck, Lang thought. "No, Susan," he said sincerely, "I can guarantee that *that's* not it. He isn't cooling on you, believe me."

"No?" Susan asked, eyeing him dubiously.

"Absolutely not," he said firmly.

"Then . . . how come I feel like I can't get close to him? How come I feel more connection just sitting here talking to you than I have on the two dates John and I have had?" Susan's eyes were earnest and a little hurt.

"Here's your water," the waitress smacked the glass down on the table in front of Lang, spilling some over the edges.

He was happy to have the momentary reprieve.

"Come on, Ray, talk to me," she said. "You guys are so tight, you must have a theory or something about this."

Lang ran his hand hesitantly through his hair, the cuffs jangling unnervingly.

"Well," he said, "that's hard to . . . you know, it's hard to really explain stuff like that." That, he told himself, was somewhere beyond feeble in the response category.

Susan sighed. "I have the worst luck with guys," she said mournfully.

"You do?" Lang was surprised. She was pretty, she was sweet, she was caring. Oh, right, he thought, with those qualities, she probably falls for every sad sack in the world. She's probably a mark for every schmuck with a hard luck story.

"Uh huh," Susan said. "And I have to admit that it really used to be my own fault. I had this speech impediment . . . I couldn't say no." She looked up and laughed ruefully. "Well, having Bonnie cured me of *that* problem! Actually, it cured me of a lot of things."

"She's a cute kid," Lang said offhandedly. Even if she did like Mel Gibson better than Nick Lang.

Susan's eyes sparkled. "You like kids, don't you?" she asked.

Lang nodded. "Yeah, sure. Kids are great," he said.

"They feel it coming from you," Susan assured him. "You were a big hit with Bonnie last night."

Lang shrugged. "It's not hard to get along with someone whose biggest demands in life are the right kind of pizza," he said.

Susan seemed to gaze inward for a moment. "You know," she said with a sigh, "this is all such new territory for me. I mean, I *never* thought I would ever date a cop. They always used to be the bad guys, you know what I mean?"

Lang nodded.

"Oh well," she said with a shrug, "times change, and so do people. John's the first one I ever dated." She paused. "So, what's it like?"

Lang grinned. "I don't know, I've never dated a cop, either."

Susan giggled. It was a nice change of mood, and it lit up her face.

"Nooo . . . ," she said, "come *on*. *Being* a cop, that's what I meant, what does it feel like?"

Lang paused and stared down at the table. What did being a cop feel like? How the hell would he know? John Moss wouldn't give him half a chance to find out! Then he remembered what Moss had said, the speech that had impressed him so much the day before.

He looked up and stared Susan straight in the eye. "It's . . . kinda tough to put into words," he said modestly.

"Just try," Susan urged him. "Please. I really want to understand."

"Okay," he agreed, "I'll try." He paused again. "I mean, you have to understand one thing about cops. We live the job. It's something we *are*, not something we *do*."

"That must be so intense," Susan murmured.

More of Moss's diatribe was coming back to Lang, and as he spoke the words, he could feel himself becoming the part, becoming Moss.

"When you're a cop," he told Susan, "fear is just a part of your life. Every time you walk up to give someone a speeding ticket, you know that you might have to kill them or be killed yourself." He made his eyes go steely and dark. "All people know about this job is what they see in the movies. But in the movies, they can have seventeen takes to get it right. We don't *get* seventeen takes, Susan. We get just one, and it lasts our whole life. We mess it up and we're dead."

He saw the way Susan was staring at him, and he realized that she was mesmerized, openly moved by his words—moved in precisely the manner that he hoped to move audiences with his coveted portrayal of a cop. It gave him a jolt of confidence. Tony DiBennedetti, he thought, you're gonna be mine.

"Ray, that is so . . . eloquent. It defines the whole job, and the person who does it," Susan said. Then she sighed. "Why can't John ever say things like that? I know he must feel that way, too, don't you think?"

Lang felt an unexpected, sharp pang of guilt. Suddenly, he wanted to admit that those weren't his words at all, that John had said it just like that and, in fact, had said it first. But he couldn't. Instead, he settled for smiling uncomfortably.

"I'm sure he does," he said weakly.

Susan leaned forward and put her hand over his. "I have a feeling that you're one special policeman, Ray," she said.

"Oh, well . . . " Lang shrugged modestly. "I'm no different than anyone else."

Susan looked at him earnestly. "I don't think that's true," she said. Then she looked at her watch. "Oops!" she said. "I didn't realize it had gotten this late . . . Gotta go."

"Me, too," said Lang. "Come on. I'll catch a cab with you."

Susan stared at him oddly for a moment, and then she laughed. "A cab?" she repeated. "On my salary? On yours? Very funny, Ray."

Oops, Lang thought. Nearly blew it again. "Ha ha," he said. "Just kidding."

EIGHTEEN

"DON'T YOU HAVE ANY TOKENS?" SUSAN INQUIRED.

"Tokens . . . ," Lang said blankly.

He had never been in a subway in his entire life, and he had simply been following Susan's lead so far. Pushed and shoved by a crowd eager to get somewhere, they'd trekked down a large, dank flight of stairs to a cavern filled with graffiti, rumbling noises, and people of every conceivable type. He was almost entranced by it. It was so full of *humanity*. It was so *authentic*.

"Uh . . . " He pretended to fumble around in his pockets. "I must've left them."

"Oh, never mind," Susan said, pressing one into his palm, "it's my treat."

Lang followed obediently as she dropped the token into a turnstile and hurried through it and onto the platform. He did the same, acting as though he did this every day of his life.

"Honestly," Susan said, shaking her head in affectionate dismay, "you and John . . . "

"Me and John what?" Lang asked. John Moss never had subway tokens either?

"Oh, you know. Both of you are like that—it's as if the day-to-day stuff doesn't occur to you, you know, without being reminded. The real life stuff . . . But I suppose that's because you both have bigger problems on your mind all the time."

"That must be it," Lang agreed absently, staring in complete fascination as a train rumbled rapidly out of the dark tunnel to the right and came to a screeching halt in front of them. *The Taking of Pelham 1,2,3*, he thought. Wow!

The pneumatic doors whooshed open, and Susan hurried into the train. Lang did the same, keeping close to her. They found seats easily in the half-filled car, and Lang looked around him in wonder, taking it all in—the scrawled-over ads along the sides, the graffitied doors, blasé passengers hanging onto straps and reading at the same time. And then the darkness enveloped them as the train pulled out of the station and began to gather speed again. You're so strangely isolated here, Lang mused, surrounded by humanity but so cut off from the world above.

"I like this," Susan remarked, smiling at him.

"What's that?" Lang asked, jerked back to reality by her words.

"Getting a police escort," Susan said. "I think I could get used to it."

"Susan, that's no joke, not really," Lang admonished her. "I really don't think you should ride these things alone; it's dangerous." He'd seen enough movies to know *that* much.

Susan laughed. "Ray, that's so sweet," she said. "But so impractical." She studied him. "You know, if I'd met someone like you—someone so concerned and decent—say, fifteen years ago, I might have straightened out my life a lot sooner."

Lang felt a growing sense of discomfort. Susan's conversation topics seemed all to lead in one direction, and that direction, Lang thought, seemed to be . . . romance. It wasn't as though she was putting moves on him, not directly, that is; it was more as if, frustrated by her efforts to get close to John Moss, she was turning to the person she believed to be closest to Moss—his partner—and seeing in that person what she wanted to see in Moss. That wasn't so good.

It wasn't, Lang told himself, as though women didn't fall all over him anyway. He was used to that. And it wasn't

138

as if those women didn't occasionally mix him up with the characters he played on screen. It was just that this woman was different, and these circumstances were different.

Lang decided that it was his responsibility to take the situation in hand, switch things around, make Susan focus on the *real* object of her affection again.

"Look, Susan," he said seriously, "it's really important to me that this works out. You and John, that is."

Susan looked curiously at him for a moment. "Why?" she asked finally.

"Because I can tell he really cares about you," Lang said firmly.

"Oh?" Susan seemed skeptical. "Then I guess you must see more than I do."

"Maybe," Lang agreed. "But you have to believe me, he really does. He just has a hard time showing it."

"I'll say." Susan bit her lip. "I just get such . . . mixed signals from him."

"Give him a little time, Susan," Lang urged her. "It's not fair to give up on him so soon."

"It isn't?" Susan sighed. "I don't know, I guess I'm just being self-protective," she said. "I don't want to get hurt any more, not at this point in my life. I don't think of it as giving up, Ray," she said, shrugging. "I guess it's more like . . . well, just keeping my options open. Don't you understand?"

"Yes," Lang said slowly, "I do. But if you really want something, I believe you have to go for it all the way, a hundred-and-fifteen percent. Not just drop out when the going gets tough."

Susan was quiet for a few minutes; she seemed to be thinking about what he had said.

Then the train came to a squealing halt at another station, the doors opened, and more passengers crowded on. Two of them were obvious trouble—and everyone in the car seemed to sense it immediately, staring, then trying not to stare, not to draw any attention to themselves.

They were large teenagers, bulky and belligerent, stoned

139

on something, no doubt, and wearing the colors of their gang. Lang, like everyone else on the car, shrank back, hoping to blend in with the woodwork and become invisible.

He cringed even more when he heard Susan whispering to the woman next to her. "Don't worry," Susan was assuring her, "the man I'm with is a cop."

Lang elbowed Susan in the ribs. "Listen," he hissed, "this really isn't my jurisdiction."

"What does that matter?" Susan shot back, surprised. "You're still a cop."

Lang thought quickly. "I'm serious," he hissed, "the transit police get really bent out of shape if we butt in on their busts."

Susan threw him a look of astonishment, then turned away to see what was happening.

The teenaged thugs had picked out their first victim. She was a tiny, neatly dressed old lady who was traveling alone. The huge needlepoint purse on her lap would be hard to miss, and it was a perfect target for the young muggers. The two young thugs gave each other the eye, then swaggered over to the old lady, looming above her in order to make her well aware of their threatening presence. The elderly woman seemed to fold up, to shrink under their ferocious gaze. Smiling nastily, the two sat down, one on either side of her, crowding her. She looked from one to the other, obviously petrified.

The train began to slow down as it approached another station.

"I'll hop off and flag the transit cops," Lang told Susan.

"What's in the big bag, Gramma?" one of the muggers asked the lady.

The old lady gazed straight ahead, refusing to acknowledge their presence or the question they had asked. She clutched the bag tightly on her lap.

"It looks way too big for you," the thug continued.

"Yeah," the other thug agreed. "Looks way too heavy for you to be carrying alone. Like maybe you might need some help."

"Ray!" Susan hissed sharply. "For God's sake, do something!"

The train hissed to a gliding stop and the doors opened. The young toughs exchanged more eye signals, and then the one on the lady's left moved swiftly toward the door. The one on the right snatched the bag from the woman and followed his friend.

"Help!" yelled the lady. "Somebody help me!"

"Ray, for heaven's sake, what are you waiting for?" demanded Susan.

Lang realized he no longer had a choice: if he didn't begin to act like a cop, Susan was going to discover—and blow—his cover. He swallowed hard, took a deep breath, and whipped out his phony badge. Brandishing it like a silver cross meant to ward off a vampire, Lang leapt right into the muggers' line of escape, blocking them, and flashed the badge.

"Police officer," he said loudly. "Hold it right there."

The two thieves froze momentarily. Then one of them whipped a gun out from under his jacket and began to brandish it wildly. Even in his own panicked state, Lang could see that the mugger was shaking—almost as much as he was.

"Don't *you* move from this train," the mugger ordered Lang, shoving him roughly to the side. "Pig!"

Then the two thieves began to back out of the car. Without warning, the gun in the thief's hand went off, a terrifying boom in the confined space; the shot went into the ceiling and screams began in earnest.

Lang watched with stunned amazement as a variety of guns, knives, mace, and makeshift weapons suddenly appeared, pulled from the passengers' purses and pockets. Jesus, he thought irrelevantly, people didn't exaggerate about New York. A couple of the angrier gunslingers fired after the retreating thieves, as they scrambled rapidly from the car. Lang saw people dive to the floor as two windows were shattered by gunshots. The metal sides of the train were punctured with more shots. And all hell broke loose—

people were ducking, hiding, shooting, screaming—anything to get out of the way of—or join in—the dangerous fracas.

The muggers took advantage of the widespread panic to flee, and all eyes turned to Lang and his badge as the teenagers ran down the station platform.

"Are you a cop or *aren't* you?" one furious woman screamed at him. "Why don't you do something?"

Lang darted a swift glance at Susan, who was staring at him—or rather, at his lack of definitive action—with growing horror. There was no way out of this, he realized. If he didn't stay in character, this research trip was history. Besides, *somebody* had to get that poor old lady's purse back.

Lang darted out of the car and headed in the direction of the retreating thieves. Legs and arms pumping, adrenaline flowing, he raced down the subway platform. Ahead of him, he saw the unarmed mugger go crashing into a startled bystander, and then both of them went tumbling to the ground.

Lang tried to pull the useless rubber gun from his pocket, but he got it tangled with the still-attached cuffs and gave up before the muggers had time to put any more space between him and themselves. He continued to race awkwardly down the platform, dodging stunned, gaping passengers. Just as he approached the downed mugger and bystander, Lang tripped and went flying right on top of the thief.

"Okay," breathed Lang, "I've got you—come on, you're under arrest!"

And pow—a fist in the face launched Lang backward, seeing the proverbial stars.

"Hey . . . ," he protested weakly.

The mugger scrambled to his feet, and pausing just long enough to kick Lang twice in the stomach, he ran off. Lang lay there, gasping for breath, then made a feeble attempt to climb to a standing position. Winded and in pain, he rested for a moment on his hands and knees.

Then he scrambled all the way up, his head and belly throbbing. He could see from the way the panicked crowd was parting up ahead that the two muggers had reached a dead end in the tunnel and, now panicked themselves, were heading back in his direction.

"Oh, shit!" Lang gasped.

They were getting closer. Lang's mind darted quickly through his possible choices, but it all boiled down to only one: he had to stand his ground.

Managing to untangle the handcuffs from the rubber gun, he yanked it from his pocket. Then, assuming the two-handed, straight-ahead stance he had practiced in the mirror back at Moss's apartment, he pointed it at the oncoming thieves.

"Freeze!" he yelled, but it came out as a cracked whisper. "Freeze!" This time, it was a more authoritative yell.

The muggers skidded to a halt, and the one who was armed raised his gun hand.

"Oh, sweet Jesus," Lang said, and went diving to one side as the thief fired directly at him.

Lang curled up and rolled himself behind a temporary barricade.

Boom! He heard the report of the pistol, and half of his barricade—a rickety newsstand—shattered from the impact, sending magazines and newspapers crashing to the floor all around him.

Boom! The terrifying sound came again. More of the newsstand splintered apart, and Lang saw issues of *Hustler*, *PC World*, *The New Yorker* go flying, shredded to bits.

Lang peered desperately around, hoping against hope that someone—anyone—would appear armed and on his side. But he realized that the vigilantes from the subway weren't about to venture from the relative safety of their position. He was on his own.

Boom! The sound came again, and the rest of the newsstand was gone. Lang dove behind a concrete pillar. From this position, he could see a group of terrified people huddled together down the platform.

"Hey!" Lang screamed toward them. "Somebody call the police!" Then he added, "More of them, I mean, other police, besides *me*! Backup!" Preferably, he thought, ones who carried *real* guns, not rubber replicas.

NINETEEN

CROUCHING LOW, SUSAN SCURRIED ALONG THE wall of the station, trying to get as far away as she could from the terrifying sound of gunshots. She dashed up to the street in quest of a pay phone, taking the stairs two at a time. But when she reached the top of the stairs, out of breath and frightened, she saw that a number of blue-and-whites had already converged on the scene, brakes screeching, sirens howling, red lights flashing.

"Thank God," she said to herself.

Cops streamed out of the cars, holding their rifles at ready. Susan was surprised to spot John Moss among them.

"John!" she yelled. "Over here!"

She saw him look around in confusion.

"John!" She ran to him. "Oh, John, thank God you're here!"

"Susan." His look was concerned. "Jesus! What are you doing here?"

She grasped his arm. "Hurry, John, you've got to hurry! Ray's pinned down by a couple of muggers—they've got guns, but I don't think Ray can fire back at them—there are too many people around, it's too dangerous!" The words tumbled breathlessly from her lips.

There was no mistaking the urgency in her voice, but Moss didn't register the danger of the situation as quickly as he did the implication of it. "Ray . . . ," he said, " . . . and you?"

"Hurry!" Susan urged him, oblivious to what he was really asking.

Moss's cop-mind clicked into gear. This wasn't the time or place to wonder what the hell his girl and Nick Lang were doing on the same subway at the same time. Along with a group of uniformed cops, he started down the stairs to the scene.

Down in the tunnel, Moss went automatically into a crouching stance and began to creep along the wall in much the same way Susan had. The sound of sporadic gunshots echoed through the station, and Moss cocked his head, listening, then headed in their direction.

As he rounded a corner, he could see Lang up ahead, kneeling behind a thick pillar. Well, at least the little rat had the sense to find himself a safe hiding place, Moss thought grudgingly. Then he noticed the rubber gun dangling from Lang's hand. Even in this potentially lethal situation, Moss found he had to hold himself back from laughing.

But his silent mirth faded as abruptly as it had begun when farther down the platform, beyond Lang, Moss could see the armed young mugger. The kid had a lethal-looking gun in his grasp, and even from a distance, Moss thought he seemed hopped up and frightened—a potentially deadly combination.

Moss flattened himself against the wall, preparing for the crack of a fired pistol as he saw the thief take aim and squeeze the trigger.

But it never came. Instead, there was just a flat sounding click, and the mugger looked down at his weapon in consternation.

"He's out of bullets," Moss heard Lang whisper jubilantly. "He's out of bullets!"

"Then go get him, Hollywood," Moss said softly.

Lang whirled around, then let out a sigh of relief when he saw who had spoken. "Jesus," he said softly, "am I ever glad to see you."

Moss eyed the handcuffs dangling from Lang's wrist. "Really?" he said dubiously.

146

"Listen, Moss . . . ," Lang began.

"Shut up and get out of my way," Moss said succinctly, walking around Lang and out into the open.

"What are you doing?" he heard Lang hiss. "Are you nuts?"

"You're the one who said he was out of bullets," Moss said calmly.

"Yeah, but . . . "

Moss ignored Lang. Standing up straight and tall, he showed himself to the mugger. His gun was held lightly at his side. He looked oddly loose, almost relaxed as he moved steadily toward his quarry.

As Moss got closer, he could see he'd been right: there was a mixture of fear and anger in the mugger's eyes.

"Easy," Moss said, "and no one will get hurt. Just toss the gun on the floor."

The mugger stared down at the weapon he was holding. "Fuck no," he said.

"Come on," Moss said reasonably, "you don't want to add murdering a policeman to the charges, do you?"

"Fuck you."

"Special circumstances, you know about that, don't you?" Moss said, still advancing slowly, steadily, toward the thief. "That means you fry—no parole, no hearings, just the chair."

"Stay back, man!" the mugger shouted. "I mean it, you stay away from me!"

The gun was shaking in the thief's hand, but Moss had no doubt the man was serious. It was a situation of bluff and bluff again. Whoever was the better bluffer won; whoever wasn't, lost. And loss could mean anything from arrest to death.

Moss's mind clicked rapidly through the situation, thought about the age of his adversary, and took a calculated risk. He brought his own gun up from where it dangled casually at his side to face straight ahead, eye level. He kept walking forward.

"I'm warnin' you . . . ," said the mugger.

There was a trickle of ice down Moss's back. He kept walk ing. He was so close he could see the perspiration beading th mugger's forehead, could see his hand shaking as he tried raise the gun he was holding. It was as if his arm refused obey his brain—the gun stayed pointed down at the floor.

"Stay back, man, I mean it!" the mugger screamed. "I blow you away!"

But Moss just kept on going. Slowly, deliberately, as if had all the time in the world. And then he was there, standing unblinking, toe to toe with the thief. He stared directly in the young man's dangerous eyes. Then Moss raised his gu and put it against the mugger's trembling upper lip.

"Thanks for the warning," Moss said. "But we seem to at a standoff here. What do you think we should do about it?"

He saw the panic and anger in the mugger's face chang to a look of surrender. Then Moss simply reached out an took the gun from the mugger's hand. The weapon droppe loosely, heavily, into his palm.

Then, suddenly, there was activity all around them. Fo uniformed cops rushed in from their hiding places and lea on the mugger. He put up no resistance as they threw hi roughly to the ground, cuffing his hands in back. Someor frisked him head to toe for other weapons. Someone el began to read him his rights.

Moss breathed a sigh of relief and reholstered his ov gun. He examined the mugger's weapon, which he still he in his hand.

Lang crept around from behind the pillar and came up Moss, eyeing the mugger's gun with some trepidation.

"Whew!" said Lang. "That was close."

"Was it?" asked Moss, sighting down the barrel of the gu

"Well, hell yes!" said Lang heartily. He reached for the g and Moss let him have it. "See, I was right," Lang said prou ly, after a cursory examination of the weapon. "No bullets.

"May I?" Moss said politely, holding his hand out for th gun.

Lang handed it back to him, and Moss banged it sharply against the wall. Then he pulled the trigger, and the gun fired loudly into the tunnel.

Moss looked at Lang and shook his head. "Nope," he said, "you were wrong. It was a misfire." He turned and walked away.

Lang felt his knees buckle weakly under him as he realized how close he had come to getting killed. His pants were wet. "Oh, Christ," he muttered. "Perfect." This was not his day for bathroom etiquette. He looked hurriedly around and grabbed a partially intact newspaper; holding it in front of his crotch, he hurried up the steps and out into the daylight, where Moss was giving details to another cop.

Susan spotted him and left Moss's side to come running over to him. "Ray, are you all right?" she asked, worry in her voice.

"Sure." Lang waved the whole thing off, trying to keep the newspaper in place.

"God," Susan said with admiration, "you were terrific! That was so brave!"

"It was?" Lang said, amazed.

"Well, yes, of course it was!" Susan said, looking at him oddly. "Look at the way you handled that incredibly dangerous situation! I mean, it's exactly what we were talking about before."

"And just how *did* he handle that incredibly dangerous situation that he told you about before?" Moss appeared beside them.

What Lang saw in his eyes was neither admiration nor worry. Sarcasm and barely contained anger dripped from his words.

"What . . . what do you mean, John?" Susan asked, bewildered by his blatant belligerence. "You were right there, you saw—"

Moss interrupted her in mid-sentence. "All right!" he snapped. "Would either of you like to tell me just what the hell is going on here?"

149

Susan looked at him blankly.

John looked from the embarrassed Lang to Susan and bac
again. "Oh, right," he said, "I get it. I suppose you're goin
to say that this was just a coincidence, that *you*" —he directe
a burning look at Lang— "just wanted to experience the sub
ways, and out of all the millions of subways you could hav
picked, you just *happened* to pick the one Susan was on."

"Hey," said Susan.

Moss wasn't listening. "And you just *happened* to win
up in the same car."

"Hey!" This time, Susan shouted, and it got Moss's atter
tion. "I asked Ray to lunch," she said.

Moss's jaw dropped. "You *what*?" he said incredulous
ly.

"I asked Ray to lunch," Susan repeated firmly.

"I can explain . . . ," Lang started to say, but Susan cu
him off with an angry gesture.

"There's nothing *to* explain," she said, her temper rising
"What is this, the Neanderthal routine or something? Ju:
what the hell do either of you—"

"There sure as hell *is* something to explain!" Moss ex
claimed angrily.

"I can explain . . . ," Lang began again, but no one wa
listening to him. The argument was now between John an
Susan.

"First," Moss said, seething, "he butts in on our date la:
night, and then he leaves me to clean up a mess while h
waltzes off with you and Bonnie."

"Waltzes *off*?" Lang said in amazement. "I was just try
ing—"

"You shut up!" John snapped. "I'm not finished. So," h
said, turning to Susan again, "that's last night. And then, ne>
thing I know, the very next day, you two are having lunch!

"Well, you don't have to make it sound like you caug!
us in an X-rated motel!" Susan snapped back at him. "An
now that you've said your little piece, I've got a few thing
to get off my chest, too!" She stared at John, her eyes narro>

and angry. "You can just cut the jealousy bit, John, because you've got no right acting that way with me!"

"Oh, I don't . . . "

"Shut up and listen!" Susan said. "You know, John, I'm sure this is the last thing you want to hear, but I'm going to say it anyway. You could take a few *pointers* from a guy like Ray."

Moss groaned. Lang groaned silently.

"It's true!" Susan continued doggedly. "At least he knows how to deal with people. It doesn't get in the way of his being a cop! And he knows what it means to be a cop, too! While you were off . . . I don't know, probably trashing another pizza parlor and booking some dangerous drunks, he was here, handling some *real* felons, without losing his head!" She took a quick breath and wound up triumphantly, "And Ray didn't even fire a single shot!"

Susan lifted her chin haughtily, turned around, and stalked off.

Moss stared balefully at Lang. "Didn't fire a single shot, huh?" He yanked the newspaper away from Lang's crotch. "Yes, he did."

But Susan had already disappeared into the crowd, and Moss was left to wonder once again if she had also just disappeared right out of his life.

TWENTY

MOSS BURST THROUGH THE DOOR TO CAPTAIN Brix's office as if the hounds of hell were after him. Brix didn't even have a chance to protest; Moss was already talking a mile a minute.

"Okay," he said, warding off the Captain's response, "I know, I *know*! I left him on his own, guilty as charged, mea culpa, all that crap. But hey, come on! For Christ's sake, nothing really happened, well, anyway, the guy *is* okay, not that that's any kind of valid excuse, I *know* that, and I know that it's probably not music to your ears to hear that this whole mess happened while I was working on the Party Crasher case, which I know I wasn't supposed to be doing, but before you start, before you even take a breath to say what you have every right to say—even though I know what it's going to be—just listen to one thing, okay?"

Brix got the chance to nod silently, but he had no idea if Moss had even noted the response.

"I know where the Crasher's going to be tonight. This is the real thing. I know when, I know where; now all we have to do is mobilize every available man for this thing right now, and we can call the shots ourselves—we can at last drop this guy cold!"

Moss finally paused for a breath, steeling himself for Brix's onslaught.

Brix studied him coolly, carefully. "How?" was all he said.

Moss blinked, startled. Then he recovered himself. "He's picking up the gun tonight, from this guy Terranova who I . . . well, never mind that part of it. Anyway, I know when this is going down, so we'll just have to get there first. Captain," he continued earnestly, "this is it—this is our only real shot."

Brix looked at him for what seemed to Moss to be an eternity. Finally, he nodded his head. Then he pressed his intercom button and spoke.

"Get Cain," he told his secretary, "get Grainy and China, Billy . . . anyone else you can round up, get them in here immediately."

Moss expelled a long sigh of relief. "That's great, Captain," he said. "*Thank* you. And about that other little problem, we can just get someone else to baby-sit Lang while I'm . . ."

This time, Brix shook his head negatively. "Moss," he said, "I'm afraid that's out of the question. You know when this assignment came down it was you, *specifically*, he requested, and it was you *specifically* that the Mayor asked for. I can't do anything about that, and you know it. Lang stays with you."

"But, Captain," Moss protested, "this could be—no, it's *going* to be dangerous."

"And that's precisely why you are going to stay out of it."

"What?"

"You heard me," Captain Brix continued calmly. "Until Lang goes home, he's not leaving your sight." He looked warningly at Moss. "Not to brush his teeth, clip his toenails, *nothing*. And if the two of you go near anything more dangerous than a coffee shop, you are back in uniform and your ass is mine!"

Moss could feel himself getting red in the face, feel himself getting ready to blow. But he knew that wouldn't change things. He controlled himself and simply said, "Yes, sir."

Lang was in the squad room waiting for Moss to emerge from his meeting with Captain Brix. He was sitting restlessly, trying to be congenial near the pot of coffee the cops had on hand.

"So," Lang said to an extremely tall cop, who was pouring a cup for himself, "what is it about cops and bad coffee?"

The man glanced over at him. "What do you mean?"

"I mean," Lang continued, "why do we always have to drink warmed-over sludge? If it's in the manual, I never read about it."

The cop said stonily, "I made this coffee."

"And it's *terrific* coffee," Lang said hastily. "That's what I mean, it's so *unusual* to find good coffee in a squad room, why can't it *always* be this good?"

The cop stared at him for a beat. "My secret is chicory," he said confidentially.

Lang opened his mouth to say something, but he was grabbed suddenly by Moss, who was striding quickly by. "Come on," said Moss, and Lang went.

Moss was quiet until they got into a blue-and-white car. After they had pulled out of the police garage and were in heavy traffic, he turned to Lang.

"Listen, Lang," he said, "since you're riding in this car with me, you've got a right to know something."

"Okay," Lang said obligingly, "shoot." He caught Moss's peculiar look. "I didn't mean, *shoot* shoot," Lang corrected himself, "I meant . . . " He shrugged helplessly and stared out at the falling dusk.

Moss waved off the explanation. "No time for that," he said brusquely. "Here's the bottom line—I'm not giving up on this case; I don't really give a damn *what* Brix says."

Lang nodded encouragingly. "I understand completely," he said. "When you're obsessed with something, sort of like I am with getting this part—"

"Would you please just shut up and listen?" Moss snapped. "This is important, this is real life!" He glanced sideways and saw Lang nod again. "Okay, this guy's got to be stopped," he continued grimly. "*I* tracked him down today, *me*, and if it turns into anything, I'm going to be there when he's caught.

With you, without you, it doesn't make one bit of difference to me. Are you reading me?"

"Yes," Lang said meekly.

"Good," said Moss.

"Listen, John," Lang said. "There's something I've got to say, too . . . about Susan."

Moss stared straight ahead, his eyes icy. "I don't want to hear about it," he said.

Lang believed him. He changed the subject. "So," he said, "what's this Party Crasher's M.O.?" He saw Moss throw him a look of disbelief. "Okay, okay . . . never mind the M., uh, never mind. But if I'm going to ride along with you, I might as well have all the facts."

Moss thought about it for a moment, then nodded grudgingly. "It's hard to tell exactly what this fruitcake thinks he's doing," he said, "except that all his victims, so far, are bad guys. A pimp, a racketeer, a drug dealer, an inside trader . . . "

"Whew!" Lang whistled. "Inside trader, that's pretty sophisticated."

Moss smiled grimly. "Yeah," he agreed. "And he likes to off them in front of the police." He was silent, thoughtful for a moment. "Like he's . . . showing us up, maybe."

Lang nodded in agreement.

Just then, the radio crackled into life. Through the static, Lang and Moss heard, "All Crasher Task Force units, male caller states Party Crasher is located in abandoned apartments at 1412 Second. Repeat, this may be the Party Crasher . . . Units responding?"

"That's only six blocks from here!" Moss exclaimed, speeding off into traffic.

Still driving, he leaned across Lang and popped open the glove compartment. He pulled out a lethal-looking .38 and handed it to Lang.

"What . . . ," Lang began.

"This one's loaded," Moss assured him grimly. "This whole thing is bullshit, Lang, and we both know it. I don't

156

like you being here, I don't like playing wet nurse, but the fact is that you could have been killed on that subway today. So, if you're going to be here, tagging along where you have no business being, then you have the right to protect yourself."

Moss tossed the gun to Lang. Lang looked at it as if it was a snake. "Okay . . . ," he said.

"By the way," Moss said, pointing, "*that's* the trigger."

It was almost completely dark when they pulled silently into an alley that backed along several rickety tenement buildings. They came to a stop beside some broken crates and garbage cans, near a side entrance to the decrepit building Moss was heading for.

Moss turned to Lang. "*Do not move* from this car," he said emphatically. "We're not playing now. You just sit here and watch that door, and if you see him come out, you stay right where you are until *I* come out, and then you tell me which way he went. You do *not* pursue him, you don't do *anything*. That is an order, get it?"

"Got it," Lang replied, nodding.

"And that gun?" Moss pointed at it. "That is *only* for *emergencies*."

Lang could barely make out Moss's features in the gathering gloom, but he nodded again. "I know," he whispered.

Then Moss was out of the car. Lang saw him move cautiously along the filthy wall, then disappear into the building.

The minutes seemed to stretch into weeks as Lang, gun in his hand, peered through the darkness, waiting to see a sign of Moss reappearing, waiting to see another patrol car, waiting for something to happen. But the alley remained nerve-wrackingly quiet and deserted. Lang realized his foot was tapping rapidly of its own accord, and he forced himself to stop the nervous action. "Get a grip," he muttered to himself.

But he couldn't seem to calm down. He checked his watch for the umpteenth time. Nearly eight minutes had elapsed since Moss had gone into the building. It was too long.

Justifying his action with the thought that something should have happened by now, Lang climbed tentatively out of the patrol car, gun in hand. He crept quietly up to the open doorway that led to the abandoned residential hotel and paused to listen. Nothing. He peered cautiously into the dark building, but he couldn't see or hear a thing. Dammit, he thought nervously, this was all wrong. Where the hell was Moss? Where the hell was some backup?

Suddenly, footsteps that seemed as loud as gunshots clattered down the stairway, echoing loudly in the deserted building. Lang jumped a foot, then forced himself to stand still. He heard what sounded like people scuffling and realized some sort of confrontation must be happening. He had to help Moss . . .

Lang moved carefully into the building, pausing just inside the doorway. Then, without warning, the dark place seemed to spring into violent life. Lang panicked as he heard the loud report of a pistol going off, once, twice . . .

Then he heard Moss's voice, from somewhere deep in the recesses of the place, yelling something indecipherable.

And then there were footsteps coming directly at him, getting louder and louder, and he froze, unable to move or think. Don't panic, he told himself, help Moss. "Moss!" he shouted, "*Moss!* Where are you? Are you all right?"

"Get the hell out of here!" Moss's voice came back as a scream.

The footsteps were getting closer. "Moss!" he shouted again. "Are you all right?" No reply. "Moss, is it . . . *him*?"

There was a pause, and then Lang heard, "Lang, get the hell out of here! *Now!*"

Lang panicked. His legs felt like jelly. Finally, the sound of the footsteps almost upon him, he turned and bolted through the door and into the alley, looking frantically around for backup, somebody, *anybody* to help. In the dark alley, he felt himself trip and sprawl against the brick wall. The gun went spinning out of his grasp.

"Oh, Jesus!" he gasped, going down on his knees, searching frantically through the garbage. "Oh, please!" His hand finally made contact with the gun. He grasped it thankfully, then raised it, just as a man exploded out of the doorway, running right at him. Lang shut his eyes, prayed, and squeezed the trigger. When he reopened his eyes, he saw his attacker stumbling, falling to the ground, blood pouring from his chest.

Lang felt as though time was standing still, as if everything around him was happening in slow motion. After what seemed to be an eternity, Moss came panting through the doorway. He stopped dead in his tracks, taking in the scene— the stunned Lang, still crouching on the pavement, and the fallen man, who was now bleeding from his mouth.

"Oh, Christ, Lang!" Moss gasped in horror. "What did you do?"

Lang could barely register the words. "What . . . "

Even in the darkness, Moss seemed pale. "You . . . got the wrong guy," he said softly.

" . . . wrong guy?" Lang echoed blankly. "*What* wrong guy?"

"Where's the guy with the *gun*?" Moss demanded. "The guy that was *shooting*?" Lang was silent, stunned beyond words. "Shit!" Moss said, nodding toward the now-motionless figure on the ground. "This was just some street bum; he was just trying to get out of the *way*! Jesus *Christ*, Lang!"

"But . . . you didn't tell me there was more than one guy," Lang protested feebly.

"This guy doesn't even have a gun," Moss replied grimly. "Didn't you *look*?"

Moss squatted down beside the fallen man and put two fingers on the side of his neck.

"Well?" Lang ventured.

Moss shook his head. "He's dead," he said.

"Dead?" Lang said, dazed. "Are you sure?"

"Oh, yeah, Lang," Moss replied softly, "I'm sure."

Lang could feel himself begin to hyperventilate. "No! Oh, God! Oh, God!" he moaned. "Oh, Jesus, what am I going to do?"

Moss was silent; he seemed to be lost in some private train of thought.

"This is *it*!" Lang exclaimed, babbling, on the verge of hysteria. "This is the end of everything I've worked for, my whole life . . . " Then he paused, flinching at the implication of his own words. "God," he said more softly, "what am I talking about? I killed a man, Moss. I killed an *unarmed man*." Lang slumped against the wall, his entire body shaking.

Moss got up from his crouching position and strode purposefully over to him. He bent down and yanked Lang to his feet. "Stand up," he said, "and give me the gun."

"What?" Lang said.

"The gun!" Moss repeated impatiently. He reached over and took the weapon from Lang's shaking hands. "Get in the car," he ordered him.

"Are you arresting me?" Lang asked dully.

"Shut up and let me think!" Moss snapped. "Just get yourself in the car, okay?"

On trembling legs, Lang barely managed to propel himself into the front seat, trying not to look at the dead man in the alleyway. Inside the car, dizzy and sick with fear, he bent over and put his head between his legs to keep himself from fainting.

A moment later, he heard Moss say, "Get up, Lang!"

Lang lifted his head and tried to quell a wave of dizziness that threatened to sweep over him. "What?" he asked, confused.

"Get up! Just sit up and take some deep breaths—I can't afford to have you passing out now!"

Lang, dulled by what had occurred, did as he was told. "What are we going to do?" he asked plaintively.

Moss just looked annoyed and frazzled. "Shut up and let me think, would you!" he barked.

Lang heard Moss whistling softly, an atonal, nerve-wracking sound. Finally, he spoke. "Okay," he said. "You're a civilian." His tone was calm and rational. "You're a civilian who just shot an unarmed man with a police-issue weapon. And *I* let you do it." He paused thoughtfully. "Now, the thing is, if I let you take the rap for this, we both lose our careers."

"Oh, God," Lang whispered, visions of Hollywood black-balling, jail time, *hard* time, dancing through his head.

"But," Moss continued coolly, "if I tell them *I* was the one who shot this guy, maybe I can make it look a little more . . . real. A little more justified, a little more . . . he-roic."

The direction Moss was taking began to dawn on Lang. He stared up at Moss, aghast. "Are you kidding?" he asked. "You'd take the fall for this? *Why?*"

Moss looked over at him with cool derision. "Don't think I'm doing this for you, Hollywood," he said. "My ass is on the line here, too."

Lang nodded slowly, his brain beginning to work again. "Yes," he agreed, "it is."

"My fingerprints are on the gun," Moss continued. "And Lang," he said, fixing Lang with a sharp, cold look, "get this straight. You weren't ever here. You were . . . at my place."

"Doing what?" Lang enquired. "Captain Brix is going to want to know."

"You leave Captain Brix to me," Moss snapped. "You were . . . You had enough, you got all you needed for the part and, uh . . . well, that's enough."

"You think?" Lang said dubiously.

"I know," Moss replied decisively. "You leave *everything* to me."

Lang cast one last glance at the pitiful, crumpled figure lying in the alley. "Okay," he whispered.

TWENTY-ONE

LANG WAS OBVIOUSLY SEVERELY TRAUMATIZED; he remained quiet for a longer amount of time than John Moss had thought possible. All the way back to his apartment, Lang simply sat, mute, staring out the window of the patrol car, into the dark night. He didn't babble; he didn't get excited about seeing hookers or drug dealers on Manhattan street corners; he didn't talk at all about "real life" and his perception of it. Moss figured he must have just had the single worst 'real life' experience he could have had, and it had literally shocked the ebullient actor into silence.

Back at his apartment, Moss helped Lang throw his clothing into his leather tote and coached him again on keeping his mouth shut about what had happened. He reassured the actor that he could handle it by himself much more easily and expeditiously than would be possible if anyone got wind of the fact that there had actually been two of them at the scene of the deadly shooting.

For his part, Lang was still numb, and pathetically grateful that Moss was handling everything for him—from making sure his toothbrush was packed to calling the airports to find out who had the soonest flight leaving for Los Angeles. In his dazed state, Lang thought this must be the shock that people talked about after a severe trauma of any kind—a car accident, a death in the family, a . . . death. Oh, God, Lang thought, a wave of shakiness washing over him, a real death.

He tried to force himself to push the memory of the bum's bleeding body from his mind.

They made it to Newark Airport in record time, and using his cop ID, Lang parked in a restricted zone and got out, hurrying around to Lang's side.

"Well, come on," he said impatiently, sticking his head down beside the passenger window. "What are you waiting for?"

Lang climbed out of the car slowly, feeling like a tired old man. "Moss," he said tentatively, "are you absolutely certain . . ."

Moss nodded impatiently and grabbed Lang's bag from the trunk. "I'm sure," he said firmly. "All *you* have to do is get yourself on that plane and get the hell out of this town. You're *out* of it, Lang, you're clean and safe."

They headed quickly for the escalator that led to security clearance. Lang blinked in the glare of the fluorescent terminal lighting. His complexion was pale, his eyes glazed over. As they reached the bottom of the moving stairs, he faltered, but Moss grabbed his arm and propelled him aside onto steady ground.

"Come on, Lang," Moss said softly. "You're an actor, so act."

"Wha-what?" Lang replied, confused.

"*Act*," Moss repeated firmly. "Pretend nothing ever happened."

Lang shook his head miserably. "I don't know how I can . . ."

"You are going to get on that plane," Moss directed him. "You're going to fly home to flaky old Los Angeles, and you are going to just keep on doing what you've been doing all along. Host a couple of charity balls for some liberal cause, blow up an offshore oil rig, save some whales or dolphins or something . . . Come *on*, Lang, are you reading me?"

Lang nodded reluctantly. "Yes," he said quietly.

"Do whatever it takes to make it okay in your own head, including talking to your shrink—no, wait a second, better

164

not do that; they just ruled badly on that one in your looney-tunes state, some teenage millionaire murderers case. Yeah, forget the shrink. Don't tell *anybody*, just get yourself over it!"

"I don't know . . . ," Lang said again.

"Well I *do*," Moss replied. "Get through it, get over it, and forget it!"

Lang looked at him, his hazel eyes troubled. "How can I forget?" he asked softly.

"You just . . . do," Moss told him.

They walked together in silence for a few more yards, then Lang turned to Moss again. "But . . . there'll be an investigation," he said, "won't there?"

Moss nodded, then shrugged. "I've been through it before," he assured the actor.

"But . . . "

"No, Lang," Moss said firmly. "I'll handle my end here, and you just work on handling yourself and getting past this. Trust me, it's the only sensible way to deal with this. I'm a cop; cops make mistakes and people forgive them. But you . . . ," he trailed off as he eyed Lang meaningfully, "well, even as popular as you are, I don't think your career could survive *this*."

They were now only a few yards away from the security clearance lines, with their attendants and metal detectors.

Moss stopped and pulled Lang to the side. "This is where I get off," he said. "I don't want to show my badge to get the gun through the detectors . . . I don't want to take a chance on anyone maybe remembering that I was here. Okay?"

Lang nodded mutely. After a moment, he spoke. "Moss, why are you doing this?"

Moss paused a moment, too. Finally, he shrugged again. "I don't know," he admitted.

Lang felt an overwhelming surge of grateful emotion wash over him. He grabbed Moss and gave him a huge bear hug. Moss stood stiffly until Lang finally broke away.

"Listen," Lang said in a low voice, "if you need anything,

John, and I mean *anything*—uh, money, a good lawyer, a new suit for the trial . . ."

Moss shook his head negatively. "I'll handle it," he insisted.

"Okay," Lang said reluctantly. "I'll call when I get back."

"No!" Moss exclaimed, his expression panicky. "I mean, uh, don't call, you don't want to have anyone connect the two of us! As far as Captain Brix is concerned, I'll tell him Nick Lang got bored and decided to split. And Ray Cazenov . . . well, I'll just tell everyone he got a chance to work with Internal Affairs or something." Moss pointed to the detectors. "Now you just get on that plane and don't look back."

Lang took a deep breath, straightened his shoulders, and nodded. Then he walked away.

Moss took a deep breath and expelled it. "Jesus," he said softly, then turned and left the airport.

It was early the next morning when Lang awoke, cramped and uncomfortable, still in the boarding area. He was surrounded by people who had obviously been there all night, too.

"We'd like to apologize for our delay," a flight attendant was saying over the loudspeaker. "At this time, Continental flight 76 to Los Angeles is ready for boarding. Any passengers with small children or special needs, as well as first class passengers, may proceed to the gate at this time."

Lang roused himself and yawned, stretching his cramped arms and legs. He responded on automatic pilot—first class, he thought, that's me. Then, suddenly, the events of the night before hit him like a brick. He got up slowly, grabbing his bag, and walked toward the flight attendant who was collecting tickets with a bright smile that belied the overnight wait.

As Lang handed his ticket to the young woman, something inside him balked. How the hell could he do this? He hesitated, then grabbed the ticket back and turned away.

"Sir?" said the flight attendant, with concern in her voice. "Don't you want to board?"

Lang froze for a moment. Good question. Part of him did, he thought; part of him wanted to put the whole ghastly mess behind him, sluff it off on someone else, run back to L.A. and his safe haven there. But he couldn't. He was responsible, he realized, and the someone else who would shoulder the blame for him was John Moss. What the hell was he doing, he chided himself, thinking he could walk away from this?

"No," he told the flight attendant, "I have to take care of some unfinished business." Then, without waiting for her reaction, he walked out of the terminal, a new purpose in his stride.

Lang burst through the doors of the precinct a determined man. It was the usual chaos, he noted briefly—hookers and johns being booked, a man with a knife wound swearing out a complaint, somebody throwing up noisily in the corner. Lang paid no attention to any of it. He looked around for someone he knew but didn't see any familiar faces.

"Anyone seen Moss?" he yelled over the babble and confusion.

The watch commander shrugged. Lang wondered if, right at this moment, Moss was swearing to some bullshit confession that would save his—Lang's—hide. Suddenly, he spotted China coming through the door to the stairs. He pushed and shoved his way through the crowd.

"China!" he said breathlessly. "Where's Moss?"

China looked at him peculiarly. "He's out," she said.

"Where?" Lang demanded.

China shrugged. "I don't know," she replied.

Lang felt a wave of panic wash over him. "Well," he said, his words coming out in a rush, "whatever he said he did, he did for me, and he didn't really do it at all. I did, and we've got to tell somebody before . . ."

China's eyes were wide and puzzled. "What the hell are you talking about, Ray?" she asked. "No, never mind, if it has to do with John, I don't even really want to know."

She began to move away, but Moss tagged along beside

her, still talking a mile a minute. "China, listen, you've got to listen to me," he said. "It's a matter of life and . . . no, never mind that. Just, uh, get a stenographer, uh, a court reporter or something, even a tape recorder!"

China just looked at him as if he was crazy. "What's wrong with you?" she said, still moving.

"I waive my right to an attorney," Lang said insistently. "I want to make a full confession!"

"To what?" China said with a smile. "Being too short?"

"Don't bother trying to talk me out of it," Lang said, not hearing a word she said, "my mind's made up, and nothing, not even Moss's concern, is going to stop me."

China shrugged. "Whatever," she said.

They were standing outside the squad room, and Lang could hear laughter from within. "I'm going to find the Captain," he said firmly and started off. Then he stopped in his tracks as the conversation from behind the door became clear and distinct.

"So, you shoulda seen it," he heard an unfamiliar voice say. "This guy's knees are like rubber, he's about to shit a brick, and he's screaming . . ."— and here, his voice went up an octave— "Moss! Jesus, Moss! Help! He's coming right at me!"

Lang felt a sudden cold chill of suspicion wash over him. China, unaware of the drama being played out, went through the door to the squad room. Lang caught it quietly as it began to close, and unseen, he peered into the room.

Several officers were gathered around the storyteller, having a good laugh at whatever he was saying. Lang caught a good look at the man and felt the cold chill turn to shock and confusion. The speaker's voice wasn't familiar, but his face certainly was. Lang stared at the man whom he had last seen dressed in the clothing of a street bum, lying dead in an alley outside a deserted residential hotel. The man he believed he had killed. He was very much alive. And he was quite obviously a cop, having a very good laugh at Lang's expense.

The confusion gave way to a hot rush of humiliation.

168

Lang kept his mouth shut and continued to listen to the storyteller.

"So I come through this door into the dark alley, loaded for bear, and here's this bozo that Moss got stuck with, I mean, his eyes are actually *closed*, and he somehow manages to squeeze off a shot . . . "

At this point, the cop-turned-actor got up and acted the scene out for the amusement of his fellow officers. He slapped his hand onto his chest and staggered, while talking. "I bonk my chest, hard, bust the condom, and all this ketchup spurts out . . . and I fall flat on my face, then writhe around a little so my head is turned up—so's when I bite down on the capsule, this turkey can see the blood dribbling out of my mouth . . . "

Here, he laughed heartily, as did his audience. Lang thought his head was going to burst from the effort of keeping silent.

"I'm telling you, I thought this guy was gonna check out on the spot!" the cop continued. "I'm glassy-eyed, I swear, I'm holdin' my *breath* to keep from laughing, and Moss is giving this *intense* performance—that guy oughtta go on the stage! He's sayin', 'It's gonna be all right, I'll take the fall for ya, you just gotta get the hell outta town!' Like this is some Jimmy Cagney gangster movie or something! So anyway, later he tells me, he stuck the schmuck on a plane. The guy is finally out of Moss's hair, and he's back on the Party Crasher case . . . and say, that reminds me, you know they got some kinda sting set up for tonight? In the park?"

The cop looked around at his audience and suddenly came to a complete stop in his speech as his eyes locked with Nick Lang's.

All heads turned to see what the cop was staring at. And Lang, humiliated beyond what he would have believed possible, stared back. They stayed like that, a frozen tableau, for what seemed to Lang to be forever. Then, as his anger took over where the humiliation had been, Lang turned on his heel and marched rapidly down the hallway.

One part of him couldn't believe that such a trick had been played on him. The other part had already decided to get even.

TWENTY-TWO

THE UNOBTRUSIVE VAN HAD A NEWLY PAINTED LOGO that proclaimed that New York City's Con Ed people were hard at work, so please excuse the delay. But it wasn't Con Ed, it was the NYPD hard at work inside. The van was parked inconspicuously in the shadows across from the gas station lot, and should anybody on the street care to look, it was impossible to see in through its windows. But there were no people on the street—at least, no one who didn't know exactly why the van was there in the dead of night.

Inside the van, Moss waited, outwardly cool but inwardly as jumpy as a cat on a windy night. Would the Party Crasher show? Would Terranova be able to pull it off? Was anyone going to get hurt in this sting; was anyone going to be . . . killed? It was difficult not to think about that kind of eventuality where the Crasher was concerned. It was almost as difficult as not smoking.

Moss pulled a cigarette from the pack in his pocket and stuck it in his mouth without lighting it.

"Christ, Moss," Grainy said, "that is the stupidest way to quit that I've ever seen."

"If it works . . . " Moss's shrug was eloquent.

"Quiet," Cain whispered as he motioned them to keep it down, "I thought I saw something."

All three of them peered through the darkened windows of the van, over at the parking lot of the gas station, where

Terranova and the Crasher had set up their meet. Terranova's van—the mobile armory, as Moss had nicknamed it—was parked a short distance away from the gas pump islands, which shed the only light on the scene. The whole effect was eerie, Moss thought—the deserted gas station, the dark van, the fluorescent light—it looked like something from an Edward Hopper painting. Except, he added mentally, more menacing.

He picked up a pair of sophisticated binoculars equipped with special infrared night vision lenses and scanned the nearby shadows and buildings, checking on the whereabouts of the officers hidden in strategic positions. He could see China crouching on a rooftop, Billy nearby, huddled on a fire escape. Two other sharpshooters knelt behind a dumpster. There were more of them around, Moss knew, more who couldn't be seen. It should have been a comforting thought.

Suddenly, they heard Terranova's voice, speaking softly and nervously into the wire attached to his chest. "He's a half an hour late," Terranova whispered. "I don't like it."

Grainy picked up the van's mike and spoke back to the weapons dealer. "I don't like it either," he said in a perfectly normal tone of voice, trying to keep Terranova calm. "I mean, I could be home watching "Wrestlemania" instead of this."

Then they retreated into their jumpy silence once again. The minutes passed. Moss reached for a pack of matches, then forced himself not to. Cain whistled tunelessly under his breath. Grainy seemed quietly preoccupied. But underneath, all three men were just waiting for the Party Crasher to arrive.

"Okay," they finally heard Terranova whisper after another interminable ten minutes had crawled by. "Here he comes."

Moss nodded tersely at Cain, who took the mike. "We have contact," he said softly to the scattered undercover cops. "Stay on your toes and wait for the signal."

Riveted to the scene in front of him, Moss peered intently through the night, and saw a tall figure, dressed all in black,

172

detach itself from the shadows along the side of the building. Backlit, ominous, unafraid, the Party Crasher walked coolly toward Terranova's van.

Moss felt a prickle of apprehension run down his spine. This is too easy, he thought briefly, then put the thought out of his head. Rational thought, logic told him that all around them, cops had their rifles raised, ready to shoot to kill at a microsecond's notice. This was no time to start second-guessing the complexity of the plan. They had gotten to Terranova, Terranova had lured the killer in, and now it was time to wrap up the package.

A dozen hidden pairs of eyes watched as the driver's door to Terranova's van was opened and the gun dealer climbed out. Through the mike attached to Terranova's wire, the men in the police van could hear Terranova's labored breath. Christ, Moss thought, Terranova was so nervous—Don't you blow it now, Moss warned him silently.

"Where's the bodyguard?"

They were the Party Crasher's first words, and the cool, deliberate sound of the killer's voice made Moss shiver.

"I, uh . . . I gave him the night off," Terranova replied. "It's Saturday."

The Crasher said nothing, but Moss thought he saw him nod.

"So . . . ," Terranova continued, "ready to do some business?"

"That's what I'm here for," replied the Party Crasher.

Terranova walked around the van and unlocked the back doors. The Crasher followed him. Terranova reached into the van and pulled out what Moss knew was another customized .45 with a laser sight. He handed it to the killer, who inspected it carefully. Moss could see him looking down the barrel, running his hands over the cool metal.

"This is good," Moss heard the Party Crasher say softly.

Cain gave Moss the thumbs-up sign; the mike was working fine, and they could hear every word.

"Perfect," the Crasher said. "And by the way," he paused thoughtfully, "I'm glad you brought company."

Moss's head jerked up in alarm, but before the cops could even begin to react to his words, the Party Crasher had swung his arm, smashing the butt of the gun directly into Terranova's face, stunning the arms dealer. Then, as Terranova reached to protect himself, Moss could see the killer, moving as swiftly as a cat, grab Terranova and pull him in front of him. With one hand, he kept the .45 pointed at Terranova's temple. With his other hand, using Terranova as a human shield, the killer reached around Terranova's chest and ripped his shirt open, exposing wire taped there.

"Lieutenant Moss," the killer said coolly, "I know you can hear me."

"Oh, Jesus," whispered Grainy.

Moss was silent, shocked and yet, somehow, not surprised at all. This killer had a maniacal intelligence; he'd known that all along.

The eerie, flat calmness of the Party Crasher's tone didn't vary. "It's about time we talked," he continued, still addressing himself to Moss exclusively. "Time we . . . got to know each other and hashed this problem out, don't you think? After all, you've made it patently clear that you don't appreciate what I'm trying to accomplish . . . do you?" He paused for a moment. "Come on down, Moss," he said genially. "Don't make me kill Terranova."

Moss started instinctively out of the police van.

"Moss!" Cain exclaimed, "Don't . . . "

Moss gestured impatiently. "There's a dozen cops out there," he said. "Just make sure they're awake!"

Moss stepped all the way out of the van, holding his arms away from his sides to let the killer see that he wasn't aiming a gun at him.

"Okay," he shouted, "I'm comin'." As he walked into the lights of the station, he could see the man's deadpan face, his cold eyes. He could see the terrified expression Terranova wore.

As Moss got closer, the Party Crasher backed up, dragging Terranova with him. He came to a halt by the gas pumps.

"Glad you could make it," Moss," the Party Crasher said genially. "You can stop right there . . . Don't come any closer."

Moss did as he was told, halting about twenty feet away from the killer and his captive. Moss did his best to appear composed, unthreatening.

"You know," the Crasher said conversationally, "I've really been looking forward to this."

"To what?" Moss said with a calmness he was far from feeling. If he could just keep the psycho talking long enough for someone to draw a bead on him from behind . . .

"To *what*?" the Crasher repeated mockingly. "To *this*, Lieutenant Moss. To standing face to face with you." He smiled a strange smile. "A dialogue, Moss, an intimate chat, just the two of us, one major player to another. Although," he added thoughtfully, "I have a feeling there are a lot more people here than that." He tapped the gun butt hard into Terranova's forehead. "Not even counting this . . . scumbag."

Jesus, Moss thought, what's next? He didn't have to wait long to find out.

Keeping his one arm hooked around Terranova, the Crasher reached in back of him and unhooked first one, then the other gas pump nozzle from its receptacle. He let them fall in front of him, down to the blacktop, then flipped up the levers that turned them on.

Oh, no, Moss thought, as the area began to flood with gas, as the pungent stench of it filled the night air. Oh, no. He didn't have to see his backup to know that every cop watching him had just lowered his or her weapon. One spark and the station would be a raging inferno sending them all to hell.

"Why *are* you doing this, Lieutenant?" the Party Crasher asked. "I'm really curious."

The viscous liquid snaked toward Moss, reached him, and puddled thickly around his feet. "Doing what, exactly?" Moss countered.

"Treating me like a criminal." The killer's voice was matter-of-fact.

"I don't know." Moss shrugged. Then, deliberately baiting him, he said, "Maybe because . . . you *are* one?"

"I am not!" the Crasher hissed.

Moss felt himself flinch. Wrong approach to this breathing time bomb.

"You're a policeman," the Crasher said. "You should be able to understand what I'm trying to do."

Moss suddenly had a glimmer of insight about where this line of conversation might be heading.

"I should?" he said mildly. His shoes were soaked in gasoline. He couldn't even think about it, not now. "Why is that?"

"Because we're on the same side," the Party Crasher told him. He managed to make the statement sound perfectly rational. "I haven't done anything bad, Moss. *You* know that. Think about it—I killed a pimp, a drug dealer . . . the kinds of people who make your job so tough. People who I know you'd really love to see just . . . gone. But you can't do it that way—you're all bogged down in petty bureaucratic rules and procedures. But I'm not. I can just . . . "—he snapped his fingers and laughed—"make them disappear, gone off the face of the earth." He laughed again, a chilling sound in the night.

Gone off the face of the earth is right, Moss thought. That's exactly what *you* are, spinning around some other unnamed planet. But he kept his mouth shut and let the killer ramble.

"Maybe it makes you mad," the Crasher continued thoughtfully, "that I'm doing your job for you. And doing it better." There was that eerie laugh again. "Pop psychology, but it's kind of interesting, don't you think?"

"What's that?" Moss said cautiously.

" . . . I'm not 'acceptable' enough to wear your uniform," the Crasher said. Suddenly, it was as if a different man was talking; the killer's voice was now bitter and angry. "But

176

the truth, Lieutenant Moss, the *truth* . . . is that I'm really a better cop than anyone else here. I'm better than you."

Oh, sweet Jesus, Moss thought, so *that's* what this was all about! "You want to be a cop?" he asked calmly. "Maybe, you know, it's not too late. Maybe we could work something out. I could . . . put in a word for you."

"Lieutenant," the Crasher interrrupted him sharply, "stop it. Just how crazy do you think I am? Crazy enough to fall for that line? Sorry."

Moss swallowed hard, trying not to breathe in the noxious fumes that swirled around him, trying not to think of the lake of gas that was growing and growing.

"I don't even know why I bother to help you," the Party Crasher said softly, almost sadly.

"Listen . . . ," Moss began.

But his words were cut off by the crack of the .45 the Party Crasher held, and Moss watched helplessly as a dark hole blossomed in Terranova's chest. The gun dealer fell to the ground, dead.

"Don't shoot!" Moss shouted. "Don't shoot! He'll blow us all up!"

"Calling off your backup, Lieutenant?" the Party Crasher asked. "Pity."

Moss saw him reach into his pocket and pull out a cheap butane lighter. He flicked it and a small flame spurted up, a tiny beacon of death in the dark night. Holding the lighter like a candle, the killer walked calmly toward Terranova's van, which stood, engine idling, a few safe feet from the lake of gasoline.

The Party Crasher climbed into the van. He slammed the door shut behind him, holding the lighter aloft out the open window.

The killer's eyes met Moss's. "Looks like only one of the good guys gets to ride off into the sunset this time," he said.

As he screeched away, he tossed the lighter casually over his shoulder. With a whoosh the lot became an instant inferno, flames licking the ground in all directions.

177

But Moss was already gone, running out of the pool of gasoline and diving for the back door of the van as it peeled away. Hanging on for dear life, he was dragged out of range of the fire just as the flames reached the pumps. Moss cringed, while behind him there was a deafening explosion as the pumps blew, sending what used to be the gas station into the night in a terrifying roar of a fireball.

TWENTY-THREE

DESPITE THE HOURS THAT HAD PASSED SINCE THE incident, Lang couldn't stop fuming. No, he thought, it was stronger than that. He was furious, he was boiling over with anger, anger at Moss, anger at the cop who had helped him in his little ruse, anger at everyone. No one treated Nick Lang this way, *no one*!

The look of realization on the cop's face as the alleged "dead bum" caught sight of Lang in the doorway of the squad room had told the whole story: he'd been set up, he'd been made a complete patsy . . . he'd been made to look like a stupid fool. And now everyone in the precinct knew it, too.

Lang didn't know precisely what he intended to do. He was too angry to think logically. But somehow, he knew, he had to get back at John Moss. Somehow, he had to prove that he was as smart, as macho, as Moss. As any cop on the force, for that matter.

Lang had hightailed it away from the squad room after he'd been seen and, almost by instinct, headed for the subterranean police garage beneath the precinct house. Without really planning his action out, he automatically identified himself as Ray Cazenov, Moss's new partner, and said he needed a patrol car, pronto. The officer on duty just nodded and handed him a set of keys, almost bored. No one got down there unless they were supposed to, so the officer had simply allowed Lang to check out a patrol car and cruise on out into the

179

streets. Procedure, plain and simple.

And that was exactly what Lang had done—cruise fo hours on end, driving around Manhattan numbly, relivin; his humiliation again and again. Jesus, Moss, he though bitterly, what did I ever do to *you*? Okay, maybe he ha gotten in the way of Moss's goddam investigation, but s *what*? After all, there were plenty of *other* cops working o the case, too. It wasn't as if Moss was the only one wh could catch this lunatic.

Lang stopped and sighed. He had to admit it—he di understand. Moss wanted the Party Crasher as much a he wanted the part of Tony DiBennedetti. It was sort of personal quest. And Lang seemed to be th one obstacle that had to be removed before that coul happen.

Still, he was pissed.

Driving moodily along, Lang stared out the window watching the endless foot traffic of colorful character parading by. He wondered if he should head for Moss' apartment, or maybe to Susan's, tell her the whole thing get some sympathy at least.

Suddenly, the radio in the patrol car crackled into life. Th dispatcher's voice was matter-of-fact, but the facts she relaye were anything but ordinary. "All units heading west on Forty first, pursuit of the Party Crasher in a gray van with tinte windows, partial plate, SQM . . . Repeat, all units . . . "

Lang started as he heard the information. Then he real ized that he was well within range. Without giving himsel a chance to reconsider, he automatically yanked the wheel t the right, screeching around the corner and heading towar the pursuit. Exactly what he would *do* if he actually caugh up with the killer didn't even enter his mind. Laying on th horn, he sped through traffic, heading for where he was sur Moss would be.

With his one good arm, John Moss clung tenaciously t the handle on the rear door of the commandeered van as th crazed driver squealed out of the parking lot, leaving a blazing inferno in his wake.

"Goddam it!" Moss shouted, but he knew there was no way he could be heard above the screeching of the tires and the noise of traffic all around them. Not that his shouting was likely to stop this madman anyway.

He managed to get one foot up onto the rear bumper and to keep himself precariously balanced as the Party Crasher wove through the night, scattering cars and pedestrians in his path.

Moss winced as they sideswiped a sedan, its angry driver blasting his horn and shouting something unintelligible after them. Moss tried desperately to yank himself all the way up so that he could pull himself into the back of the van, but gravity seemed to be working against him. All he could do was hold on and hope that the Party Crasher didn't annihilate them both in some hideous head-on.

He heard the incessant, staccato honking of the van's horn turn into one long blare as the Crasher leaned on it. Uh-oh, Moss thought, bracing himself. This was it. Collision time.

With an ear-splitting, brake-squealing screech and the sudden cacophonous crunch of metal, the van went smashing into a large produce truck in its path. Moss felt himself jolted, then thrown to the ground like a rag doll. The impact seared through his body, and with the wind knocked out of him, he lay there for a moment, dazed. Then he picked himself up and ran around the now-stalled van, only to see the killer running down the street, a limp not hampering his progress as much as Moss would have hoped.

Moss pulled his gun and ran after him, but they were on a busy street, and, conscious of innocent bystanders, who parted in confusion as the two men went flying past, he was forced to keep the weapon down at his side.

"Police!" Moss kept shouting, frustrated. "Get out of my fucking way!"

Up ahead, halfway down the block, he saw the Party Crasher veer abruptly to his left and duck into a movie theater.

"Shit!" Moss muttered to himself, dashing after him. A crowded, dark movie house. Just what he needed.

Lang's patrol car came careening around the corner with its sirens blaring and its lights flashing. Lang peered intently around him, searching for Moss, for the killer, for the gray van. But the only one he saw was sitting, obviously disabled, crumpled up against a large truck in the middle of the street.

Then, out of the corner of his eye, he spotted a man running and realized it was Moss. "There you are, you sonovabitch!" he exclaimed.

Lang stomped viciously on the brakes, and the patrol car did a sudden, 180-degree turn in the middle of the street, landing half on the sidewalk, and knocking over a fire hydrant as it went. Lang flung the door open, and, ignoring the outraged screams of pedestrians and the geyser of water that jetted into the air, he abandoned the car where it was.

Lang shoved through the confused crowd after his quarry. Up ahead, he saw Moss turn abruptly into a movie theater and dashed toward it, screaming, "Moss! You shitheel, stop!"

Moss didn't hear him. He ran as fast as he could through the double glass doors of the theater and flashed his badge at the confused ticket taker who had just witnessed another desperate-looking man, dressed all in black, knock three people down as he ran into the building without stopping to buy a ticket.

"What's going on?" the ticket taker demanded.

"Police!" Moss yelled wihtout stopping. "Which way did he go?"

The ticket taker just shook his head in confusion, and Moss knew he'd be wasting his time trying to get information here. Inside the lobby, he took a cursory look around, almost certain that the Party Crasher wouldn't pause there, under the bright lights. He quickly checked the men's room, then the ladies', earning an outraged protest from a woman there.

"Sorry," Moss said hastily as he backed out.

Jesus, he thought, he could *really* use some backup now. But there was no chance of that, he thought with a sinking feeling; the entire Party Crasher squad was back at the blazing gas station. In this entire, huge theater, packed with people, he was the only cop in sight. And he had a feeling that the Party Crasher—despite his claim of killing only the bad guys—wouldn't hesitate to take a few innocent people out with him if it came down to that.

Moss pulled the door to the auditorium open as little as possible and slid through, trying not to draw any attention to his presence. He kept very low, moving at a crouch, his keen eyes sweeping over row after row of moviegoers who seemed to be fascinated by what was on the screen. Moss was only peripherally conscious of ominous music as a backdrop.

Suddenly, he spotted sitting near the aisle a man who looked as if he was the right height and build. He was dressed in dark colors. Moss felt the deadly weight of the pistol he held and took a deep breath. Moving silently up behind him, Moss seized the dark-garbed man by the shoulders, got a choke hold on him, and whipped him around.

"Sorry," Moss whispered to the confused, bearded patron.

Before the man could even protest, Moss was gone, slinking forward, peering down row after row, trying not to draw any attention to himself. He could feel the tension mounting palpably as he moved.

"I'm over here . . . ," a loud, taunting voice announced, and Moss whipped around.

Then he realized the voice had come from the screen, and he looked up. What he saw there was another unpleasant shock: the voice belonged to a trenchcoated Nick Lang, playing super-hero Joe Gunn. His too-familiar face stared at Moss in a huge close-up, filling the screen. "You didn't think you could get rid of me that easily, did you . . . ?" asked Joe Gunn.

Oh yes, I did, Moss thought. Jesus, what luck! What timing! He tried just to dismiss the pesky actor's screen presence as he went on with his search, but it was more difficult than he had thought. The music score seemed to crescendo, getting louder, more dramatic, as Nick Lang–Joe Gunn fought Ninja after Ninja on the screen, as he ducked deadly martial-arts weapons and fire-breathing dragons in his quest to rescue the scantily clad leading lady. The audience responded on cue with gasps and cheers and boos.

That was good, Moss thought, as he concentrated on his own mission; the crowd's noisy reactions might distract the killer. But he was getting very close to the front of the theater, and there was still no sign of his quarry. Moss kept on going.

Lang darted across the street, through traffic, causing several screeching stops and a lot of yelling and swearing. He ran through the doors to the theater, the same doors he had seen Moss disappear through.

"Hey!" yelled the outraged ticket taker.

"Police!" Lang shot back.

"Where the hell's your badge?" the ticket taker screamed. "Hey . . ." Lang went barreling through the doors into the lobby. The ticket taker shrugged and shook his head, then signaled to a couple of ushers inside.

Lang darted toward the darkened auditorium, only to find his way barred by the same two young ushers.

"Oh, jeez," he muttered, and promptly reversed course, taking the stairs to the balcony two at a time.

He pushed his way through the doors to the balcony and stopped dead in his tracks, confronted by his own huge screen image, swinging in slow motion across a spike-laden pit, to rescue the lovely Holly.

Then, from the audience below, Lang heard several outraged voices.

"Outta the way, shithead!"

"Hey, buddy, get down!"

"For seven bucks, I didn't pay to see your butt!"

Lang slid quietly to the side of the balcony, trying not to disturb the crowd there, and peered over the low front wall. A man was moving determinedly across the very front of the movie house, not only blocking the front row, but getting in the way of most of the audience's view of the screen.

Moss, Lang thought grimly. Hah! I've got you where I want you now!

Just at that moment, Lang's attention was caught by something out of place in the theater balcony. With a prickle of fear running down the back of his neck, he turned his head and saw a man crouching in back of the balcony wall—a man dressed all in black, a man with a . . . gun. And he was drawing a bead on Moss, who was perfectly silhouetted by the light of the silver screen behind him.

"Moss," Lang screamed, "look out!"

Just at that moment, the Party Crasher fired, but it was too late: Lang's shout had sent Moss diving down, flattening himself before the front row as the Crasher's bullet hit the stage.

Infuriated at this intrusion on his perfect opportunity, the Party Crasher whirled and fired again and again at Lang, who was already in the process of fleeing through the doors.

Down below, Moss was still lying on the floor.

"Missed me, scumbag," Joe Gunn said triumphantly.

Another gunshot echoed off the plaster walls in the balcony, and suddenly the crowd of moviegoers seemed to realize that they were in the middle of a real-life shoot-out. The panic was immediate, and it swept like wildfire through the audience. People arose, screaming, and ran for the exits, nearly trampling each other in an effort to escape.

Lang was sprawled on the stairs to the lobby when two of the more vigilant ushers came after him.

"Look, buddy," one of them said sternly, "if you don't have a ticket, you're gonna have to—"

But his words were cut short as the doors burst open, and a tidal wave of frenzied people exploded out of them. Lang managed to roll to one side and saw both ushers knocked over by the crowd.

Lang got up. "Nobody gets Moss," he said, speaking more to himself than anybody else, "not before I get *my* hands on him!"

185

TWENTY-FOUR

MOSS WAS MENTALLY REELING. HE COULDN'T *BE-lieve* he had actually heard what he *thought* he had heard; but he also couldn't take the time to wonder where in *hell* Nick Lang had come from, or where he had gone after his shouted warning. It was, however, perfectly clear that the actor had just saved his ass.

As people fled from the auditorium in a panicked stampede, Moss just tried to keep himself low and invisible while he continued to sweep the balcony with his eyes, looking for a sign of the Party Crasher. He brought the gun at his side up into firing position, just waiting for the right opportunity. This was it; this was the showdown that both of them had been waiting for.

In the screaming, churning panic reaction that the Crasher's shots had set off among the viewing audience, it was difficult to see or hear, but Moss kept moving, staying low and looking up in the direction the shots had come from. He thought he had finally spotted the killer when he caught a movement that didn't belong with the crowd, a movement away from the doors. Moss struggled to keep the figure in sight amidst all the chaotic movement.

It *was* the killer, he thought triumphantly, as the man leapt from the balcony to a narrow ledge near it. But that feeling faded immediately as Moss realized that the ledge, which was nearly perpendicular to the balcony, gave the shooter an even better sweeping view of the auditorium than he'd had before. On the ledge were two large, decorative urns for the Crasher to hide behind, and even though they wouldn't provide much protection, Moss realized they would serve as a good screen for the man intent on killing him. Moss knew that in the emptying auditorium he was a perfect target.

But there was no way he was letting the Party Crasher get away again. He had to take a chance on forcing the killer into a confrontation now, even though there were still plenty of people around. He lifted his gun and pointed, but couldn't fire: every time he had a clear shot at the ledge, someone got in the way.

"Get down!" Moss shouted at the people blocking his shot. "Get out of my way!"

His words didn't have the desired effect; a woman directly in front of him saw his gun and began to scream in panic.

Moss yelled, "Dammit, lady, I'm a cop!"

As people around him ducked and fled screaming out of his way, Moss saw the Crasher's head appear briefly from behind one of the urns, and knew that this was the moment. He took quick, careful aim and fired, then dove to the floor again as the Crasher, apparently uninjured, fired two shots back at him.

Moss wiggled down between the rows, trying to keep out of the line of fire, as the Party Crasher fired off shot after booming shot. The bullets pinged around Moss; a tear ripped through a plush seat right next to his cheek.

"Shit," Moss muttered, as he popped up in the fifth row and fired off a couple of shots in return. He saw part of the urn explode with the impact of the bullets, but surprisingly, it still stood. Jesus, Moss thought, what does it take to kill this guy?

In the meantime, Lang had brushed off the ushers. Pushing himself in the opposite direction of the swirling crowd, he then crept back into the now-empty balcony. He heard the gunfire and crouched; then he slipped down the side of the aisle, keeping himself in the shadows, moving as stealthily as he could toward the front of the balcony. What he would do if he somehow managed to sneak up on the killer was something he didn't even think about. But where *was* the killer?

Lang heard the crack of gunfire again and visually followed the line of the shots. Peering over the balcony rail, he could just make out the outline of a man hunched between a couple of rows near the front of the auditorium. It had to be Moss, he thought, hiding, trapped. But if he could see him, so could his attacker. Lang crawled to one side, then spotted the Crasher crouched behind one of two large urns on a side ledge.

From Lang's point of view it was obvious that the killer had Moss pinned, that Moss didn't stand a chance. . . . Somebody had to do something . . . and until police backup arrived, it looked as though Lang was the only posse in town.

His heart in his mouth, Lang steeled himself, then vaulted the rail that separated the balcony seats from the ledge where the killer hid. As he landed on the ledge, he bumped into the second of the two urns, sending it crashing to the floor below.

The Party Crasher whirled in surprise and promptly fired at Lang, who reacted with pure survival instinct: he dove over the side of the ledge and then grabbed for the edge. He hung there, swinging in midair.

"What the fu—" Moss muttered, as he saw a second man leap onto the ledge and then tumble over the side. He peered up through the gloom of the theater and focused on the man swinging from the ledge. Then he realized what was happening.

"Lang . . . ," he muttered. Of course, he thought, the actor couldn't leave well enough alone. Not Lang—a verbal warning wasn't enough; he had to prove he was a real-life hero!

There wasn't any choice. Now it was Moss's turn to save the actor's ass. He leapt to his feet, took quick aim, and fired off several ringing shots in the killer's direction. The ploy worked well enough to distract the Party Crasher from Nick Lang's presence—exactly what Moss had hoped to do. Christ, Moss thought fleetingly, that's all we need—to have Nick Lang's murder touted as the fault of the NYPD.

Jesus, Lang thought, his legs dangling in midair over the seats below, this was incredible, this was the real thing, all right. And it was terrifying . . .

The Party Crasher, now panicked by the attack, which seemed to be coming from both sides, looked wildly around for any kind of escape. Suddenly, he spotted a gaudy decorative pole painted with gold-and-silver stripes, which stretched nearly to the balcony.

Gauging the distance instantly in his mind, he went for it, grabbing the top of the pole with his hands and kicking hard off the tiny ledge, throwing the weight of his body into the leap. He held on tightly as the pole bent and then arced toward the stage. At the last possible moment, the killer leapt from the wild ride and landed heavily on the stage, right in front of the screen. Acting on pure instinct, he ducked swiftly around the corner of the screen, fleeing to the backstage area, Moss's shots ringing at his heels. Too bad, Moss, the killer thought mockingly, you haven't come close to hitting me yet. A bizarre sense of invincibility was his.

Moss rushed after the killer, up the stairs to the stage. Then he flattened himself against the screen and slid quickly around it. In the dim backstage area, he could just make out the killer's shape as the armed man fled toward an exit door. Moss squeezed off a round that echoed loudly in the cavernous area, then ducked as the killer turned and fired back.

Moss took refuge behind a stack of crates, and the killer ducked behind some old theatrical posters. The two men used anything they could find backstage—janitorial equipment, stacked boxes of food concession supplies—to camouflage their positions as they fired off round after deadly round at one another.

Where the hell was his backup? Moss wondered as he crouched in the shadows.

Where the hell was the backup? Lang wondered, clinging precariously to the ledge.

'Wasn't this where they were supposed to show up? The muscles in Lang's hands and arms were beginning to cramp and strain, and he knew he couldn't just dangle there in mid-air for very much longer. He eyed the pole that the Party Crasher had used to get away and formulated a plan. With a burst of willful athletic determination, Lang forced himself to move. Hand over cramped hand he went in the direction the killer had taken. It was agonizingly slow work, pulling himself along the edge; he wasn't certain he could make it.

"Come on," he muttered to himself, "just *do* it!"

At last, the pole was within his reach. Lang grabbed at it gratefully. Then he attempted to kick off the way the killer had, but his awkward position limited his momentum. The pole swayed wildly for a few moments, with Lang like a monkey clinging to it, and then it bent slowly toward the side of the stage. He wasn't going to make it, Lang thought as the pole seemed to hesitate. He grabbed desperately for the heavy red velvet curtain that separated front stage from back.

The material wasn't as strong as it looked. As Lang flung himself on it, his weight caused the dusty curtain to rip apart, and suddenly his momentum picked up, and he found himself swinging feet-first, heading right into the screen. And just as he realized what was happening, Lang saw that the film was still running; his real-life feet were going to collide with his own larger-than-life Joe Gunn face!

"Nooo!" screamed Joe Gunn as Nick Lang swung help-lessly toward the screen.

"Nooo!" screamed Lang as his feet punctured Gunn's nose. There was a crash and a rip as the screen split apart, depositing Lang in an unceremonious heap backstage.

Just at that moment, the door that led backstage from the alley flew open, and a phalanx of uniformed and plainclothes cops spilled into the building. From his position on the floor, Lang saw the Crasher run back past him, leap through the split screen, and head for a side exit.

"That way . . . ," Lang gasped.

But the directions were unnecessary: Moss was right behind the Crasher, and the killer knew it.

As he whirled to take one last shot at Moss, the two men, killer and cop, shared a split second of eye contact and deadly intent. Moss was quicker. He took fast, accurate aim and fired.

The bullet was a direct hit to the upper chest. With a look of surprise on his face, the Party Crasher dropped his gun and tumbled to the floor, blood gushing from the wound. Uniformed cops rushed up, guns drawn.

"We got him! He's down!" one of them shouted triumphantly.

Lang just stared from the crumpled figure of the killer to Moss and back again. He couldn't believe it was finally over. He couldn't believe he'd been there to witness it. Still struggling to untangle himself from the mess of curtain and screen he lay in, he looked up and saw John Moss reaching out a hand to help him.

"What the hell are you doing here?" Moss demanded, yanking him to his feet. "For Christ's sake, Lang, that guy is a multiple murderer, and you don't even have a gun."

Moss's torrent of words stopped abruptly as Nick Lang reached up and punched him square in the face, sending the cop reeling in pain and surprise.

"Wha—" said Moss, clutching at his jaw.

"You," Lang seethed, "are a dead man."

"What the hell are you talking about?" Moss rubbed his chin, looking genuinely puzzled.

Lang stared belligerently at him. "It'll be easy, right, Moss? After all, I've killed *once*; the second time should be a picnic!"

Suddenly, Lang's verbal powers seemed to desert him again, and all he wanted to do was beat the living daylights out of Moss. He leapt on Moss and banged away maniacally, hitting him in the stomach, the ribs . . .

"Ouch!" Moss protested. "Careful, my ribs . . . stop it!"

192

He tried to push Lang away. "Come on . . . ," he yelled, shielding his head, "I didn't mean anything, Lang. I was going to leave a message on your machine when you got home."

Lang glared crazily at him. "You made me think I *killed* someone, Moss!" he yelled. "You really pulled it off, you should be congratulating yourself—I tried to turn myself in for *murder*!" All of his outrage rose up again, and Lang threw a hard right hook, connecting solidly with Moss's jaw.

Hurt and fed up, Moss instinctively hit back, throwing a stinging punch at Lang, which sent the actor reeling back in his tracks.

"Quit hitting me in the face, you little shit!" Moss yelled. "It was just a joke! And besides, it probably did you some good, woke you up!"

"Oh, yeah?" Lang said belligerently.

"Yeah!" Moss said. "Maybe it's about time you got a little reality dose, Lang! Maybe you understand now that some things in life can actually be worse than staying in the tanning booth too long or missing a call from your agent!"

Moss turned and started to stalk away, but Lang wasn't finished. He grabbed Moss by the shoulders and whirled him back around to face him.

"You bastard!" Lang yelled.

"Enough!" Moss said, shaking him off like an annoying gnat. He tried to walk away again, but Lang flew at his retreating figure and knocked him into a pile of boxes, which came crashing down around both of them.

"What the hell is wrong with you, Moss?" Lang demanded. "Are you even human? I just wanted your help, goddammit!"

Moss's eyes got hard and steely. "Oh, really?" he shot back. "Is that what justified screwing up an entire investigation? Is that what justified you coming into my life and taking it over? You just 'wanted a little help'?" he mocked sarcastically.

"I wanted to learn something from you," Lang said more quietly.

"Is that right?" Moss retorted, his voice rising. "And what about Susan? What the hell were you learning from *her*?"

Lang stared and shook his head in disbelief—so *that* was what this was really all about. "She just wanted some advice from your *best friend*, Moss. She wanted to find out . . . ," and suddenly his voice was shaking with anger, "why you are such a colossal *asshole*!"

Then they were at it again, Lang shaking Moss by the shoulders and pounding him ineffectually. Moss, even more infuriated by Lang's explanation about Susan, grabbed him and, with an unexpected burst of force, threw him to the floor.

Lang looked up, stunned. "You really *are* an asshole, you know?" he said. "You made me think I took a man's life. Do you have any idea how that feels?"

"That's what you *wanted*, isn't it?" Moss shot back. "You wanted to know what it 'feels' like to be a cop, right? You wanted to method-act your whole fucking *life* out; you wanted to know what it *feels* like to kill someone." His glare was glacial, his voice dripping with contempt. "Well now you know, Lang. Or at least for a couple of hours you did. You know it feels like shit. So why don't you just go on back to Hollywood where you belong and *use* it?"

Lang stared at him with utter disbelief. Finally, he got up, dusting himself off. His tone steely and calm, he spoke. "I also found out what it feels like to be you, Moss. It's miserable." He stared back at Moss, his look just as glacial and just as contemptuous. "Susan, me, we have some idealized picture of you. Maybe we *do* want to be like you—but maybe that's the problem—we *can't* be like you, because being like you means never letting anyone *in*." He stopped and shook his head. When he spoke again, his voice was calmer. "Maybe that really is a part of being a cop," he said, "but if it is, you can keep it."

Lang turned and walked away. Moss stood and stared after him.

TWENTY-FIVE

THE YOUNG POLICEMAN'S NAME WAS KEVIN MAHO-
ney, and he was new to the force. Although he came from
a long family line of cops, nothing had really prepared him
for the experience of seeing a man bleeding from a gaping
wound, lying unconscious, facedown on a stretcher. As he
climbed into the ambulance, Kevin steeled himself.

The paramedics were a whole different story; they saw this
kind of thing every day, sometimes more than once a day. It
was all business to them, and the business was keeping the
human wreck in front of them alive long enough to get it to
the emergency room. They tended not to look at the victims
as people so much as individual challenges. Sometimes they
met the challenge and won; sometimes the person died, and
then everybody lost. It didn't matter whether the person was
the Party Crasher, an Upper East Side heart attack victim, or
a bowery bum—the problem was the same.

"Hmmm," said one of the paramedics, a wiry Hispanic
called Raldo, "this guy don't look so good. I think we gotta
flip him over, officer."

Kevin Mahoney looked dubiously down at the Party Crasher, who lay unmoving, facedown, his hands cuffed behind his
back. "You sure?" he asked.

"Yeah," the other medic agreed. "We gotta turn him on his
back," he said, confirming Raldo's assessment. He looked at
Mahoney. "No problem, just cuff the guy in front instead of

back." Then he glanced briefly down at the unconscious form on the stretcher. "He isn't going anywhere, believe me."

Still, Kevin hesitated. He thought about calling in a superior officer, but Raldo said, "Come on, let's just do it. He's losin' a lot of blood, and I think you want this one alive for the trial."

Kevin Mahoney, like every other cop on the force, had ambivalent feelings about that particular subject. After all, a trial could go either way, and if the Party Crasher got himself some fancy mouthpiece, Mahoney knew he might walk away with an insanity defense that netted him a couple of easy years in some upstate loony bin, instead of what he really deserved.

Still, as he looked at the helpless, bleeding form in front of him, his conscience won the battle. He pulled out his key, then reached over and unlocked the cuffs. He started to give the two paramedics a hand as they shifted the Crasher's dead weight in order to turn him over.

Just as they were about to flip the killer, all hell broke loose.

The Party Crasher was far from unconscious; he had heard every word they said and knew this was a God-sent opportunity to act. He sat abruptly up and, taking advantage of the others' surprise, clubbed one of the paramedics across the face. The man went reeling backward, crashing into the side of the ambulance, and the Crasher leapt to his feet.

Raldo took a brutal knee to the stomach, which doubled him over; a vicious, efficient chop to the back of his neck sent him sprawling down. The killer, pumped up and maniacal, leapt on the shocked Kevin Mahoney, before he could even draw his gun, and smashed him in the kidneys. Then, as Kevin bent over, the killer grabbed his hair and pulled him forward, getting Kevin in a headlock.

"I'll take this," said the Crasher, reaching around and grabbing Kevin's gun.

"Gimme the keys," he rasped to Raldo, then reached to grab them for himself, still keeping Kevin immobilized. He pushed Kevin hard across the little space in the vehicle and trained the gun on all three of them. No one moved a muscle as the Crasher backed out the double door and slammed it shut, locking it behind him.

The two paramedics and the cop came alive, pounding and shouting for someone to let them out, as the killer disappeared into the crowd that still milled around the scene.

Inside the theater, Moss was completely unaware of the events transpiring out front. He was in the lobby, telling China what had gone down, when they heard a patrol car screech away from the curb, burning rubber as it went.

"What the hell . . . ," Moss said.

They looked in the direction of the noise and saw Lang, furious and intent, at the wheel of the car. Onlookers had the sense to scatter as he drove.

"Gee," said China, deadpan, "I think he might still be a little upset."

"Screw him if he can't take a joke." Moss shrugged flippantly, but he was a little uneasy about it nonetheless. Lang had been really upset, and both of them had said things that Moss was now beginning to regret.

"He's not so bad, John," China said to him. "I mean, he really *did* try to save your ass."

"I know," Moss said gruffly. "Do you think we could change the subject?" he added abruptly. "Maybe just talk about what happened here?" He didn't want to hear about Nick Lang, not now and not anytime in the near future either.

"Sure." China shrugged. "Why not . . . After all, it's all over now."

Lang squealed out of his illegal parking spot and drove, with no idea where he was going. "Damn Moss," he muttered to himself. "Damned nerve of him . . . "

He was only two blocks from the theater when he heard a voice from the backseat say, "Keep driving."

The startled Lang looked in the rearview mirror and saw an apparition: the Party Crasher, bruised and bleeding, holding a gun to Lang's head. The killer's eyes were bright and manic.

Lang felt the blood drain from his face. He began to hyperventilate, and his mind went reeling. This couldn't be happening, he thought. But it was. It really *was*.

"I'll tell you where to turn," the killer rasped, "and you don't do anything *except* what I tell you, got it?"

Lang started to nod, aware of the cool metal barrel not an inch from his temple. He forced himself not to panic; that wouldn't help anything. Lang summoned up every ounce of courage he had and faced grimly forward, trying to figure out a way to get out of this. Then, suddenly, he had an idea. It was risky, but no more risky than this little jaunt was already proving to be. He thought he knew the way to handle this situation—do it as the screen heroes did it.

His hazel eyes met the killer's crazed ones in the mirror. "You talkin' to me?" Lang snarled. "Well," he demanded, "you talkin' to *me*?"

The Crasher looked momentarily confused. "Just shut up and keep driving!" he ordered Lang.

But Nick Lang wasn't Nick Lang anymore. He was Joe Gunn, Travis Bickle, and Harry Callahan all rolled up into one. And Joe/Travis/Harry didn't take orders from *anyone*. "I fuckin' hate it when people don't say 'please,' " Lang growled, as he stomped on the accelerator as hard as he could.

The patrol car lurched forward and began to weave dangerously through traffic, sideswiping cars nearby in the process.

"Hey!" the Party Crasher protested, brandishing the gun. "Slow down!" There was no response from Lang except a crazy-sounding laugh. "Slow down!" the killer repeated.

Lang shrugged and kept the petal floored. "Or what?" he said cynically. "Or I'll be scrapin' my brains off the dashboard?" His eyes met the killer's again. "Sorry, pal," he said, "you picked the wrong chauffeur." And with that, he stomped on the brakes and sent both of them flying forward. " 'Cause I just don't give a shit," Lang informed the killer.

The car screeched around in a one-eighty and slammed into a parking meter, jolting the killer in his seat.

"Lookit that," Lang mused, "and everybody's always complaining about how you can't find a parking space in this city." He laughed, then turned around to face the Crasher, with a crazed look on his face. "Got some change for the meter?" he said and laughed. Then he threw the car into reverse and stomped on the accelerator again.

This time, the impact threw the Crasher backward in his seat, as the car backed off the bent meter. "What the hell are you doing?" he shouted.

"Oh, you don't like this?" Lang said quizzically. He promptly threw the car into gear and lurched forward again, roaring off into traffic.

"Stop it!" screamed the Crasher, as the car bounced off the side of a parked vehicle and careened around a corner. "Slow down! You're gonna kill us both!"

"Big deal," Lang said. "I always wanted to go out in a blaze of glory, didn't you?" He accelerated dangerously through an intersection, barely missing being broadsided by a huge moving van. "Hey," Lang said conversationally, "isn't this where we just were?" He jerked a thumb toward the theater, where cops and ambulances were still in evidence. "Wanna go back?"

Then he laughed and screeched away.

Inside the theater lobby, Moss and China watched as Lang's patrol car screeched crazily by.

"I guess he's *real* upset," China remarked.

"No," Moss said, catching a glimpse of a figure in the backseat of the car. All of a sudden he realized exactly what was happening. "Oh, shit!" Moss exclaimed, grabbing China by the arm. "He's got company, and I think I know who it is."

Running outside, they were just in time to see Kevin Mahoney and the two paramedics, looking battered and frightened, being let out of the back of the ambulance.

"Shit," Moss muttered, taking in the scene. "It's as bad as I thought!" Then he ran for a patrol car.

"See this?" Lang said, holding up a bottle of antacid mints he'd found on the front seat. "This is nitrocarbonate-aminocin." He grinned crazily at the Crasher. "I got this growth on my brain, you know? Like the size of a summer squash . . . They tell me it's terminal, and I gotta take these every hour to keep from losin' my mind altogether. But tonight," he said as he shrugged and tossed the bottle out onto the street, "who cares? I mean, this is the way to do it, the way to go out, don't you think?"

"Hey!" screamed the Crasher, panic in his voice. "Lemme out of here—you're nuts!"

"Maybe," Lang mused. "Brain tumors can do that to you. Anyway, the doctors say I've got three months, but *I* say I'll check out when I goddam well please! And tonight looks . . . auspicious."

As if to match his words with action, he headed up a one-way street the wrong way. As the patrol car veered into oncoming traffic, cars careened right and left to avoid them.

"You damn maniac!" the Crasher screamed as the sounds of blaring horns and crunching metal filled the air.

"Well, jeez," Lang said in a wounded voice, "don't you kinda' think that's the pot calling the kettle black?"

"Pull over or I'll shoot!" the Crasher screamed frantically.

Lang shrugged. "Go ahead," he said, "shoot." He checked the speedometer. "I'm goin' about sixty right now. What happens when no one's at the wheel?"

"Pull over, goddammit!"

"See," Lang continued thoughtfully, as all around them cars going in the opposite direction continued to crash into each other in an effort to get out of Lang's way, "I've really got nothing to lose. My warranty's about to run out, buster, and I'm ready to be fitted for a body bag."

"Pull over!"

"Get rid of the gun and I'll think about it," Lang said, smashing into the side of a parked van and screeching away.

The Crasher threw himself at the door, but it was wedged shut from the impact of the van. "Pull over!" he screamed again.

"Get rid of the gun," Lang repeated. He veered up onto the curb, taking a fire hydrant with him. As water gushed twenty feet in the air, he screeched back into traffic.

Horn blaring, an oncoming car crashed head-first into their right front bumper, and the impact sent Lang's car up over a parked car's fender. The front end of the patrol car went up, then sickeningly down, and both men were thrown violently to the side.

Lang recovered first, grabbing both the wheel and the gun, which had flipped out of the Crasher's hand and landed in the front seat of the car.

"Well, well," he said jovially, "I knew that eventually you'd have to see it my way."

Holding the gun triumphantly, he grinned and reached for the mike. "Hello, NYPD," Lang said cockily into the mike. "Ten-four! It's book 'em Danno time, boys and girls! This is Officer Cazenov, and I've got a present for you . . . The Party Crasher's in the back of my unit, and I'll be delivering him to you, gift-wrapped and safe. No need to thank me; it's just a part of the gig." He smiled at his reflection in the mirror. "Not bad for an actor, huh?"

But Lang's smug attitude promptly worked against him. Instead of his own reflection, he should have paid attention to the road. As he turned his eyes to the front, he heard the Crasher scream incoherently from the backseat, and with complete shock, Lang suddenly realized their patrol car was barreling up the empty back of a huge auto transport carrier.

"Ahh!" Lang screamed as they crashed with a sickening crunch of metallic sounds into the cab of the truck.

Lang was tossed violently forward and his head cracked against the windshield, dazing him for a moment. When he

201

managed to shake the fog loose and look around, the windshield was spiderwebbed from the impact of his skull, and the killer was climbing hastily out the side window of the patrol car, on his way to freedom again.

TWENTY-SIX

THE NEXT MORNING, THE WIDE CONCRETE STEPS leading up to the doors of the precinct were crowded to overflowing with cameramen, reporters, and curiosity seekers. When Nick Lang finally appeared to spontaneous applause, he was sporting a bandaged forehead and a sling on one arm, both the result of his interaction with the patrol car windshield and steering wheel the day before.

But otherwise, the old Nick Lang, the *real* Nick Lang, was back in full, charismatic force. The cocky, charming grin, the twinkling hazel eyes, the offhanded, humorous attitude—these were in high gear, and they marked him as a star, not a cop. There was no mistaking one for the other, not today.

The media had been alerted the day before, when the Party Crasher had escaped the police again, and their attention had focused on the theater and what had happened there. The dangerous pursuit in the crowded theater, the wild car chase outside, the hail of bullets—it was all front-page stuff. But as if all *that* wasn't enough to please the readers, there was the extra, added, utterly delightful fact that the "cop" who had swung, feet-first, into the screen showing *Smoking Gunn II* was none other than the real-life Joe Gunn, the movie star Nick Lang. It was better than any fiction they could have dreamed up on their own, and they were having a field day with it.

Once the initial furor died down and the problems of interview scheduling were being haggled over, Nick Lang was content to let them hold their press conference at the station. He'd spent what was left of the previous night in the emergency room and gotten a clean bill of health. Other than a slight concussion and a sprained wrist, he was fine. He was free to go and meet his public.

And it couldn't have turned out any better, he thought. Well, he amended the thought, that wasn't quite true. It could have been even more spectacular if only he'd been able to complete his mission, to bring the killer in. Still, he mused, he couldn't have bought better publicity than this. And publicity, he hoped—along with the convincing bruises he sported—would persuade the director that he should play Tony DiBennedetti.

He walked out into the sunlight and posed graciously for the cameras, fielding questions the reporters threw at him. Yes, he admitted, he *had* disguised himself in order to pass for a policeman. No, he agreed, it certainly *wasn't* an easy job—the men and women who did it every day should be congratulated. Yes, he was heading back to Hollywood this very afternoon. Yes, it was frightening being in a car with the Party Crasher. And yes, he had every confidence that the NYPD would catch the man.

The main event over, Lang stepped up next to local anchorwoman Tammy Bennett, ready to do the exclusive interview the distraught but pragmatic Angie had promised her the night before. Angie, he thought with a shudder, who was ready to kill him for what she called "that incredibly stupid stunt" he had pulled. Well, he thought, Angie would change her tune when he won . . . the Oscar.

Tammy, her blond hair perfectly coiffed, her bland, pretty face perfectly made-up, smiled into the camera. "A little real-life glamour found its way into the 46th Precinct today."

The camera pulled back to include Lang, who also smiled broadly.

"I'm standing here with Nick Lang," Tammy said, "silver-screen hero of the new box-office smash *Smoking Gunn II*.

Lang spent last night at West Side Hospital after a life-and-death struggle with the notorious serial killer known to law enforcement only as 'The Party Crasher.' " She turned to Lang and held the mike out for him. "Is it true you were nearly killed, Mr. Lang?" she asked, turning her perky smile into a suitably serious look of concern.

"Well," Lang shrugged modestly, "it had its moments. I suppose some people might call it a brush with danger that's a little too close for comfort." Like my agent, he wanted to add.

"The man called the Party Crasher," Tammy said somberly "has claimed five victims so far, including the latest, reputed gun dealer Tony Terranova, last night. But the killer is still on the loose. How do you feel about that?"

"Well, gosh," Lang said, "I wish I'd been able to bring him in. But I guess these fine men and women," he added, gesturing magnanimously around at the eager crowd of cops who'd gathered to watch the interview, "will be doing that pretty soon."

Tammy faced the camera again. "Lang had been riding undercover with Lieutenant John Moss, who, you may remember, was also wounded in an earlier battle with the killer. We tried to contact Lieutenant Moss, but he was unavailable for comment."

Right, thought Lang—more likely, he'd had a few pithy and unprintable words for the journalists.

Tammy turned toward Lang again. "Was this action of yours what we've been told?" she continued. "Was it really research for an upcoming role?"

Lang nodded. "That's right," he replied. "And you couldn't get a quicker, tougher, more realistic lesson anywhere."

Tammy nodded. "So . . . what was it like, actually being face to face with a *real* villain?"

Lang looked directly into the camera. "It was not a lot of fun," he said seriously. Then, with that charming smile lighting up his face, he joked, "I just kept waiting for someone to yell 'Cut!' " He winked at the camera and Tammy laughed. She knew when it was time to call it quits.

205

"That's all for 'Action News at Noon,' " she said. She made a throat-slitting gesture to her cameraman. "It's a wrap," she called out. "We're gonna make the national news, kids." Then she turned to Lang. "So," she said, "off the record, what do you think about Lieutenant Moss? I mean, I tried to interview him about this killer, and he came off like a real assho—uh, hardcase."

"Moss?" Nick Lang said, trying to look surprised. "Gee, you must've caught him on a bad day." He did a quick survey of the cops milling around and saw that Moss wasn't there. It was no surprise, but he realized that he actually felt a little disappointed all the same.

Lang pleaded other pressing commitments, said a hasty good-bye to Tammy, and then edged his way slowly into the station. Every few feet it seemed, someone stopped him to congratulate him, to shake his hand, to ask for his autograph.

Outside the squad room, he bumped into China, who shook her head ruefully. "I *knew* you looked like Nick Lang," she said with a laugh.

"Well . . . " Lang shrugged.

"But you *are* shorter!" She grinned again. "At least, shorter than you look up there on the screen. Oh, Moss is in there," she added. "I mean," she said hastily, "if you were *looking* . . . "

It was Lang's turn to smile. "Thanks, China," he said.

Inside the packed squad room, he was still stopped by admirers and autograph seekers. It was slow going, but he finally made his way across the room, to the spot where Moss lounged against his desk, watching the commotion with an unreadable expression on his face. The other cops, sensing the tension between the two men, seemed to fade away from the immediate vicinity.

"Moss," Lang said. He found himself unexpectedly tongue-tied. "Uh . . . I wanted to say . . . well . . . well, anyway, I'm leaving. I'm flying out tonight, six o'clock, uh . . . so I guess I'll finally be out of your hair."

Lang paused and waited for Moss to say something, anything to fill the space between them. But Moss just stood there, as silent and remote as a sphinx.

"Look," Lang said, "I know what you're thinking . . . "

"Do you?" Moss asked dryly.

"I know, I know," Lang said with a gesture. "I had him, I even got his gun, and I let him get away . . . "

Moss was silent. Finally, he shrugged and looked at a spot somewhere to the left of Lang's head. "You're alive," he said. "And that's a lot to say after five minutes with that guy."

Lang was shocked into silence. He was actually not getting any shit from John Moss. No, even better than that, he was . . . maybe . . . being complimented. He studied Moss's face for a sign, something that would enable him to believe that Moss wasn't actually furious at him. There was no sign, but the absence of anger seemed to indicate that it was all right to at least stand there and try to have a conversation.

"Well," Lang said finally, clearing his throat. "So . . . what's the next step? I mean, where do you look for this maniac now?"

Moss shrugged wearily. "He's too damned smart," he said. "I hate to admit it, but we don't have any idea where to look. I guess we just have to wait until *he* decides to communicate."

"With a bullet or what?" Lang asked dryly.

Moss shrugged again. "Maybe he's hurt badly enough to try to get help from a doctor," he said. "We've alerted all the hospitals in the area."

There was another awkward pause, which threatened to stretch into a really long, uncomfortable silence. Lang struggled to think of something to say, but for once, Moss beat him to the punch.

"Listen," Moss said, then seemed to hesitate. Finally, he took his gaze off the wall and looked Lang straight in the eye. "The thing is," he began, then seemed to run out of words

207

again. "The thing is," he repeated, "I've been meaning to tell you something."

"What?" Lang asked, surprised. The taciturn Moss had been thinking about talking?

"Yeah, well . . . " Moss sighed. "About you thinking that . . . that you killed that guy who ran out of the building, you know, that whole setup the other night."

"What about it?" Lang prodded. Life-threatening situation or no, he was still angry about that.

"Well," Moss looked at him soberly. "It really took some stones to come back here and confess."

Lang laughed in surprise, but it was a laugh that was tinged with bitterness. "Thanks," he said curtly. He really didn't want to be reminded of that nasty little episode, and even Moss's grudging admiration and left-handed compliment didn't take the sting out of the incident for him.

Lang shrugged. "So . . . I guess this is it," he said. "I've got a plane to catch." He turned to leave but was stopped by Moss's voice.

"Lang," Moss said quietly.

Nick Lang turned again. Moss was still slouching at the desk, his arms crossed over his chest. But he looked as though some emotion was trying to surface.

"Look," Moss said, "I'm lousy with thank-yous and stuff like that . . . "

"I hadn't noticed," Lang said dryly.

"But," Moss plowed resolutely on, determined to set the record straight, "I *do* pay attention." His dark, intense gaze met Lang's. "And *you* know and *I* know that if you hadn't been in that balcony at just that minute, and if you hadn't seen what was going down and yelled out to me, without even thinking about your own hide . . . well, he'd probably have hit me with that shot."

"Maybe," Lang agreed cautiously, wondering where all this could be leading.

"So . . . the thing is, I owe you, and I didn't want you

to split thinking that I didn't know that I did. So . . . thank you."

Lang shook his head and smiled a smile of disbelief. "Careful, Moss," he said, "you're on the verge of gushing."

One eyebrow went up. "Yeah, well," Moss said, retreating back to normal form, "don't let it go to your head or anything. You're still a major pain in the ass, Hollywood."

Lang smiled. "Better than being the ass, Copper."

A spontaneous look of humorous, mutual respect passed between them then, and at that moment, Nick Lang finally felt as though John Moss had actually acknowledged him as a human being, for the first—and probably last—time in their short, stormy acquaintance.

There didn't seem to be anything left to say.

"So . . . ," Lang said. He shrugged again. "See ya."

"Yeah," Moss said, looking steadily at him. "See ya."

Moss stood and watched as Nick Lang made his way back through the squad room, still stopping to autograph a piece of paper, to say hello or good-bye. But he left without looking back again, and strangely, Moss wasn't all that happy to see him go.

TWENTY-SEVEN

MOSS HAD FINALLY MANAGED TO ANSWER EVERY-
body's curious questions, finish up the paperwork on the Party Crasher's latest getaway, and leave the precinct. Then he
retreated to the quiet privacy of his place.

Now devoid of Nick Lang's intrusive presence, his pos-
sessions and his prying, the place was neat and pleasant once
again. Well, Moss thought, except for the ruined sofabed,
which he had put back together but not too well, a couple
of broken lamps, the black scrape marks on the walls, and
one end table that had lost its battle with the manacled actor.
Moss sighed as he looked around and straightened up the
books on his bookcase. He'd done as much as he could do,
he realized. Then he went into the kitchen and pulled a frozen
dinner from the freezer.

Ah, peace and quiet, he thought gratefully, popping it into
the microwave and setting the timer. Tomorrow he'd get some
real shopping done, make himself a nice dinner, fresh salad.
Maybe, if he got up the nerve, he might call and see if Susan
was even still speaking to him. What were the odds on that,
he wondered.

He sighed again and wandered over to the window, looking out into the night. Then he shook his head and laughed
ruefully. Nick Lang's *Smoking Gunn II* billboard was still
staring into his window, bigger than life. "I guess I'll never
get rid of you, will I?" John asked the billboard.

He sat down at his dining room table and put Nick Lang and Susan resolutely out of his mind as he studied the written reports and the photos from the Party Crasher case. How the hell could this guy get away so *often*? he asked himself. The killer seemed to have the devil's own luck, Moss mused, wondering for the first time if he'd ever really be able to catch the man. Moss didn't usually have self-doubts, not about work at least, and the brief uncertainty was unnerving.

There had to be *something* here, he told himself, poring over the papers and pictures, *something*, in all this information, that added up to a clue to the killer's identity. But he couldn't seem to find it. He let his mind drift off into visualizing his encounters with the Crasher, searching back over his own memory for something, some hint, some pointer.

The knock on the door that startled Moss out of his reverie was sharp and businesslike, and completely unexpected. He got up, went to the door, and looked through the keyhole, then threw the door open.

"Susan . . . ," he said, happily surprised. "Come on—"

He didn't get to finish the invitation. Susan marched briskly on by him and planted herself in the middle of the living room. Then she just stood there, tapping one foot impatiently, her arms crossed over her chest. Her dark eyes snapped with some emotion John thought *might* be anger.

"So, John," she said pointedly, "I'd like you to tell me something—what the *hell* is going on?"

Yup, it was anger all right. Moss opened his mouth to answer.

But she didn't even give him a chance to reply. "Just *tell* me, John. What is it?" she demanded. "What's with this little charade?"

"What charade?" Moss asked.

"What *charade*?" Susan repeated furiously. "Very funny, John. Maybe you should take up stand-up comedy as a sideline!"

"Oh," said Moss, "you mean . . . "

212

"I mean the one with you and your so-called *partner*, John! *You* know, the one named Ray Cazenov!" She glared at him. "Or *should* I call him your best box-office buddy, Nick Lang?"

"Look, Susan," Moss began, "I wanted to talk to you about that, I was *going* to talk to you about it. I'm really sorry."

"You lied to me, John!" Susan snapped, interrupting him in mid-apology. "*He* lied to me!"

"But I . . . we . . . " Moss fumbled for the right words, but they didn't come quickly enough.

"I know we haven't been going out for very long, but I thought," Susan said, banking down to a smolder, "that *maybe* I meant a little more to you than that."

"You *do*."

But Susan had her piece to say, and she wasn't about to let him off the hook that easily. "I thought that he was just this really nice, sensitive cop, and he wanted to help us out, and then, suddenly, on the *news*," she glared at him as she emphasized the word, "I have to find out that you're both playing some asinine juvenile game!" Her eyes reflected the hurt she felt as well as the anger that was in her voice. "Was this all supposed to be some kind of big macho joke or *what*?"

"Susan," Moss said earnestly, "believe me, it wasn't a joke at all."

"Then what was it?" she demanded. "I don't understand."

"It was just something that . . . got out of hand. I can explain it if you'll let me." Susan arched a cynical eyebrow at him. "I really *was* going to tell you anyway," Moss repeated. "Honest."

Susan snorted, but she appeared to have calmed down a little in response to his apology. Moss saw it, and he took her arm gently. "Come on," he said, leading her to the lopsided couch, "please just sit down here for a minute and listen to me, okay?"

Susan nodded reluctantly. They sat side by side on the couch, Moss bent forward, his arms clasped between his knees, Susan upright and guarded.

Choosing his words carefully, Moss looked over at her. "First off, none of this was my idea," he told her. "The Captain foisted Lang off on me—he, you know, Lang saw me interviewed on the news and thought he could model some damned policeman *character* he's going to play in a movie after me . . . So he just pulled some political strings and got what he wanted . . . Well, he got *me* at any rate." Moss shook his head in disbelief. "Brix ordered me not to tell *anyone* who he really was. I still can't believe it happened, it was so . . . weird!"

"And?" Susan inquired.

"And . . . well, I just didn't think I'd have to explain it to you. I never thought the two of you would even meet each other." He glanced over at her. "Let alone that you'd wind up . . . asking him out to *lunch* with you," he added snidely.

"Oh, for heaven's sake!" Susan said angrily, with a dismissive wave of her hand. "What's the big deal? Lunch! What did you think, that I was making a play for him over a sandwich?"

Moss shrugged. "I don't know what I thought," he said. "But it made me jealous, and besides, Lang told me that you thought I was an asshole."

Susan looked surprised, then embarrassed. "I didn't say that," she said, "at least, not exactly in those words."

Moss nodded. "Well, maybe I *was* acting a little like one," he admitted. "But this kind of stuff is just . . . hard for me."

"What stuff?" Susan asked in a gentler tone.

Moss shrugged, suddenly feeling shy. "I guess I've never been the kind of person who opened up to other people very much . . . It's always been a problem, and it's probably what screwed up my marriage. When I meet someone I like . . . like you"— his dark gaze held hers briefly, then he looked away—"well, I kind of clam up. I don't know how to act, or if I'm doing or saying the wrong thing. I get . . . nervous."

"Don't be nervous," Susan said softly. "There isn't any right way to act. There's only how you feel."

Moss took a breath and looked directly at her. "Well, that's the thing," he said. "You're the first person who's made me feel . . . the way I feel . . . in a very long time, Susan." He paused. "And if I haven't blown it completely, I'd really like another chance."

Susan stared at him for a long moment, then nodded. "I left Bonnie with a sitter," she said softly, "so, you know, if . . . I thought we might want to talk this out . . . a little more."

Moss leaned closer and nodded. "Oh, yeah," he said, his lips almost on hers, "I think we should."

A loud, frantic banging at the door startled both of them, and they jumped apart.

"Moss! Goddam it, Moss, it's me!" It was Nick Lang's unmistakable voice, shouting at him from the hallway. "Moss! This is important, you've got to let me in!"

Furious at the interruption, Moss was up and across the room in four angry strides. He flung the door open and saw Lang, panting and distressed.

"What the hell . . . "

Lang rushed in past him. "You've to get out, now, Moss!" he exclaimed. "I've got it figured out. He's coming here, the Party Crasher, he's coming after *you*!" He noticed Susan. "Oh, Susan! Jesus, you've *both* got to get out of here, now!"

"Lang, what the hell are you talking about?" Moss demanded.

"Revenge!" Lang replied emphatically. "He's going to come after the cop who shot him, don't you see?"

Moss was utterly baffled. "No! I'm afraid I don't see at all! Why the hell do you think *that*?" he demanded.

"Because they always do," Lang replied. "The psycho *always* shows up at the cop's house!"

Moss took Lang's arm and tried to propel him toward the door. "Is that in Hoyle's?" he asked. "Because I didn't know there was a rule book for psycho behavior, but personally, *I* think the psycho is already here," he said with a grim smile.

Lang shook his grip off impatiently. "Goddam it, listen to

215

me! He feels a . . . well, a personal *connection* with you, Moss. Think about it! You were on the tow truck; you were at the stock exchange and the nightclub. For Christ's sake, he called you by *name* at the van stakeout! China told me! And at the theater, you're the one who shot him, Moss. Are you listening?"

Moss nodded slowly. It was something to think about. But not now.

"Okay." Lang breathed a sigh of relief. "Now get out of here. He'll be coming for you; I *know* he will. He'd come after me if this was one of my movies," he finished triumphantly.

"But this isn't one of your movies," Moss reminded him, grabbing his elbow again and moving toward the door. "It's my apartment, which is not listed in the Manhattan directory, and which, at the moment, is being used for something very personal, something very *private*, and," he finished in a hiss, "you happen to be right up there next to the Party Crasher on the list of people who don't belong here right now!"

They were almost at the door, but Lang broke loose again and stubbornly stood his ground. "You're making a mistake, Moss," he said evenly, "and you're making it with Susan here."

That took Moss aback for a moment.

"I know what I'm talking about," Lang said firmly. "I don't care if you think I'm as crazy as a loon, at least take some precautions! Keep your gun handy and close that window in the bedroom."

Moss stiffened suddenly, looking down the hall at the window Lang was talking about. "I didn't leave that window open," he said softly. "I never do."

He whirled away from Lang and grabbed Susan, pulling her off the sofa and pushing her out into the hallway. "Go down to Mrs. Keppler's, in 7B," he whispered urgently. "Call 911 and tell them the Crasher is here. Then stay put!"

"But . . . ," Susan began.

"No buts, just go!" he said, and the look in his eyes told her this was very serious.

Moss whirled and hissed to Lang, "Go with her!"

"What are you going to do?" Lang said urgently.

"Die."

The voice was calm, expressionless. Moss and Lang turned slowly to see the Party Crasher advancing at them from the hallway. In his hand, pointing at them, was a gun that proved his words weren't an idle threat.

"You're going to die," he said again, then added, "both of you."

Moss felt Lang freeze at his side. "I told you he'd come," he whispered.

The Party Crasher looked briefly at Lang, hatred in his eyes. "You were actually a big help, movie star."

"Me?" Lang gulped.

"Sure." The killer grinned at them. The blood from the gunshot wound, the cuts and bruises, made him look like a ghoul when he smiled. "You've got such a big mouth; you like publicity so much. You're an easy target." He winked, looking more sinister than ever. "You said on the news that you were going home to Hollywood tonight. All I had to do was wait at the airport. I was going to . . . ask . . . for Moss's address right before I killed you, but," the Crasher said, shrugging and never wavering with the gun, "you left too fast. But that's all right—I just followed you here."

Moss could feel Nick Lang shrink with chagrin beside him. He glanced quickly across the room, to the place where his jacket and his holstered gun hung over the back of a chair. Too far, he knew; even if he could get to it, by the time he did, Lang would be dead.

The Party Crasher seemed to be in a chatty mood. He looked at Lang with contempt. "You know," he said, "I hate your movies."

"What?" Lang said, stung.

Oh, great, Moss thought, now we're going to get into film criticism. Still, it was all right—the longer they kept the Party

Crasher talking, the better chance they had of finding some way out of this deadly mess.

"They're garbage," the killer said. "They appeal to the lowest common denominator—to people's worst instincts." He paused and stared hard at Lang. "You're not even a real hero," he said.

"Hey!" Lang said.

The Party Crasher lifted the gun and sighted down the barrel. "Lieutenant," he said, "you're in the way." His smile was ghastly. "I want to do you last."

Just at that moment, the loud ring of the microwave timer sounded, startling all of them. The Party Crasher spun around and automatically fired at the noise, blowing the oven to smithereens.

It was the split second Moss needed, and he acted instantly, grabbing the nearest chair and raising it up in the air. He brought it crashing down on the killer's head with all the force he could muster, sending the Crasher reeling from the impact. The killer's gun went skidding across the floor and slid beneath the couch.

Moss hesitated for a moment, trying to gauge the time it would take him to get to his own gun. The moment was lost when the killer regained his footing and leapt on Moss, trying to pull him to the floor, his hands on Moss's neck. Moss struggled to thrust the man off, but the Party Crasher slapped him aside with a brutal backhand and fled from the apartment.

Moss scrambled up and went for his gun, then ran after the fleeing killer. He brushed by the dazed Lang with a warning look.

"I know, I *know*," Lang called after Moss as he raced down the hallway, "you want me to stay."

TWENTY-EIGHT

GUN IN HAND, MOSS CLATTERED DOWN THE HALL
in pursuit and was just in time to see the Party Crasher clam-
ber out a window that led to the fire escape. Moss climbed
quickly out after him, then paused on the iron escape and
glanced down. No trace of the killer that way. Moss knew he
must have headed for the roof. With a silent groan, he reached
for the metal rung above his head and began his own ascent,
trying to ignore the pain radiating from his ribs and arm.
Climbing with one arm in a cast was slow and awkward.

As Moss reached the flat, tarred expanse of the roof and
pulled himself up, he could just make out the killer's figure,
a dim shape in the dark night, vaulting agilely over the low
retaining wall that led to the next building's roof. Moss raced
to the wall and leapt over it.

He felt his heart plummet as he discovered in midair that
the rooftop next door was a full story lower than the one
on his building. He landed hard, lost his balance, and rolled
head-over-heels. His side felt as if it was ready to split open,
but Moss bounced to his feet and continued running in the
direction the killer had taken. He could barely make out the
form of the man he pursued, but with dogged persistence,
Moss kept going, keeping a firm grip on his revolver. This
time, he vowed, the son of a bitch wasn't going to escape.

Like a monkey the killer scrambled down the ladder, Moss
hard on his heels. Moss felt himself stumble then regain his

balance, and he cursed the extra fifteen yards the Crasher had just gained. He saw the killer leap out into what seemed to be thin air. When Moss reached the spot, it proved to be an air passage between two buildings. Breathing hard, Moss told himself not to look down, just forward. The jump was only three feet, but he knew that if he didn't make it, the fall would be five long stories down to the pavement below.

His injuries and his awkward landings spelled trouble for Moss: the killer was gaining distance. Swearing under his breath, Moss forced himself to take that same flying leap. He landed hard on the next rooftop, just in time to see the killer disappear behind a large duct. Approaching cautiously, gun ready, Moss crept silently up to the duct, then slid around it, his heartbeat rapid; but the killer was already moving toward the edge of the roof. There, he leapt, catlike, onto the next roof and ran toward a huge metal scaffolding. For a man as beaten and wounded as the Party Crasher, Moss thought grimly, he was in awfully good shape.

Moss ran toward the scaffolding and clambered awkwardly up the ladder, which scaled the giant erector-set beams of the structure. Just as he reached the catwalk halfway up, he saw the killer disappear into some sort of utility shed. A door slammed shut after him. Moss ran after him, throwing his weight against the door. It didn't budge. The killer had locked him out. But Moss was determined; panting and aching, he hurled himself against the door again. It still didn't give an inch.

Moss drew back, took aim, and blew the handle and lock off the door. The shot echoed in the night as Moss kicked the door open and entered the dark space inside.

It was an eerie place, filled with dim shadows and a constant, unidentifiable mechanical noise. Keeping himself as low and silent as possible, Moss crept carefully toward an opening at the other end of the room, then stared down. The staircase spiraled down into more moving things. Moss peered carefully, and he realized suddenly where he was and what was making the mechanical noises: this was the back

220

of a billboard above Times Square, and both levels of this shed were used to house the pipes, pulleys, and gears, all the mechanical apparatus that worked in tandem to keep something on the front of the billboard moving.

Suddenly, Moss heard something above him. He whirled too late as the Crasher dropped bodily onto him from the rafters where he'd been hiding. He swung into Moss with enough force to knock the wind out of his lungs and the gun out of his hand. Moss heard a sickening clatter as it dropped to the machinery below.

Grunting with exertion, the killer launched an assault on Moss's face and body, kicking and punching and gouging. Moss tried desperately to defend himself from the Crasher's blows, but his own pain and the killer's almost superhuman strength combined to make it a losing battle. Already debilitated and hampered by his injuries, Moss felt his strength slipping, and he wondered fleetingly if he could last much longer.

Then the killer made a mistake, dropping his hands just long enough to give Moss the opening he needed. Moss pulled swiftly back and swung his plaster cast across the killer's face with all the power he could muster, knocking the man off balance. It bought just enough time to give Moss the advantage—at least temporarily. Moss threw himself on top of the killer, barely aware of the huge, dangerous gears grinding and turning right next to them.

The two men fought viciously, exchanging blow after blow. The killer's face was a bloody mess, and Moss thought his must look just as bad. Suddenly, the killer was on top, Moss bent at an awkward angle. The man seized Moss's injured arm and bent it backward.

An excruciating pain shot through Moss, and he heard the horrifying sound of the plaster being ground up—Moss realized that his arm was caught in the gears. Instinctively, he hurled himself forward, but not before the gears got ahold of the cast, ripping it in two. Moss just barely managed to yank his arm free before the plaster cast was chewed up by the machinery.

A metal pipe came swinging at Moss's head. Moss threw himself sideways, crashing into a door, which sprang open, sending Moss tumbling out onto the face of the billboard. He found himself clinging to a ridge six stories above Times Square. The people and traffic below were doll-sized from up here. Moss felt dizzy from the combination of blows and height.

With a giddy feeling of unreality, he saw that what he was clinging to was actually the brim of a giant hat, the hat that belonged to Nick Lang in his *Smoking Gunn II* billboard, the very same billboard that stared into his own apartment!

There was no time to appreciate the irony of the situation. The Party Crasher flew out the door and was on him again, with murder in his eyes. Grappling unsteadily, Moss managed to grab the end of the pipe being swung at him; then, with tremendous effort, he wrenched it from the killer's hands. But his triumph was short-lived: the impact of that action threw them both off balance, and together, they went tumbling over the brim of the hat.

Moss grabbed frantically out into thin air, just catching onto the steel supports that made up the underside of the billboard. He clung grimly there, dangling sixty feet in the air, while the Crasher, who was hanging on a higher beam, kicked out at him, trying to dislodge Moss's grip and send him tumbling to his death. The killer aimed a particularly vicious kick right into Moss's broken ribs.

"You psycho!" Moss gasped, writhing in pain.

With a bloody smile on his face, the Crasher took advantage of Moss's inability to fight back. Clawing and shinnying, he managed to pulled himself up onto the brim. Then he grabbed for the pipe again.

This is it, Moss thought dizzily. He knew the Crasher was going to start beating the pipe on his wearying fingers and sooner, rather than later, send him flying off into space. But just as the first blow began to come down, the killer stopped in mid-arc, startled by something in back of him.

The door of the utility shed banged open, and Nick Lang burst through, gun in hand.

"Hey!" he shouted. "Put that down!"

The Crasher whirled around, and Lang aimed the gun at him. "Put the pipe down," he screamed. "Don't make me shoot you!"

The Crasher seemed oblivious to his words. He was staring at the gun in Lang's hand. Calmly, coldly, he moved forward, every step a menacing approach. He held the metal pipe out in front of him, brandishing it like a shield.

"I mean it!" Lang shouted, trying to keep his voice from shaking. "I'll do it, I swear I will!"

"You won't do dick," sneered the killer. He was five feet away from Lang.

The gun shook in Lang's hand. "One more step," Lang said, "and you're history."

The Party Crasher looked Lang straight in the eye. "So shoot me," he said calmly.

Lang froze.

"You don't have the balls," the Crasher told him coldly, and wham, the pipe swung viciously around, smashing into Lang's ribs and sending him sprawling backward. He moaned as the gun, knocked from his shaky grasp, went clattering out of reach.

Using more strength than he thought he still possessed, Moss managed to pull himself up just in time to see Lang take the hit. Moss saw the killer swing the pipe up over his head and knew instinctively that the Crasher was going to bring it down on the actor and just keep on hitting until Lang was dead.

Completely ignoring his own pain, Moss pulled himself to his feet and, with a roar of anger, threw himself onto the Crasher's back. Together, they went down in a tumbling, rolling heap, the force launching them both out onto the hat brim again.

Moss felt himself grappling wildly for some sort of support, and then, suddenly, Lang was in the melee, jumping

223

on top of the Crasher and sending all three of them tumbling to the very edge again. There was a startling cracking sound, and with a heart-stopping jolt, Moss realized that the flimsy wood brim had broken under all their combined weight and they were about to fall.

Moss found himself sliding precipitously down, then once again dangling in midair. The killer was half over the edge. Lang was the only one who managed to scramble all the way to relative safety.

"Come on, Moss," he shouted urgently, reaching out to pull him up.

"I can't," Moss gasped, the pain and fatigue finally taking over. "I can't move."

"Yes you *can*, goddammit!" Lang snapped, reaching perilously forward to grab ahold of Moss's hand. "Come on, Moss, you've got to *help*!"

Just as the seam that fastened the brim to the hat ripped with a sickening sound, Moss summoned up his last vestige of energy and, letting Lang pull from above, managed to find a foothold and scramble over the edge of the brim onto the crown.

Just as Lang pulled Moss to safety, the killer threw himself up and over the edge. He scrabbled backward, away from his adversaries, and suddenly seemed to disappear in a bank of fog. No, Moss realized as his eyes began to water, it wasn't fog—it was smoke. Something, perhaps his gun, Moss thought briefly, had gotten caught in the mechanism of the billboard and was causing a malfunction. Smoke was now pouring not just from the giant cigarette, but from everywhere: nose, eyes, mouth.

Moss coughed violently. He bent over, gasping, and brushed a hand across his watering eyes. When he looked up again, through the billowing smoke, he could just make out the figures of Lang and the killer, grappling wildly with each other.

Moss staggered toward them. He thought he saw Lang, caught in the killer's grasp, bring his knee up hard into the

224

killer's crotch. The Crasher bent over, screaming in pain, leaving Lang free to keep on hitting and punching and kicking; but Moss knew Lang was no match for the demented killer.

Moss pulled himself shakily along the jagged, broken brim, toward the fight. Every part of his body felt battered and useless, but grimly, Moss forced himself to keep moving. Suddenly, he tripped over an object and realized it was the metal pipe the killer had been wielding.

"Thank you, God!" Moss gasped. With a surge of energy, he swung the pipe over his head and brought it down with a crack onto the Party Crasher's shoulders.

The impact jerked the killer off balance, and before Moss or Lang could move, the Party Crasher went tumbling over the edge of the hat and screaming into the night. Coughing and choking, Moss approached the edge of the crown and peered cautiously over. Through the smoke and darkness, he could just make out the unmoving form of the killer, sprawled on what was left of the brim.

Moss looked at Lang, who was slumped in pain, and Lang stared back, exhausted.

"You okay?" Moss said after a few moments.

Lang, drained, managed a thumbs up. Then he pulled himself up and limped slowly over to join Moss at the edge, the smoke now completely obscuring their view.

"Jeez," Lang said between gasps.

"You said it," Moss agreed.

"We did it," Lang gasped. "Didn't we?"

Moss nodded.

"And we saved the taxpayers . . . ," Lang said, coughing, "a whole shitload of money."

Moss started to smile. "Yes, we did," he agreed hoarsely.

"No," they heard a voice say, "you didn't."

They both whirled to see the specter of the Crasher, holding Lang's gun. Hidden in the dense smoke, the killer, still very much alive, had managed to pull himself up and silently approach Moss and Lang.

"Lang," said Moss, "get out of the way."

But Lang did quite the opposite. As if in slow motion, Moss saw Lang throw himself in front of him, saw the killer's trigger finger press back, saw the flash of light, heard the crack of the gunfire.

"Nooo!" Moss screamed as time sped up and Lang, now hit, went stumbling forward in the line of fire, blocking the killer's path to Moss.

As Lang fell to one side, Moss threw himself at the killer, determined to get the bastard. Moss's hands went for the Crasher's throat, but just as he reached him, the man tripped, reeling backward. He seemed to slip just out of Moss's grasp as the impact of their bodily collision forced him over the edge again.

"Help me!" the Crasher screamed, clinging desperately to the edge.

But Moss just stared, stunned and immobilized, as, with one final scream, the Crasher fell into the darkness.

This time, Moss knew he'd finished the killer off. He stared vacantly down as, six stories below, a crowd began to gather around the corpse. Moss shuddered. It was over. It was finally over.

Then he turned and saw Lang lying in a heap.

"Oh, Christ," Moss whispered. He knelt by the actor, cradling him in his arms. "You stupid son of a bitch," Moss said, "why'd you have to go and do that?"

Lang's eyes fluttered open. He coughed weakly. "I don't . . . know," he gasped, "I just did it."

"Hang on, Lang," Moss said grimly, "I'm going to get some help."

"No, don't . . . leave me," Lang said, his chest heaving. A coughing spasm shook his entire body.

Moss was surprised to feel the moisture in his eyes. "Dammit, Lang," he said softly, "why the hell can't you do what you're told? Why didn't you get on that plane to L.A.? None of this would have happened; you'd be safe in your own world again."

"My world," Lang repeated softly, as if the thought of that

world was very far away. "You think . . . ," Lang coughed, "I would have gotten the part?"

"Hell, yes," Moss replied. "I *know* you would have."

"What about . . . Do you think . . . I could have been a cop—a *real* cop?" Lang's voice was getting weaker and weaker, but there was no mistaking how important the question was to him.

"Yeah, Nick," Moss said as one lone tear rolled down his cheek, "you'd have been a fine cop. You've got . . . you've got the balls."

Another coughing spasm shook Lang. "I'm . . . getting so . . . cold."

So this was it, Moss thought fleetingly. This was where it was all going to end. What a waste, what a tragedy. What, Moss thought, a pointless loss. He held Lang tighter, determined not to let the actor go into the night alone. He could see Lang's pale face, see his eyes flutter, then close.

"No," Moss whispered, his voice cracking. He stared down at Lang's still form.

Suddenly, Lang's eyes popped open. They were clear and quizzical and very much alive. "Did you mean that?" he demanded. "You really think I've got balls?" he asked happily.

Moss yelped in indignation. "What the hell . . . ," he said, dropping Lang from his arms.

Lang promptly sat up and smiled. "Not bad, huh?" asked the actor.

"Goddammit!" Moss yelled. "What the *hell* are you *doing*?"

"A death scene," Lang said matter of factly. "They *never* let me die in my movies—they say it's bad for my character. I've *always* wanted to play one of those, and let's face it, this was a golden opportunity." He winked at Moss. "By the way," he added, "I found that gun, the one with the blanks that you gave me when you set me up."

Moss groaned. "Great," he muttered, "so you went after a killer with a gun full of blanks. Very smart."

Lang scrambled to his feet and brushed himself off. "Well," he said, "it worked. I thought I could at least bluff the Crasher with it." He peered over the edge. "He *is* dead this time, isn't he?"

"He'd better be," Moss replied.

Lang grinned. "I didn't realize my early demise would affect you so strongly," he said.

"You son of a bitch!" Moss said wonderingly.

"Oh, come on, Moss," Lang said, "admit it—you deserved it."

To his surprise, Moss realized he wasn't really angry at all—he was simply very, very relieved that Lang was alive. And then he couldn't hold back a smile that started to surface. "You little shit," he said, shaking his head in admiration. He looked at Lang and laughed.

Lang shrugged. "So what do you think?" he asked. "You gonna arrest me for interfering? Gonna ball me out? Gonna tell your pals what a schmuck I am?"

Moss stared at him and shook his head slowly. "No, Lang," he said. "None of the above. I think I'm just going to say thank you for helping me out."

Lang stared at him, delight struggling with disbelief on his mobile face. Finally, he settled for a casual shrug. "All in a day's work," he said offhandedly.

Moss got up and brushed himself off as best he could. He was sore in more places than he would have believed possible. His castless arm throbbed. "All in a day's work, huh?" he asked. "For who—Joe Gunn?"

Lang looked around at the ruined billboard. The hat was in pieces; the cigarette dangled brokenly. Joe Gunn was a mess. Lang laughed. "Who knows?" he said. "Maybe this *is* the real me."

"Come on," Moss said, nodding toward the door to the utility shed, "let's get the hell out of here."

"Okay," Lang agreed.

But still, they stood there for a long moment, side by side, surveying the scene that could have spelled death for both of them. The thought seemed to reach them at the same time, and a look of acknowledgment passed between them.

Moss knew then that despite their very real differences, a bond had been forged, a bond that, after this, wouldn't be easily broken. "Come on," he said again.

"Yeah," Lang said, his old jaunty self again. "Let's blow this pop stand."

"Oh, for Christ's sake, Lang," Moss said crossly, "I haven't heard a cop say that in fifteen years."

Together, the two men walked toward the utility shed and the ladder that would lead them down. Moss threw an affectionate arm across Lang's shoulders. "So, how does the real you feel about filling out lots of real paperwork?" he asked pointedly.

Lang laughed again and shrugged. "Well," he said, "it's all part of the gig, isn't it?"

EPILOGUE

THE GRUNGY, TIRED-LOOKING COP WORE A THREE-day stubble of a beard and raggedy clothes. He looked mean and purposeful, and as he ran down the crowded New York street, people parted to let him through. He headed quickly down the dirty pavement stairs and reached the subway station below. It was grimy, filled with tattered posters, graffiti, and tired, unhappy people.

The cop didn't seem to notice—he was intent on something else. He glanced quickly around, then vaulted a turnstile and ducked behind a pillar. Up ahead of him, he spotted the green rookie huddled behind a magazine stand, frozen with fear, while a vicious-looking thug fired shot after shot at him. The rookie was bleeding from an arm wound.

The tough cop brought his own gun up and fired into the air, drawing the thug's attention to him. Then he somersaulted out of the way of a return shot that went whizzing by his ear, chipping off pieces of stone. He took aim again and fired off a couple of rounds. The thug did the same.

The gunfire sent the crowds scattering, screaming, but the tough cop heard more than the cacophonous sounds of panic. He looked up alertly as he heard the unmistakable sound of an empty chamber clicking. The thug was out of bullets.

Without hesitating, the cop barreled across the expanse of open space and yanked the gun from the startled thug, just as he was shoving a fresh clip into place. With one swift, brutal punch to the jaw, the cop knocked the thug to the ground and efficiently handcuffed him to the nearest pillar.

"Stay," was all he said.

Then he walked over to the trembling rookie, fire in his eyes. The tough cop gave a cursory glance to the kid's wound—it was nothing to worry about. He yanked the rookie to his feet.

"You happy now?" he snarled, his face an inch away from the rookie's. "Are you? You gotta be a hotshot, you gotta do it on your own, you're so *ready* to be a cop!" He shook his head in disgust, while the rookie dropped his eyes in shame. "Listen to me, shithead!" the cop said coldly. "And look at me when you listen to me. *This* is what being a cop is all about. *Real* bad guys, *real* bullets, *real* blood, and sometimes, if you don't pay careful attention or maybe your number's just up, *real dead*!"

"I'm sorry . . . ," the rookie began.

"Shut up!" the tough cop shouted. "Sorry means absolutely *nothing* here—there's no such word! You got some stupid-ass idea that we're *playin'* here, but we're *not*! This isn't like cops and robbers in the movies, this isn't about heroes and supermen and Dirty Harry, this is about puttin' your life on the line every day! Those assholes in the movies get seventeen takes to get it right, but *you don't*! You only get *one* take, kid, and if you mess it up, you're history!"

John Moss started in his seat as tough cop Tony DiBennedetti went into his harangue. Moss had a frog dog in his hand. Susan was on one side of him, and Bonnie was half-asleep on his other shoulder. Moss's eyes narrowed intently as the speech went on and on.

It was the New York premiere of *Hollow Victory*, starring Nick Lang in what the critics were already calling his breakthrough role. Moss, Susan, Bonnie, and most of the precinct members were there, all in a row, all transfixed by the screen presence Lang had managed to evoke. All except Moss.

"That's *my* line," he whispered angrily to Susan. "That's exactly what I said! Half this *movie* is something I said to him . . . Goddammit, Susan, that little sonovabitch *stole my life*!"

Susan patted him understandingly on the arm and tried to suppress a grin. The couple in front of them, upset by John's hissing, turned and shushed him.

Moss snorted but settled down. Then he tapped the couple on the shoulder, and when they turned, he gestured up toward the screen.

"You know," he said smugly, "he's a lot shorter in person."

The couple gave him a look of utter bewilderment and turned to the movie again.

Susan giggled. "Do you feel better now?" she whispered.

Up on the screen, Tony DiBennedetti was being chewed out by his Captain.

"Yeah," Moss said grudgingly, slumping back in his seat. He watched silently for a few moments. Then he said, "He's not so bad, is he?"

"No," Susan agreed. "He's not so bad."